AN ALMOST PURRFECT MURDER

JACQUELINE VICK

An Almost Perfect Murder

A Frankie Chandler Pet Psychic Mystery Book 3

ISBN-13: 978-1-945403-36-1 (Paperback)

ISBN-13: 978-1-945403-17-0 (Ebook)

Cover Art by GoOnWrite

For Ambi and all her kitties.

ONE

"I thought it would be overcast."

I clutched the ship's guardrail in sweating hands and wondered how I, Frankie Chandler, had allowed myself to be talked into leaving sunny, ocean-free Arizona for a floating deathtrap. The pointless comment I'd just made was an attempt to keep my brain from noticing how far we were from land. Safe, dry land.

Penny Newcombe, my best friend since first grade and the optimistic half of our friendship, snorted a laugh through her nose. "Why would you think that?"

In my view from the back of the ship—the stern if you're a sailor and want to get picky about it—Seattle, Washington, had shrunk into a tiny, gray blob with miles of freezing cold water in between. Kill-you-in-seconds-if-you-fall-in cold. Okay. Maybe minutes, but the farther north we traveled, the deadlier the water temperature would get.

"I looked it up," I said, referring to my point about the weather. "They get so much rain in Washington it's the suicide capital of the world."

1

Penny snorted again. "A state can't be a capital."

"And they breed serial killers there. I think I read that all serial killers are born in Washington. The depressing weather drives them mad. What if some of them got on the ship? We'll be trapped for the next seven days with the Manson brothers."

Penny let loose a laugh, squeezed my shoulders, and told me I was a card. Nothing short of murder could dampen her mood. We were on one of Finlander's finest cruise ships, the *Iso Kala*, on our way to Alaska, and in three days, my friend would step into a white dress and walk down the aisle to become Mrs. Kemper Mohr.

The decision to hold a destination wedding had come after stressful months spent trying to decide whose family to appease; Penny's kin lived in Wisconsin, Kemper's in New York. They went through pre-Cana at their own parish, St. Mel's in Wolf Creek, Arizona, and then, with Monsignor Robert's permission, they contacted the Apostleship of the Sea to find the name of the priest who would be on board the September sailing of the *Iso Kala*. When asked if he would be willing to perform the ceremony, Father Basil Zimmerman responded with an enthusiastic thumbs up.

Because of the expense involved, the wedding would be an intimate affair, but afterward, the happy Mister and Missus would fly back to their home states in turn and have a reception for each set of family members and friends.

Lost in thought, I'd been staring at the white trail of turbulence that stretched out behind the ship without really seeing it, but then Penny gave a cry of joy and pointed to a school of dolphins keeping pace with us. Once again it came home to me I was chugging through water that would be over my head should I fall in. I could swim, but so could large, carnivorous fish and creepy things you wouldn't find in a sweet little pond, or even a lake.

"Have any of the Finlander cruise ships ever sunk?"

"No-ahh!" Penny's response turned into a shriek as a tall man with the same shade of blond hair as my friend wrapped his arms around her shoulders, and leaning back, lifted her off her feet. She kicked and giggled, and when he put her down, she spun to face him.

"Robby!"

While he enveloped her in a bear hug, Robby Newcombe studied me through aqua-blue eyes. I felt my face flush. He had changed a lot in sixteen years. The lanky college kid who had remained in Illinois after graduation to work in banking had developed into a solid specimen with a square jaw and deep dimples.

"This *can't* be little annoying Frances." All of Penny's family, including Penny, called me by my full name instead of my nickname, Frankie.

I grinned. "In person."

He pushed Penny aside and opened his arms wide. "Move over, little sister, and make room for a huggable female who isn't related to me."

When he lifted me off my feet, my face met with a solid chest, and as the cold air blowing off the ocean had covered my skin with tiny water droplets, I snuggled in to soak up the warmth.

"Marry me, Frances," he growled. "Everything has been paid for, so we can have a double wedding, cheap."

"You goof," Penny said, punching his arm. "Release my maid of honor."

He complied. "At least you can dance with me to celebrate my little sister's matrimonial bliss. Has anybody warned Kemper what he's in for?"

"We can do that now," Penny said as she hooked her arm through Robby's. "Mom and Dad said everyone should meet on the Lido Deck."

We took the elevator to the 9th floor, and the minute I stepped out onto the carpeting, I knew I'd found my home away from home.

TWO

The Lido Deck was the food haven of the ship. Penny had used it as leverage to coax me into leaving dry land, something I wouldn't have considered if it weren't for the idea of an entire floor dedicated to offering me every kind of food imaginable 24-hours a day, free of charge. It worked.

The smells of sustenance wafted through the air and made me forget that I was one iceberg away from being fish food. I moved to enter the dining area, but Penny stopped me and pointed to a small sanitization station.

"I don't want anyone getting sick," she said with the sternness of a determined bride-to-be, so I squirted sanitizer onto my hands and rubbed them dry before returning my attention to the room that might turn this trip into Heaven.

Beige-and-brown diamond-patterned carpeting stretched out as far as my eyes could see, separated down the middle by food stations manned by employees dressed in white kitchen outfits. Guests filled the tables and booths, and people stood in line at each station and clutched plates and browsed the selections. My feet moved forward, ready to join them, when I heard "Yoo-hoo!"

Penny's mom, Judy Doud, stood up and waved us over to two small, square tables that had been pushed together. She was a pint-sized woman with gray in her curly blond hair, but her small stature never stopped her from being the chief organizer and executor of any gathering. She had the energy and drive typical of a farm woman. And the dress code. Her polyester navy-blue pants, matching vest, and long-sleeved blouse covered in large blue flowers were most likely sold as a set from the Country Delights catalog.

I recognized Penny's stepfather, Frank Doud, a large, husky man in beige slacks and a red golf shirt, and of course long, lanky Kemper, the groom. A man in his thirties sat on the other side of Judy. He hunched his shoulders, and his curly brown hair stuck to his forehead in a damp sweat.

"What's wrong with him?" I whispered to Robby.

"That's the best man, Tommy. He's seasick."

"Already? He must have a sensitive tummy."

One woman sat with her back to me. Long reddish-blond hair hung down past the back of her seat, and when she leaned forward to catch something Kemper was saying, I caught a glimpse of her profile. I stopped walking.

"Gina."

That one word conveyed all the dread I had stored up in anticipation of my first encounter in decades with Penny's cousin, Gina Bradley. Just shy of six feet in seventh grade, she'd made every effort to make fun of me and my little side business reading my classmates' pets. This was long before I discovered I had an ability to receive messages from animals. At the time, I was only using common sense to come up with my spectacular conclusions—but come on. If my customers were willing to pay a dollar for the privilege of not thinking for themselves, who was she to interfere? Then, in eighth grade, she'd stolen my boyfriend, and if her family hadn't moved away when she was a freshman, she would have destroyed my high school memories, too.

Gina looked over her shoulder at us, and I saw that the years had been uncommonly kind to her. The smattering of freckles on her ivory complexion gave her a wholesome look, and there wasn't a split end present in her silky hair. As she stood and spread her arms wide, I saw she hadn't gained an ounce since high school, and her bust line hadn't dropped an inch with age.

"Frances!" she called out, and my eyes popped open in surprise. I had assumed the stretched-out arms and wiggling fingers, beckoning the fly to enter the spider's web, were for Robby or Penny.

"Who's that?" Robby asked.

"Gina," I answered, plastering a smile on my face before I approached the table. This was Penny's big trip, so I would have to play nice. When she pulled me close, I had to turn my head to avoid a face-full of boob.

"I can't believe it's you!" She shoved me back to take a good look, and I straightened my shoulders, which is supposed to take off five pounds. She looked over my shoulder at Robby and shoved me aside to hug her next victim.

"Look at you! You're finally taller than I am."

Robby grinned down at her. "Wow. You look great."

She flipped her hair over her shoulder. "You're not so bad yourself, cousin. How long has it been?"

They launched into a comparison of which family events they'd each missed, since they had both resided in other states, and finally determined it had been ten years since they'd laid eyes on each other. I grabbed the opportunity to get away, but Gina hooked her hand around my arm and stopped me. She had never shied away from physical

7

contact, which was just one of the many reasons I avoided her.

"I've heard rumors," she sang out, wagging a slender finger at me. "Someone's had an exciting few years, and I want to hear all about them."

As she led me back to the table, I tried to decide if she was talking about the public failure of my one serious relationship two years ago, my pet psychic business, or the two murders I'd inadvertently become involved with. None of them were topics I planned to discuss with Gina.

Sharon Bradley, Judy's ex-sister-in-law and Gina's mother, sat at the end of the table in her usual frozen-queen pose. She wore her soft, blond hair pulled back into a loose braid, and her pale-pink sweater was cashmere. Not that she harbored any ill-will toward her brother's ex or his children. She was simply a cold fish, except fish don't have finely penciled eyebrows, and Sharon did. She raised one in my direction.

Two cheery faces smiled at me from either side of Kemper, as if they had been waiting all day for the opportunity to meet me. Judy introduced them as Kemper's parents, Christina and Thomas Mohr. Kemper got his dark hair from his mother, but his six-foot tall, skinny physique matched that of his father, though Thomas had filled out with age. He wasn't fat. Just more solid-looking than his son. And he had something else Kemper lacked. A sense of humor.

After Judy said his name, Thomas shook my hand in a tight grip and said, "And I've still got my head." He followed this with a hardy laugh, and I assumed he referred to Sir Thomas M-o-r-e, martyred for his faith by King Henry VIII. I'd seen *A Man for All Seasons*.

Christina groaned and patted her husband's arm with

affection. "That joke never gets old." The thing is, I think she meant it.

I felt bad for Kemper. His side of the family was under-represented. He had a sister due any moment with her third child. She had wisely decided not to give birth at sea and would instead take part in the New York reception. Kemper's younger brother, a lieutenant in the Air Force, couldn't get leave to take part in the festivities but would hopefully be able to make an appearance in New York.

I handed out hugs to everyone present except Tommy, who with his sweaty forehead and pasty pallor had as much appeal as a plague victim, and Sharon, who wasn't the hugging type. When Gina patted the seat next to her, I dropped into it.

"What have *you* been up to?" I asked, not because I cared but because I wanted the focus on her career so she wouldn't have an opportunity to make fun of mine.

"This and that."

Judy leaned in front of Gina. "She works as an interpreter for the U.N."

"Polish," Sharon clarified, as if that made all the difference in the world, and once again I was reminded that Sharon Bradley had always struck me as a woman in need of a happy enema.

"Polish?" I said. Since she hadn't moved her critical gaze from me, I assumed she expected a response. "How...unusual."

Gina waved off her accomplishment, managing to show off her perfect manicure. "I guess that puts us in the same line of work. You translate for pets, and I handle the Poles."

She threw back her head and let loose a laugh that always reminded me of the annoying squeal of Gertie in *Oklahoma!* Penny grinned at me from across the table, and I narrowed my eyes to let her know I wasn't happy with the seating arrangement.

Kemper, who always became nervous at any mention of my pet psychic activities, darted a glance at his parents, but they hadn't heard Gina's comment. They were absorbed in conversation with Sharon Bradley about whether cruise lines should allow children. Thomas and Christina thought it depended on both the parent and the child, while Sharon voted never, with a penalty of forty lashes.

Frank cleared his throat. "Our rooms are all on the fifth floor, though they're not all together. Since we booked so many cabins, the travel agent upgraded us." He gave us a pleased grin. "We've all got balconies."

"That is *so* generous!" Sharon said, and Frank blushed, probably because the way she said it made it sound as if anything less would have been slumming.

He handed out little cards as if he were dealing a round of poker. "We got everybody a drink card. You can use it at the coffee shop in the Lookout. I'm not sure if it works at the bars. There's sixty bucks there, but if you run out, you can go to the front desk on the first floor and reload. They don't take cash on this ship."

"Thank you," I said, grateful I'd be able to have a morning latte, and everyone joined in and expressed appreciation.

Just then, an announcement came over the speaker system from a tenor voice with a slight accent. "Good afternoon. This is Captain Milo Koskela. Welcome to the *Iso Kala*. If you need anything, don't hesitate to ask any of the crew members. We want to make sure you enjoy your time with Finlander cruises without interruption, so we invite you all to the Promenade Deck—that's the third-floor deck—for a safety drill in fifteen minutes. You will report directly under your assigned lifeboat, and you can find the number of your lifeboat on your room pass. This is not optional, and anyone who doesn't show will be invited to a private session that will include laps around the Promenade Deck."

Nervous giggles followed this announcement, and the passengers moved as one to opt for the public drill. As we went with the crowd toward the lobby that held the elevator and stairs, I clutched Penny's arm. "I thought you said these ships didn't sink."

She rolled her eyes. "It's required by law, like the seatbelt in your car. It doesn't mean they'll ever *use* the lifeboats."

THREE

I will say our lifeboat looked spotless. I knew it was our boat because there was a big number twelve painted on the bottom of it. The boat hovered right above my head. I took a step back and clung to the wall. The only positive I could see was that Gina and her mother were down the hall from my room and therefore wouldn't be in my boat. At least I could die without watching Gina do it better.

"Why are you back there?" Judy said from her position at the front of our group. "Get your buns over here so you can hear the man."

I inched forward, maintaining springing distance should the boat break loose and fall. *The man* Judy referred to was a uniformed crew member who wore a life jacket, just like the one I clutched in my hand. He demonstrated how to put it on and secure it, but the instructions faded out as my face, with a will of its own, turned upward to stare at the large, heavy boat.

"Would you stop worrying?" Penny whispered.

"Did you notice they painted the numbers on the

bottom of the lifeboats? That means they expect them to capsize."

"What?!"

"How else would rescuers be able to read the number?"

Robby stepped back and put his arm around my shoulder. "I promise to save you if you go in. As long as I can do so without much effort or discomfort."

"Then we'll *both* freeze to death. I couldn't have that on my conscience. Besides. Your mother would resuscitate me so she could kill me again. Thanks anyway."

When the presentation ended, Judy suggested we go to our rooms, unpack, and relax before we changed for the wedding rehearsal. Dinner would follow in the main dining room. We had the early seating, so we had to get a move on it.

People crowded into the lobby to wait for the elevator, and just as many filled the staircases on either side. I looked at a floor plan of the ship that hung on the wall and decided to head down the hallway and use the back staircase.

As I neared the end of my trek, an inside cabin door opened. I wouldn't have bothered to look if the door had swung open and someone had stepped out laughing or chatting. This door creaked open a crack surreptitiously and then a man's face filled that crack. He had on a burgundy shirt and matching tie, short brown hair, and a crooked nose. When I turned my head to look, his eyes bugged out, and he slammed the door shut. Maybe he thought I was a member of the crew patrolling for people who skipped the safety training.

Up on the fifth floor, I had to trudge all the way back to the center lobby where the elevators were. In the hallway beyond, my room was the third door down on the left.

Penny's mother and stepfather had insisted on covering

the cost of my cruise, since the most I could have afforded would have been a tugboat tour of—did Arizona have any big lakes? I wasn't sure, having only lived there for two years.

I'd gotten the best of the bargain because, once Penny married three days from now and moved with Kemper into the Honeymoon Suite, I'd have a cabin to myself. Robby and I had both lucked out because we had been the left-overs. The Douds had a room together, and so did the Mohrs, which was only proper for married couples. Gina was sharing living quarters with her mother. On one side of my room, Kemper and Tommy were together, and on the other side was Robby.

Before I could insert my key card into the slot, Penny opened the door for me. The stewards had brought my luggage and left it on a folding stand at the end of one of two full-sized beds. The room was decorated in neutral shades—dark brown carpet and curtains, beige bedspreads, and off-white walls.

Penny had a small suitcase in which she had packed enough clothing for two days, while the rest of her luggage awaited her in the Honeymoon Suite. She pulled her dinner clothes directly from her suitcase, while I unpacked my clothes into a dresser, hung my dresses and pants in the small closet, and tucked away my empty luggage on the floor.

"I'll change in the bathroom," she said.

"Don't be silly. I'll just step outside to give you some privacy."

Past a small, plump love seat and behind the curtains, a sliding door opened onto a veranda with two deck chairs and a small table. I stepped outside and took a few gulps of fresh air. A small group of houses, shacks really, dotted a shoreline that crept past my vision. If the ship went down, and I had on warm clothes, I might even be able to swim the distance. The thought, ridiculous as it was, calmed me down.

"You could just jump into your lifeboat from here if we run into trouble."

White, wooden partitions blocked off my balcony from those of my neighbors. Robby leaned over the railing to my left and grinned at me. He was in the middle of dressing for dinner, unless he planned to wear his green dress shirt half buttoned, which wouldn't have bothered me at all. He kept fit. My gaze followed to where he pointed. One floor down from my room hung the lifeboats, covered with orange tarps and waiting for duty.

"That's comforting. Not. I'd probably knock it loose and go tumbling to my death, or else bounce off into the ocean."

"I think if you stretch out as you fall you have less chance of bouncing."

I grimaced. "Thanks. I'll be too busy screaming to remember that."

The sliding door opened, and Penny stepped outside in a long-sleeved peach dress decorated with little white flowers and matching peach-colored sling-backs. Her fine, blond hair hung straight naturally, so she never had to fuss with it. She wasn't blessed with the cowlicks that made my auburn hair impossible to tame. I had just enough natural wave to make it look like I never combed my hair.

"Your turn," she said, changing places with me on the veranda.

I told Robby I'd see him at the rehearsal and stepped back inside. The dress code for the regular dining room was dressy casual, which meant though jeans were frowned upon, I wouldn't be expected to wear a ball gown. I pulled my black knit dress and matching low heels out of the closet. It was sleeveless, but once I was dressed, I wrapped a red shawl over my shoulders, grabbed my black leather clutch purse, and called out to Penny I was ready to go.

She joined me, dripping with contagious excitement, and I forgot all about the possibility of sinking as we headed for the Queen's Lounge.

FOUR

The Douds had scheduled the wedding rehearsal in the medium-sized room where the ship's chaplain and rabbi held religious services—Mass each morning and Jewish services on Saturday, along with special events. Though Penny and Kemper were getting married in a church, this was the only place we could practice.

Twenty rows of stadium-style seating curved around three sides of an open floor. The walls, carpet and upholstery were all royal burgundy, and in the center of the floor stood an altar covered with a white cloth.

A priest with thick, white hair and a broad smile waited next to the altar with the Mohrs—including Kemper—along with Sharon Bradley, and the Douds. Gina, Tommy and Robby sat in the front row, and as I descended the steps with Penny, I understood what it felt like to be a celebrity hanger-on. Those who weren't standing stood, and everybody locked eyes on my best friend as if she had come to us from another planet.

Most of the priests who joined the Apostles of the Sea were retired, so I wasn't surprised Father Basil was in his early seventies. However, I didn't expect him to have so much energy. He clapped his hands together and made beckoning motions.

"We only have fifteen minutes before they need to set up the room for a Bar Mitzvah," he said, "so we need to work fast. I assume you're all familiar with the Mass?" Everyone nodded except Sharon, who had married an atheist, stopped practicing her faith, and refused to acknowledge her Catholic upbringing, and Gina, whose only exposure to the Mass had come from summer vacations spent on Penny's farm.

"Do you know what a homily is?" he asked the two women. Sharon admitted she did, and Gina said yes. "The Rite of Marriage takes place right after that. I'll ask you all to stand, and you'll take your places." He directed us all to our spots. "Then I'll ask the bride and groom some questions. The bride and groom will, I assume, give their consent—"

"They had better," Robby said with a grin.

"I'll bless the rings, and then I will have the privilege of introducing them as husband and wife." He glanced at his watch. "We're doing this a little backward, but let's practice your entrance. That's the part that makes most wedding parties nervous. Could I have the groom and best man and groomsman remain here while the ladies take their places at the top of the steps?"

I joined Penny and Gina to await further instructions while Father Basil positioned Kemper, Tommy, and Robby. The best man looked like he was losing the battle against an urge to topple, but he pressed his lips together and set his jaw in an effort to defeat his motion-borne affliction.

"Bridesmaid, come forward, slowly. Maid of Honor, give it a count of ten before you follow. Then, if the bride could wait until everyone is in position, the *Wedding March* will begin. Well, it will begin when there's a musician. Just imagine it for now."

Gina sashayed down the steps, her hips moving side to side. When she reached her position opposite Robby, she gave him a nervous smile. Then it was my turn. I took my time, walking one step forward and then bringing the back foot up to meet its partner before stepping forward again. It felt awkward on the steps, but once I reached level ground, it felt silly because there wasn't any music. I reached my position opposite Tommy and turned to look up at Penny. She stood still, taking it all in, and then her face crumpled, and she burst into tears.

"Sweetie!" Kemper took a step forward, but Father Basil held up a hand.

"Happens all the time. She'll be fine."

After a few sniffles, Penny straightened her shoulders and began her march. She wasn't wearing her dress, and there wasn't any music, but it still gave me shivers to watch my childhood friend walk down those steps. When she reached the bottom, she dipped her head, embarrassed, and took her place at Kemper's side.

"Then, at the appropriate time, I'll take you through your vows and the ring blessing."

Kemper pantomimed placing the ring on Penny's finger, and when he moved to kiss the bride, the priest stepped in between them and said, "And that's a wrap!"

Even Tommy seemed to forget to be seasick, at least until Frank Doud mentioned we would meet in the dining room. The best man declined, saying he didn't want to press his luck. He said he would order some broth from room service.

I left Penny and Kemper to go over last-minute details

under the watchful eyes of both sets of parents and headed in the direction of dinner, one of my favorite meals.

"Aren't you afraid you'll trip in your high heels?" Robby asked as we walked the long hallway to the other end of the ship.

"You did *not* just say that. Now I'll worry about it all night."

He grinned and put an arm around my shoulder.

"You were always so easy to play with."

I shoved him sideways, and he stumbled. "But I always found a way to get back at you."

"With the tools available to you at your tender age."

As we walked on in silence, he stuffed his hands in his pockets. I could feel his eyes on me, and when I looked, he had his head cocked as if he were working out how to get the words out.

"Spill it."

"What do you think of Gina?"

I snorted. "I try not to."

"What's wrong with her?"

I kept my shrug casual. "What's not? She's always been a thorn in my side, ever since we were in grade school. She tried to interfere with my side business."

He chuckled. "She thought you were scamming people. She has a great sense of justice."

"I was offering a service people were willing to pay for. You wouldn't cheer her on if she had knocked over my lemonade stand, would you?"

"Only if it had been strawberry lemonade. That's not natural."

"She conveniently manages to remind everyone how successful and tall and beautiful she is."

"She is." He nodded in complete agreement. "The pride of the family."

"It wasn't a compliment. I guess I should have asked why you want to know."

"I just wanted an independent opinion. I've known her for a long time, so it's hard to be objective. We haven't seen each other for a while, and she seems different somehow."

"You mean snottier than ever?"

"Ah, no." His slight smile said the conversation was over, and I wondered if I should have held back when talking about a family member, but he *had* asked my opinion.

A stream of women headed for a short hallway under a sign for the restrooms. I followed the ingrained female instinct to freshen up before dinner and told Robby I would meet him at our table.

After I used the facilities and washed my hands, I moved into the lounge area and leaned into a long mirror surrounded by little fancy light bulbs that hung over a white marble counter. My makeup hadn't slid off my face, an advantage of the cooler temperatures in Alaska. My skin had a nice, healthy glow to it, probably because of all the walking around and refreshingly chilly air. And because I was looking forward to dinner. An empty bank account meant nights eating in with something cheap, like noodles and butter. Maybe I could talk Robby into getting married next and I could feast at his parent's expense again. I gave my wrist a mental slap for being greedy, and lured by the thoughts of tonight's menu, made my way through strolling passengers to the end of the hallway.

FIVE

A small crowd gathered around a wooden podium and waited to be shown to their assigned seating by a man wearing a tuxedo, but I caught sight of Mrs. Doud in her sparkly black jacket and black pants waving both hands in the air to catch my attention. I hurried over, willing her to put her arms back by her sides where they belonged, which she did as soon as I arrived.

"It's such an enormous room and there's an upstairs and a downstairs. I was afraid you would get lost."

Penny chortled. "Frances get lost on her way to food? Not likely."

Gina had changed into a lime-green sleeveless dress and pulled her long hair into a high ponytail. The combination made her look like she was auditioning for the part of Sandy Olsson in *Grease,* except Gina was missing that wholesome quality that made you cheer for little Sandy.

She sat next to her mother in the seats closest to the window. I'd forgotten how petite Sharon Bradley was, which was even more apparent now that she sat next to her Amazon daughter. She had changed from a braid to a classy

French twist. Her long nails, painted a pale pink, matched her silk suit. Penny, Kemper, and Mrs. Doud made up the rest of that side, and there was an empty chair at the head of the table.

Across from Mrs. Doud sat Mr. Doud, followed by Robby, and three empty chairs. I took the one next to Robby, who filled my wine glass with the remains of a bottle of Pinot Noir.

I took a minute to check out my surroundings. On either side of the room, windows lined the upper half of the walls to give the guests a stunning view of the ocean. The carpet had a vintage-looking floral pattern in burgundy and brown, and in the center of the room, a carpeted staircase with gold railings wound down to the lower level. Down the middle of the room, square tables seated smaller parties. The tables along the windows, like ours, were long rectangles that stuck out into the room, and all of them sported crisp, white tablecloths and gold rimmed water glasses and place settings.

"Is Tommy going to skip dinner?" I asked. In my world, skipping a meal meant someone should call an ambulance. I kept my voice low to avoid alarming the groom, but he heard me anyway.

Kemper, who always looked solemn, drew his brows together. "I'm a little worried about Tommy. He's still feeling seasick."

"I gave him two of my motion sickness bracelets." Judy Doud toasted the air with her glass of wine. "He'll be good as new by morning."

Penny took Kemper's hand in hers and kissed it. "My little worry-wart."

Thomas and Christina Mohr joined us in time to hear Penny's comment.

"Who's worrying?" Thomas said as he scooted behind me to get to his chair. He took the one next to me and let Christina have the window seat.

"Tommy is still feeling seasick," Robby said.

Christina dug through a black purse that matched her pantsuit and pulled out two motion sickness bracelets. "These will put him right."

"My mom already got to him."

"Great minds think alike." Thomas gave his wife's shoulders a squeeze.

As she put them away, she said, "I've got these extras if anyone needs them."

I wondered if it were a coincidence both mothers were wearing black and was about to make a joke about it, but then the waiter approached, and I became focused on a single objective—my stomach. I took note of how both Penny and Gina's orders included the word *petite*. Mine did not.

People on the ship spoke of this as the *regular* dining room, implying this is where the poor schlubs hung out, but the food exceeded my expectations. I know conversation went on while we ate because I gave a few nods and grunts, but I only had eyes for my filet mignon, au gratin potatoes and baby peas.

When I set down my knife and fork with a satisfied sigh, Robby leaned over and whispered, "Do you want to lick the plate?"

I fluttered my lashes at him. "Yes, please."

Incredible as it sounds, I waved off the dessert menu. Well, maybe not so incredible, since both Gina and Penny did so after expressing a desire to fit into their dresses for the wedding. I didn't have the courage to buck the trend.

Frank Doud signed the check, but not before Thomas

Mohr insisted he pay for dinner tomorrow night. As they worked out the details, Robby suggested we walk off dinner.

"That sounds great," Gina gushed, and she turned to Sharon. "Come on, Mom."

But Sharon Bradley had other plans, and Gina decided to remain with her, though with the way she kept looking over her shoulder at us as we walked away, she would have preferred our company. I couldn't blame her.

Back in Loon Lake, Wisconsin, after-dinner walks are a tradition, and soon we were in a wide, carpeted corridor floor peppered with people who had the same idea. We passed the Photo Club, which is where passengers selected packages of photos taken by ship's photographers throughout the trip. Then the hallway forked to either side of the Atrium, a circular staircase that led down to the lower floors. The Seaside Bar extended to both sides of the Atrium, and piano music beckoned passengers to sit on the comfy couches and relax with a drink.

Farther on, there was a bend in the hallway where the two corridors converged into the shopping arcade. Dead ahead, Misty's Clothing Emporium flouted her wares like a trollop on a busy street corner. Penny paused to peek inside at the round racks of colorful clothes with Kemper tagging along like a good fiancé, but as soon as I saw the price tag on a jaunty cap covered in rhinestones—$200—I opted to stay in the hallway with Robby.

"How's it feel to have your baby sister getting married?"

He grimaced. "Makes me feel like an old man. I'll always think of you two as the little pains in my side who followed me everywhere, with you mooning over me."

It was true. I'd had a crush on him when I was in grade school and he was a high school athlete. Still, it wouldn't do to massage his ego. "Ha! That's what you think. We were bored. There wasn't much else to do other than watch the cows chew their cud."

He cocked his head and gave me a crooked grin that reminded me of Penny. "That's too bad. You've turned out pretty well for a little geek."

Penny rejoined us and announced that the top she'd been eyeing was the wrong shade of blue, and Kemper gave an audible sigh of relief.

"You got a look at the price tag," I said.

She blew her bangs out of her eyes. "You betcha."

The hallway made a bend around the General Store. Here, the corridor opened into a large space with room to showcase special sales. Against the wall, two tables covered in pristine white cloths held glass cases that sparkled with hints of red. Penny took in a breath.

"It's the Hardcastle Collection."

"The who?" I got my jewelry, what little of it I wore, from craft shows. I read the banner hung high on the wall surrounded by burgundy, gold, and white balloons. *Hardcastle Collection. Enter for your chance to win the Pure Fantasy bracelet.*

A middle-aged man and a young woman in her twenties, both in burgundy suites with burgundy shirts and ties, stood behind the tables. Their gold name tags identified them as Hannah and Art. The closest to me, Hannah, overheard my question.

"Jeremy Hardcastle appreciated fine jewels. He collected only the best, and his passion was rubies."

"His wife was a lucky woman," Penny said.

"His late wife did not share his passion. She rarely wore them."

Penny made a tsking noise, as if she couldn't believe any woman surrounded by such a beautiful selection of baubles

AN ALMOST PURRFECT MURDER

would have passed up the opportunity to fasten them around her neck and adorn her wrist and fingers.

"Think about it, Pen," I said. "She would have needed her own private military to protect her from thieves." I looked at the guard. "So, what did he do with them? Run them through his fingers in a locked room?"

The guard gave a thin smile that showed she didn't appreciate my humor. "He exhibited his private collection at exclusive parties. Guests included celebrities, politicians and even a president or two."

"So that's what they do with my tax dollars. I wondered."

She continued as if I hadn't spoken. "When he died, his children took over the estate, and they opened the shows to the public, which was very generous of them. We have replicas for sale, if you're interested."

Penny moved toward the display case in front of the male guard as if drawn by an invisible force. "I suppose even a replica would break my pocketbook."

Art took a small step forward, his eyes on Penny. If these were the real jewels, they would be worth a fortune that could keep Emily and Chauncey in premium kibble for life. I wouldn't want the responsibility of keeping sticky fingers off the cases.

"The ruby you're looking at is one of the largest," he said. "It's approximately nineteen carats."

"What's it worth?" I asked.

He looked down his nose at me in distaste, as if I were a vulgarian for asking, but lurking behind his initial sniff was pride by association. "In the setting, it's value is 2.2 million dollars."

The setting included what I assumed were genuine diamonds.

"Elizabeth Taylor!" Penny shrieked, leaning forward to gape.

"Penny, she's dead," I said, hoping the dazzling display hadn't dimmed my friend's brain cells.

"She means these bracelets were once owned by Elizabeth Taylor, the actress, and auctioned off after her death. Mr. Hardcastle was the highest bidder."

Hannah handed Penny a form. "We will have the drawing for the Pure Fantasy bracelet on the fifth night of the cruise. You just fill in this form with your personal information and return it here by the time we hit Ketchikan. The winner will also receive tickets for two to the Mermaid's Ball in Victoria, where she can show off her new jewels."

The bracelet she referred to sat on a raised platform of black velvet. Six medium-sized rubies were set into a 14-carat gold band. The display card said *the multi-faceted gems are bursting with brilliance that will warm the heart of any woman.* I've never had my heart warmed by a cold rock, but if they said so.

I leaned my head in and squinted at the way the stones sparkled in the display lighting. The pattern inside the stones reminded me of what I used to see in my childhood kaleidoscope, except the patterns in my kaleidoscope weren't flawed. I blinked. One of the facets had the tiniest chip in the right, upper corner.

Back in Wolf Creek, Arizona, where I lived, Toni Haskell, the wife of the current mayor, had explained that the imperfections in hand-spun yarn increased its value. A flaw in the natural fabric was part of its beauty. It made sense that a flaw in the gem must guarantee authenticity.

I pointed at a ring in the same case that had a pink stone set in an embellished gold setting. "I thought these were all rubies. That one is pink."

Art gave me a superior smile. "That's a ruby as well, although some people will insist on calling it a pink sapphire."

I wrinkled my brow. "I thought sapphires were blue."

Robby hooked an arm around my waist and pulled me away. "This is too complex for you, Frances. And too boring for me."

Penny joined us and turned her face up to Kemper. "Let's go dancing!"

"You guys have a good time." There were limits to what I would do for a friend. Me and my two left feet were already committed to dancing after the wedding. That was my limit.

"Why don't we catch a show?" Robby suggested. His parents wandered up in time to hear the suggestion, and they enthusiastically agreed.

"Sounds great," Judy said. "My feet are killing me from all this walking around in heels, but I'd probably cause a riot if I wore my boots."

Definitely, since they were usually covered in manure and chicken poop. The heels she referred to were one-inch high sling backs in the most neutral shade of beige I'd ever seen.

"We should tell Gina and Aunt Sharon," Robby said.

"They went to the general store for hair spray. I'll ask if they want to join us." Judy left to do so.

"What about the Mohrs?" I asked.

Penny grinned. "They're already in the Neptune Theater waiting for the show to begin."

Kemper, added with a note of pride in his voice, "They're experienced travelers. They warned me to arrive half an hour early for any show I'd like to see." He approved of their proactive and organized approach.

Sitting in a comfortable chair and resting my feet, which weren't used to dress heels, sounded ideal. "Then we had better get moving."

Penny and Kemper agreed to meet us afterward, and we went in opposite directions to our respective destinations.

SIX

The Neptune Theater was at the end of the third floor. And the fourth. The theater covered two levels. By the time we arrived, all the seats on the upper level were occupied except for two near the exit. Judy and Frank grabbed those without apology, and Robby and I took the stairs down to the lower level. We managed to find seats in the middle of the fifth row from the back, and after climbing over our fellow passengers, we dropped into our seats.

Robby pulled out a duplicate of the itinerary that was on the desk in my room. He flipped it open and ran his finger down the list of today's events.

"You're not going to believe what the first act is."

I raised my eyebrows and waited for him to fill me in, but he refolded the paper and put it away.

"I'm going to let it be a surprise."

"A magician?" I asked. He grinned and shook his head. "Singers?"

"Nope."

"Dancers?"

"Uh-uh."

31

"Singer-dancers?"

The lights went down and piped-in music burst from speakers placed around the room. The emcee, dressed in a tuxedo, bounded out from behind the blue velvet curtain and told us how glad he was to see us.

A quiet hum sounded in my ears, similar to white noise. I sat up straight. This was the noise given off by animals, but there weren't any four-legged passengers on the ship. Were there?

I craned my neck to search the room. Maybe someone had a service animal. Then I remembered a scene from a Dracula movie where the ship—or maybe it was a boat—was overrun with rats. I jerked my feet off the floor.

The emcee introduced Marvelous Marv and his Fabulous Felines and jogged off the stage as the curtains drew back. Sitting in a semi-circle on short platforms, five cats faced center stage.

I gasped in shock, wonder, and a bit of fear at what felines could accomplish once they decided to listen up and follow instructions. "Trained cats?"

Robby nodded, a huge grin on his face. "I know. Ridiculous, isn't it?"

The only thing I could get my cat Emily to do was come to her bowl after I filled it. I couldn't imagine getting a feline to perform on demand.

A woman in her fifties, optimistic about her age, pranced around the circle in a sparkling gold shirt over a black leotard, black tights and high-heeled leather hip boots. The sleeves of the shirt were layered with long fringe that swayed as she wiggled across the stage with one hand held high. Her hair, an unnatural shade of red, formed an impressive mound on top of her head. Marv introduced her as his assistant, Bitsy. Even from where I sat, I could see her shimmering gold eyeshadow when she blinked.

Marvelous Marv wore black pants and a puffy, gold-fringed shirt meant to detract from his growing belly. His dark hair, slicked back, shone with pomade. He had a stick in his hands, and it crossed my mind it might be a whip. If he cracked it at the kitties, I swore I'd climb onto the stage and beat him with it, but he only used it to point to a spot in front of a suspended ring.

A slim, gray Ocicat with the large ears typical of the breed hopped off his platform and leapt effortlessly through the loop, even after they raised it three times. His name was Sphinx, and he won a large round of applause. Then he wowed us with a game of cups. Marvelous Marv put a piece of fish under a cup while Sphinx sat with his back to the audience. I could sense the cat's boredom, which came across to me in a rumbling *Brrrrr*. Then Marv mixed up the cups. Sphinx strolled over, and without even stopping to sniff, pointed with his left front paw to the correct cup. What a smart kitty! His reward was the piece of fish.

Next, a pair of gold tabbies named Jasper and Jinx danced on their hind legs, and then a jet-black tomcat called Casper played ping pong with his paw and won against his opponent, Marvelous Marv.

Throughout the performance, I heard a light symphony in my head of rhythmic purrs punctuated by an occasional high note of pleasure and underlined by a baseline of boredom—*Brrrrr*. The only cat not into the act was a large calico. She, and I assumed it was she since most calicos are female, turned her back on Marv when he requested she join him. He hit the floor with his stick, and she licked her paw and cleaned her face.

Bitsy covered her mouth with her hand in an exaggerated expression of surprise, but Marv's eyebrows had joined into one thick line, and he wore his smile upside down. Bitsy approached the cat and made a hand gesture, repeated it, and the cat, with great reluctance, dropped to the floor and strolled over to Marv.

"Take a bow, Felix," he said with a smile in his voice, as if the show had gone as planned and he couldn't be happier if it had started raining Hardcastle rubies.

So, Felix was the one in three thousand exception. A male. A dim-witted male, because Felix just stared.

"He's not the brightest bulb," Marv said, and the audience giggled.

After two more requests, Felix took a long, slow bow, more of a stretch, and the act left the stage.

"It will be hard to beat that," Robby said. He referred to the itinerary. "Next up is a comedian."

The curtain fluttered, and from my position, I caught sight of a handsome, dark-haired man in a tuxedo standing at the edge of the stage.

"You've got to be kidding," I said.

"Nope," Robby answered. "You'll love his name. It's—"

"Sonny Street."

Taking center stage, his dimpled cheeks and dark eyes lit up with that special smile reserved for the audience, was Sonny Street, former warm-up comedian for the Baking Channel's *Blue-Ribbon Babes* television baking show...and onetime murder suspect.

SEVEN

After the show, the performers mingled with the guests in the Orca Lounge, an intimate room with a jazz ensemble providing background music. In honor of the namesake whale, the decor focused on white and black. White walls and carpet and black furniture, including the bar, and window fixtures. I made a beeline for Sonny Street, and after his initial reaction upon seeing me—to look for the closest exit—he relaxed and gave me a warm handshake.

"For a minute there, I thought you were planning to interrogate me about murder, but that's all behind us now. Tell your Aunt Gertrude what she said was right on the money!" He opened his arms to take in his surroundings. "She said the future held something big in store for my career, and you can't get much bigger than a cruise ship."

While visiting me last May, my tarot card-reading Aunt Gertrude had taken a shot at palm reading, and she had used Sonny as a guinea pig. A lucky guess, since it was a vague prediction delivered to a man who wasn't thrilled with his career at the Baking Channel, though I shouldn't knock Auntie. It was her cold reading skills that taught me to be a top-notch *fake* pet psychic before animals started to communicate with me for real.

"You certainly have moved up in the world," I said with a smile. "Congratulations."

He leaned forward and kept his voice down. "Do you remember how I paid that teenager to help me write jokes that would appeal to a younger audience? Well, the passengers on these cruises love me just as I am."

I remembered the enthusiastic claps and giggles from the *Blue-Ribbon Babes* audience members, most of whom were contemporaries of my Aunt Gertrude, and then I risked a peek at our fellow passengers. Yes, Penny and I and the wedding party hovered at the bottom of the age-range of most of the guests except for a few children and teens I'd seen at dinner. Sonny was in his element.

Penny and Kemper joined us, followed by Sharon and Gina, and I introduced the comedian to the entire gang. The bride-to-be gave him a hug as if Sonny were an old friend and said, "I've heard so much about you from Frances!" Sonny looked surprised, and Robby raised a brow in my direction.

My friend flushed. "I mean when that murder thing happened. In fact, I was at the seance Aunt Gertrude held at Frances's house. Remember? You were there."

Robby's other eyebrow joined its partner near his hairline. "Seance?"

I didn't like the direction the conversation was taking, and I wasn't the only one. Kemper had that panicked deer-in-the-headlights expression back on, and Sharon curled her upper lip back with distaste. I didn't want it to freeze in that position, so I changed the subject.

"And now Penny is getting married."

Sonny took her hands and held them up, inspecting her.

"No wonder you look so pretty. There's nothing as beautiful as a bride."

"Watch it," Robby joked. "The groom is standing right there. He might get jealous."

Kemper, his face back to its usual placid expression, looked around as if wondering if a response were required.

"Don't mind him," Penny said. "He never gets jealous."

"That's not true," he protested. "What am I supposed to do? Grab you by the hair and drag you back to your room?" He blushed at the unintended implications. "And leave you there, of course, until...you know. After the wedding."

Marvelous Marv stuck his head into our little circle. I took a step sideways to avoid the smell of his cologne, bumping into Sharon as I did.

"Sorry about that."

I don't think she noticed. Her wide-eyed gaze fixed on Marv's face, and her jaw dropped. I guess she'd never met a celebrity up close before.

Marv put his arm around Penny's small waist. "Did I hear someone is getting married? Do I get a kiss from the bride?"

And then he dipped her and planted a big one smack on her mouth. We all stared, frozen by the horror of a strange man—albeit a famous man in his own, small world—molesting the bride-to-be. Well, one person reacted.

A woman with long, black hair stood just outside our circle. She wore a filmy layered black dress and high-heeled, shiny black knee-boots. It looked as if her fondest desire was to be mistaken for a witch, especially when the corners of her thin lips, painted in blood red, dropped into a frown.

Suddenly, Kemper stepped up to Marv with his fists balled up, trembling. I thought he was going to hit the performer and so did he, but at the last minute, he reached out, pinched the skin on the back of Marv's neck and twisted. With a yell, Marv popped up fast and grabbed at his neck. Penny stumbled back into Kemper's arms and he caught her before she fell. Her face had flushed pink, and she said, "Um...well. Interesting."

"What do you think you're doing?" All signs of the order-obsessed accountant were gone. Kemper's voice cracked like a whip, and several people turned to watch. "You are man-handling my future wife!"

"Just wishing the bride-to-be luck," Marv said, still rubbing his neck. "It's a show business tradition." He gave a small bow.

A woman nearby tittered, and Kemper broke his focus long enough to see he had an audience. His arms relaxed, and he stood tall. "Well, don't do it again." His volume was still up a few decibels, so he lowered it to a mutter and added, "A stupid tradition, if you ask me."

Marv, with a quick glance at Kemper, took Penny's hand and bowed again. "I have to take my crew for a walk. Maybe I'll see you again." He shot a malicious grin at the witchy woman with the narrow eyes, and it all made sense. The performance had been for her benefit. For her detriment, really. She let her gaze wander over our group. It didn't appear as if she wanted to make friends, and she didn't even wave goodbye before she stalked off.

Before he moved to follow her, Marv paused next to Sharon and Gina.

"Hello there."

I wouldn't have described his tone as seductive, but there was some hidden meaning in the way he said those words. He meant to provoke one of them.

Sharon wrapped her arm around Gina's shoulder. "Get away from us."

He chuckled, made a slight bow toward Gina, and strolled away.

Odd that Sharon seemed just as affected by Marv's performance as Kemper and witchy woman. I didn't think she cared that much for Penny, but family is family. As she watched the back of Marv disappear out the exit, she held still, the cool, poised ice queen—all except her expression. I was glad not to be on the receiving end of her glare.

Her daughter worked for the U.N. and must have met all sorts, so Sharon's protective attitude seemed unnecessary.

I asked Gina, who had broken free of Sharon's grasp, "Has your mother ever met Marvelous Marv before?"

That earned me a horselaugh. She separated her ponytail into two sections and pulled at the ends to tighten it. "Not likely. This is Mom's first cruise."

"Congratulations, my brother-in-law in shining armor," Robby said with a snicker. "I think you upstaged Marv."

Penny's skin still had a pink flush to it, and she clasped her hands together in front of her chest. In hindsight, I'm sure it was her lingering embarrassment that made her snap at the man who had just come to her rescue.

"You shouldn't have caused a scene," she said.

Kemper gaped. "Me?" He narrowed his eyes. "Is that why you didn't fight him off?"

Her hands moved to her hips. "Are you suggesting I enjoyed being slobbered over by a stranger?"

I'm sure that had not been on his mind, and I felt sorry for him as he stood there, blinking in confusion at the sudden turn in the conversation's tone.

"Marv's okay," Sonny said, his audience smile back on his face. "Quite a joker."

"That man's an ass," Kemper said, and Penny shushed him. He shot her a dirty look.

Sonny blew out a huff of air. "Yeah. Marv's an ass. What can I say?"

"Who was the woman giving Penny the evil eye?" I asked.

"You mean Sonya? That's his girlfriend."

"The look he gave her after he kissed Penny," I said. "It was like he did it just to taunt her."

"They're at it like cats and dogs this trip." Sonny lowered his voice. "If you ask me, I think their relationship is petering out. I wouldn't be surprised if she left the ship at the end of this cruise."

"Poor thing," Penny said in the same way she might talk about a lame kitten.

"Poor thing my eye," I said. "She's got a lot of nerve getting angry at you. She must know he's an idiot, and yet she's still with him. I have no pity."

Kemper had managed to get his long arm wrapped around Penny's shoulders, and since she didn't shake him off, it looked as if all was forgiven.

"How about that walk?" Robby suggested.

"On deck? With Molesting Marv?" I snorted. "I don't think so."

Kemper agreed for them both.

"Besides," I said. "I'm beat from all the travel today."

Our little gathering broke up. Penny said she would join me soon, so I headed for the fifth floor. After pressing the button for the elevator in the lobby, I heard voices coming from the stairwell to the left. They were hissing in the way people do when they want to keep a public argument private, which as everybody knows only makes it more conspicuous. I leaned sideways and peered over the railing like a nosy parker, but when I saw who it was, I jerked back, hoping the couple hadn't spotted me.

Sharon Bradley had her finger in Marvelous Marv's face, and from her narrowed eyes and pinched lips, it looked as if it would only take one smart remark from Marv before she'd punch him. Then again, I was talking about Sharon. She'd prefer an open-palm slap to a punch. More dignified.

"If you ever open your mouth about it to her, I will kill you."

Sharon didn't like Marv, not that I could blame her. I remembered the way his thick lips had curled into a condescending smirk after he kissed Penny. I would have liked a shot at him myself. At the sound of footsteps moving my way up the stairs, I skittered to the stairway on the other side of the elevators and ran up the two flights to my floor.

When I flipped on the light to my room, I saw I wasn't alone. The stewards had made a monkey out of my towel. Literally. It hung from the curtain rod and grinned at me.

I decided to leave it there for the night, or at least until Penny got a look at it. But Penny didn't come.

I dressed for bed, chose the one closest to the veranda, turned the lights off and stretched out under the covers, eyes wide open. A bright moon shone through the sliding glass doors, and I could see the outline of my monkey-towel. I didn't want to close the curtains because that would make the room pitch dark, I had visions of people trapped on the sinking *Titanic* because they couldn't see to get out of their room. Besides, Penny might trip over something when she returned. If she returned.

The monkey gently swayed with the movement of the ship, a reminder that a dark, icy-cold grave surrounded me. And things that fed at night. Would I be able to hear the screams of their victims, like I occasionally heard the excited yipping of the coyotes hunting back in Arizona? I didn't want to know what a baby seal sounded like when it screamed. I put my second pillow over my head and pressed it into my ears. Not a practical move, since I couldn't hold that position all night, so I concentrated on getting excited about the next day.

We'd be at sea until the day after tomorrow. That gave me plenty of time to explore the ship. And eat. That Lido Deck was supposed to be open all night. It was open now.

I threw back my covers and slipped on a pair of sweatpants, a t-shirt and my tennis shoes, and then I crept out my door.

"Where are you headed?"

I spun around. Robby leaned against his door frame, grinning at me.

"I didn't have dessert," I started to explain, but he hooked his arm through mine and said:

"We must keep up our energy."

"Absolutely." I gave him a matching grin. How nice to be with a man who didn't look at night feeding as a warning sign.

We weren't the only ones with the idea of a midnight snack, although the Lido Deck was less crowded than my first visit. I had a hankering for something savory, but I was supposed to be making up for my lost dessert. I settled on a brownie. They didn't allow people to serve themselves until the ship had been at sea for a few days, a practice to keep sick passengers from spreading illnesses they brought on board with them. I would have added another brownie but was shamed by the grinning employee into keeping my request to one. And a gigantic chocolate chip cookie. And a glass of milk.

We sat at a table for two and Robby told me about his

life since I'd last seen him. Satisfactory job, meaning it paid well but kind of bored him. No one special lurking about in the wings. No pets.

"Are you happy being an Illinoisan? Or is it an Illinoisian?" I wrinkled my brow in concentration. "Illinoisite? Let's see. You're a Floridian. An Iowan. A—what are we? Wisconsonians? Sounds regal."

"You dork. We're Wisconsinites. And people from Illinois are Illinoyers or Illinoisans, silent s." He tossed a piece of cookie at me and shouted out a laugh when I caught it in my teeth and swallowed it down.

"I've been spending too much time with my dog, Chauncey."

"So. No great romance?"

That was tricky territory. Penny had always believed I had a *gift* for reading animal minds because she's sweet and gullible. My clients had assumed—wrongly—that a pet psychic must have psychic abilities, but I merely cold-read the actions, expressions and word choices of the pet owners and used animal behavior know-how to come up with solutions. Then a Golden Retriever witnessed a murder and broke through my mental barrier in a cry for help. His move let in all the other furballs, and here I was, an actual pet psychic.

That oddity had become a major stumbling block in my latest attempt at a relationship. Apparently, Detective Martin Bowers of the Wolf Creek Police found it troublesome when I, while holding his hand, transmitted a message from a pet so he *heard* it, too. We parted friends. Actually, we just parted.

"Nothing on the horizon," I said. And there wouldn't be if I didn't stop thinking about Martin Bowers.

Robby was single and good-looking. Maybe, if I could

get over the fact that he was Penny's brother, a little ship-board romance might help make Bowers a memory. I looked up at him through my lashes. Tall. Blond. Dimpled cheeks. Nice firm mouth. I thought about kissing that mouth, and I shuddered from a weird, creepy feeling. The fact that he was Penny's brother might be too large a hurdle for me.

"Are you getting cold?" he asked. "It is late." We stood and gathered our remains up and left them on a tray, and then we took the elevator down to our floor.

"Time to snuggle under the covers." He grinned. "My guess is you wear footie pajamas."

"If only they made them in my size," I said.

"With the flap in back?" Robby let loose a laugh as we stepped off the elevator and entered our hallway, but I grabbed his arm to quiet him.

"Isn't that Sharon?"

Sharon and Gina wound up in the stateroom second from the end of the long hall, so it was difficult to tell which door the woman exited. It *looked* like Sharon. As soon as the woman saw us, she ducked back inside her room.

"Where is she going this late at night?" I said.

"Maybe she's hungry, too." Robby squinted. "If it was her."

When we reached my door, I felt my pockets and swore. "I forgot my key."

I knocked softly. "Penny?" Then harder, but still no answer.

Robby looked up and down the empty corridor. "I have a couch...."

I couldn't see an alternative, so I thanked him and followed him to his room. "I feel so stupid."

"Don't worry about it."

Just as he swung open his door, a head popped out of

44

the next room down. Even under a mass of curlers, Mrs. Doud looked like a woman in charge. "What's going on?"

I felt my face flush. I had been about to enter her son's room in the middle of the night, and I could imagine the impression she might get.

"Frances left her key in her room and Penny's still out dancing with Kemper."

Mrs. Doud pushed in front of Robby, flipped on the light and headed for the phone. She dialed a number and requested a steward come and open my door for me. When she received a satisfactory answer, she hung up.

"I didn't even think of calling someone at this hour," I said.

"That's the great thing about being on a cruise. You can find help, even in the middle of the night." She crossed her arms, for warmth I assume, since she was in her nightgown and Robby had the air conditioning set on high.

"Were you out dancing with the rest of them?"

I gave her a sheepish grin. "Eating. It's like my biggest fantasy—24-hour food I don't have to make."

"It is a dream, isn't it? The nightmare begins when you get home and step on the scale."

We had left the door open, and a steward looked in and asked if he could be of assistance. He escorted me to the door, opened it, and waited until I had found my own key card before he left.

I thanked all three of them and locked my door behind me.

This time, after I settled in, I didn't mind the monkey so much. In fact, it was like having one of my pets sleeping with me. I christened him Bert and closed my eyes. But then I heard a creak. Then another. They weren't loud creaks, but they were reminders that I, that my *entire room*, was moving. I began to imagine I could feel rocking as the ship plunged through black waves of death. The people aboard the Titanic felt safe and look at what happened to them. And it happened in the middle of the night. I didn't want to die a Popsicle.

"Stop it. You're working yourself into a panic."

I took some deep breaths and closed my eyes and tried to imagine that the creaks represented the soft rocking of a hammock. To and fro. To and fro. To and WHACK!

I shot up to sitting, certain I hadn't imagined that loud thump, but what was it? Part of the ship's motor, broken off and floating in the waters behind us? I went to the window, pulled the door open, and ignoring the freezing blast of air washing over me, listened.

No panicked cries from crew members. No shrieks from hysterical passengers. I looked up. No emergency flares lighting up the sky. I slid the door closed and hurried to get back under the warm covers.

The exposure to cold air did me good. Within ten minutes, I drifted off. I didn't even hear Penny return for the night.

EIGHT

At seven a.m. the next morning, I cracked open one eye and moaned. Penny, already up and dressed in jeans and a violet sweater, said, "Good morning, sleepyhead."

I rolled over and buried my face in the pillow, mumbling, "When did you get back?"

She giggled. "Kemper and I danced until they threw us out. Then we went for a walk and talked about the wedding."

I turned onto my back with one arm over my eyes. "You're going to be sick of Kemper before you're even married."

"Not a chance." She stuffed her room key in her pocket. "I'm meeting him for breakfast. Want me to wait?"

I groaned something about needing time to make myself beautiful, and she was out the door. Now that I'd been forced awake, my only thought was to make it to the Lido Deck for breakfast. I whipped off the covers and said good morning to Bert the Chimp. Then I went to the door to see if the promised free morning newspaper waited for me in the hallway. It did, but it wasn't alone. Felix, the calico from last night's show, sat in the center of my paper. I crouched down and picked him up with a grunt. He must have weighed fifteen pounds.

"What are you doing out here?"

His fur was soft, and as I stroked his head, he purred with loud rumbles that made his entire body vibrate. His warm, snuggly body reminded me how much I missed Emily, and I buried my face in his scruff. Mistake.

In my head, I heard a man's voice cry out. *Why? Tell me why? Stop it. Please. For the love of God, don't do it!*

I jerked my arms forward in a defensive move and dropped the cat. After an offended glare, he trotted down the hallway without looking back.

I returned to my room and closed the door behind me, paper forgotten. I didn't see the room around me as I walked to the bed and dropped onto the edge. I replayed the words out loud. *Why? Stop it. Don't do it.* There had to be a scenario that would render the words benign, something that would let me forget them. When I landed on an explanation, I laughed with relief.

Some people are afraid of cats, which is not as silly as it sounds. Cats enjoy terrifying human beings if the whim hits them. Maybe Felix had run into one such person.

In my animal behavior research, I read an article that explained how people who don't like cats give off a chemical odor that attracts them. Felix simply made a beeline toward the sweet smell of fear and possibly caused a panic, and though the man's words seemed extreme to me, I didn't share his fear. That had to be the explanation, though I couldn't figure out why the calico was wandering free in the first place. After I dressed, I would search the hallways and return him to management.

I pulled back the curtains and looked out at a blue sky

and sunshine. Last night's worries seemed stupid, and I slid open the door and stepped out onto the veranda, placed my hands on the balcony, and took a deep breath of fresh air.

The shore, with the absence of houses, looked wild this morning, but in a friendly bunny-and-deer kind of way. I shook my head at my negative, nervous attitude of last night and promised myself I would embrace the day and do whatever Penny wanted. Even shop.

From the corner of my eye, I caught sight of something gold, and I leaned over my railing and looked down. Marvelous Marv stared up at me from the top of the lifeboat under my balcony, only he didn't look marvelous, not with his head twisted that way. And was that bone sticking out of his collar?

Screams filled the air, and it wasn't until I heard my name being called from the other side of the partition that I realized the screams were coming from me. Robby leaned over the rail, his hair mussed and wearing his pajama.

"Frances! What the heck is the matter?"

I closed my eyes and pointed.

"Lord have mercy!"

I opened my eyes and leaned over the railing. Judy Doud, the next balcony down from Robby's, stared at Marv's corpse for about two seconds, and then her practical nature took over.

"Frances," she shouted, "you throw on some clothes and open your door. I'll call the ship's doctor." She disappeared, but her head popped back out. "And don't let Penny see."

"She's already gone." I couldn't work up a shout, so Robby relayed the message for me.

Like an automaton, I returned to my room and pulled on my sweats in time to open the door for the ship's doctor and three medical assistants. They jogged out onto the balcony, and I was about to warn them their weight might send them crashing down on top of Marv when Robby entered the room and folded me in a hug.

I hadn't realized how big a shock I had received until I started sobbing. He rubbed my back and led me to his room. Penny and Kemper met us at the door. Her face looked like thunder. Her pert nose twitched, and she had a line between her bunched-up eyebrows.

"Frances! Not again!"

"Penny," Robby soothed. "Frances didn't have anything to do with this. Why blame her?"

Right away, my friend's expression smoothed back into one of concern, and she followed me into his room. "I'm sorry. It's just, first we find out there are animals on board, then a death happens. It's becoming a habit with you."

"Penny!"

I hadn't heard Robby's tone that sharp since we'd filled his rain boots with cow poop.

"I know. I'm sorry. I guess I've got the bridal jitters, wanting everything to be perfect."

Kemper turned to the practical. "Is everybody okay?"

"Everybody but Marvelous Marv," Penny mumbled.

"Well, since he wasn't in the wedding party, no worries." It sounded callous, but it did the trick. Penny smiled at him as if he'd just discovered calorie-free chocolate.

"You're right, honey. It's tragic, but...." She let it hang there because anything she said would sound unbelievably self-centered.

It always thrilled Penny to hear about my psychic experiences. That's why it had been so easy to fool her into thinking I had abilities before I discovered my real *gift*, as she naively called it. Gift. An assault by images from animals that could take place at any moment didn't make a good present. However, the bride was on the unstable side right now, so I decided to keep what Felix had told me strictly private.

The initial shock had passed, and my crying had subsided to sniffles. While they discussed the unscheduled surprise offered by Finlander cruise line, I separated from the herd and inched my way over to the balcony.

"Where are you going?" Penny demanded.

"I need fresh air," I said in a weak voice. "I promise not to look down."

I could hear movement from my room next door as the emergency personnel did their jobs, and I risked a peek downward. From Robby's room, the lifeboat hung to my right, but I still had a good view of the last of Marvelous Marv as a crew member zipped a body bag closed.

I tried not to think why a liner geared toward vacation fun would carry body bags, but the advanced ages of the guests should have made it clear. Instead, I focused on the position of the lifeboat. Most of the surface stuck out beyond my balcony. By leaning out and twisting my head to look up, the floors above me angled outward on the decline. It was likely Marv had hit one of the other balconies on his way down, which bounced him far enough away from the side of the ship to make a landing on the lifeboat. I shuddered. If his body had stayed closer to the wall as he fell, I might have found him *on* my balcony instead of under it.

I heard my name and returned to the room. Mrs. Doud took me by the arm and led me back to the door of my room.

"Now, Frances. They're all finished. You just straighten your spine and march back in there. After all, the body wasn't in your room. It's just something you saw *from* your room. I can't tell you the number of horrors I've witnessed in the barn. Why, once, I saw a vet with his arm all the way up a cow's patootie, but I just had to close my eyes and forget about it in time to make breakfast. Oh, shoot. Now I've got that image in my noggin again. If it makes you feel better, you can keep the curtains closed and avoid your veranda."

Her brief speech had the intended effect. "Yes, Ma'am," I said, and I stepped inside and closed the door behind me. I knew the cruise line stressed water conservation, but I felt I had earned a long, hot shower. By the time I put on my brown knit pants and baggy plaid sweater, I felt, well, like someone who hadn't just seen a dead body outside her window.

Our party met as agreed on the Lido Deck, though my enthusiasm for food had waned. The entire clan sat around a table, except Tommy, and with the way they looked up when I approached, the topic of conversation had been me. The Mohrs stared blatantly and with interest, while Kemper avoided eye contact. There was a tinge of resentment in the firm set of his mouth, which matched Sharon Bradley's expression. They both thought I was to blame for finding the body.

Penny grinned; Gina smirked. Mrs. Doud tilted her head and wrinkled her brows with pity, and when her husband greeted me, it was with the uncomfortable bluster of a host who had encountered a sticky etiquette problem.

Mr. Doud pulled out a chair for me, and I took my place. I noticed they all had the remnants of breakfast in front of them. I decided I was hungry after all, but Mrs. Doud interrupted my thoughts of pancakes and sausage.

"Let's shoo the elephant out of the room. I talked to the head of security. He thinks Mr. Marv tripped over one of his cats while taking them for their evening stroll on the Observation Deck."

I gaped. "He was walking his cats?"

Penny giggled, and then realizing what an inappropriate response this was to a man's death, pressed her lips together. "I know. When he said he was going for a walk with his crew, I thought he meant his partner, Bitsy."

Mrs. Doud silenced her with a disapproving look. "It's a tragedy." She crossed herself. "I know it sounds cruel, but it's not as if we knew the man. I want everyone to have a good time and forget all about it."

"You're right, Aunt Judy," Gina said. "This week is all about cousin Penny." Then she turned her ginger-brown eyes on me and said, "You're used to this kind of thing. Murder, I mean."

"Used to it?" I repeated. Everyone was looking at me, and my face grew warm. "That's a horrible thing to say."

"You know what I mean," she said, blinking her long, dark lashes. "You've been involved with, how many dead bodies? Penny told us, but I lost count."

I gave the blushing bride-to-be an unfriendly glare, and she returned it with a sheepish grin.

"It's that career of yours," Gina continued. "Pretending to channel the thoughts of animals, which is fraud. I'm sure it puts you in contact with some shady characters."

"Frances doesn't pretend," Penny said. Kemper got that dazed and frightened look, and Robby turned an interested gaze on me.

"It's okay, Penny. Seriously." I wanted to tell her to shut up before she said something that would embarrass me more, as if that were possible.

"Everybody's got to make a living," Thomas Mohr announced. "No shame there. I like good entertainment."

He turned to his wife. "Remember that swami guy who could guess everyone's birthday? He was good."

"I'm willing to forget anything that doesn't interfere with the wedding," his wife said, and that brought Frank Doud back to the day's agenda.

"Everyone can just relax today. If you check the itinerary, there are hamburgers out by the pool at 11:30, bingo at noon, and they're offering a lecture on Alaskan wildlife at 2:00. Dinner is back at the same table as last night at 5:30 sharp."

"I hope everyone brought their swimsuits," Judy said, "because it's going to be warm today. The captain told me we're going to be incredibly lucky with the weather."

When we finished, I noticed how everyone paired off: Judy and Frank Doud, Thomas and Christina Mohr, Kemper and Penny, and even Robby and Gina. That left me with Sharon, who was looking even more pinch-lipped than usual. I could have asked her if there was a ship-board activity that might cause her to crack a smile, like throwing rocks at seagulls, but I passed on the opportunity and went to get breakfast instead.

This was the second full day on the water, so the staff still served the food. By tomorrow morning, the buffets would be self-serve and I wouldn't have to worry about a conscientious employee keeping track of how many pancakes I consumed.

I didn't find any pancakes, but my tastes are simple. I got bacon, ham, toast, juice and a side of potatoes. I hadn't eaten an egg in a restaurant since I was a child and the waitress had served my scrambled eggs runny.

Once I had a full tummy, I realized I hadn't had any coffee. I didn't need it, since my nerves were already strained, but it would be a shame to waste the gift card

Penny's father had given me. Besides, I could always order decaf, so I made my way to the Lookout and the coffee bar.

When the elevator doors opened, there were already two passengers inside. In fact, it was headed in the opposite direction, down. A man dressed in an official white uniform stood next to Bitsy, who sobbed on his shoulder. If I had any claim on good manners, I would have taken another elevator, but I didn't. Their destination was the basement, so I pretended the bottom floor was my destination as well and hit the button to close the elevator doors.

"Oh, my gosh," I said.

She gave me a tiny nod. "I just can't believe it." Her face crumpled, and she started to sob again.

It seemed obvious to me she was maneuvering for some comfort from the man, whose name tag read Officer Robinson, Chief Security Officer. He wasn't cooperating. While she laid her forehead on his shoulder and rested her hand on his chest, he kept his own hands clasped behind his back and stared straight ahead.

"Yes, ma'am," he said. "It's difficult to believe. A tragedy."

I felt I should say something, so I squeezed her elbow— since her hand was busy clutching his shirtfront—and said, "I'm so sorry for your loss."

That perked her up. She lifted her head and dabbed her eyes. "Thank you."

I gasped.

Her eyebrows came together, and she frantically dabbed at her nose. "Do I have something on my face?"

Poor little Felix was still on the loose. I couldn't believe even murder could make me forget about a kitty's safety. "One of your cats was running loose this morning. Felix."

Bitsy gave a strangled gurgle. She clutched the front of my shirt in her hands. "Where? Where is he?"

"In the hallway on the fifth floor last I saw him, but that was over two hours ago."

She made a dive for the elevator buttons and hit number five, but Officer Robinson spoke up. "Ma'am, I need you to come to my office and go over a few things with the entertainment manager." To me, he said, "We're taking care of the cats. Thank you for reporting it."

The skin on Bitsy's face had the appearance of cream. Not the creamy complexion you hear about in romance novels, but over-processed cream. Without color.

With Marvelous Marv's violent death, it was obvious the voice I had heard in my head, the voice Felix had transmitted to me before I dropped him, belonged to Marv. I thought about his last words, which included *why* and *don't do it*. Not things you would mutter to yourself unless you were crazy. However, now wasn't the time to ask Bitsy if she'd been up on deck with him. It wasn't that I was sensitive to Bitsy's feelings. Officer Robinson might not like it, especially if she took it the wrong way.

The doors slid open and the security officer escorted Bitsy out. I hit the button for the 10th floor.

Once I had my piping hot latte in my hands, I walked through the stuffed, comfy chairs and couches and ran my finger along the selection of books packed into recessed bookshelves. Except for the back wall with the bookcases, the rest of this round room gave the occupants an almost panoramic view of the ocean.

Next to the coffee bar, desks faced each other with a divider running down the middle for privacy, and each desk came equipped with a laptop computer. I recognized the blond head opposite me and worked my way around to the other side of the tables.

"Shopping for something blue for your wedding?" I joked. Penny jumped.

"I'm emailing pictures to my friends."

"I'm the only friend that counts, and I'm here." I sat down next to her and she closed the program and stood.

"All done. I'm going to try on my dress again. One of the buttons is loose, and my mom's going to sew it on tight." She snickered. "I wouldn't want a wardrobe malfunction at my wedding."

"Maybe when you're done we can hang out. You know, just us two."

"I have to call the Prickly Pear first. I'm a little nervous leaving Monica in charge. Not that I don't trust her. It's just a lot of work, and I want to answer any questions she might have. After that we can—wait a minute. Kemper wanted me to help him pick out gifts for Tommy and Robby. Like a man, he left it to the last minute. But after that?"

I hid my disappointment with a big smile. "Sure. Great. Maybe we can catch an afternoon movie?"

She gave me a quick hug and ran off to meet her mother, and I decided to check out the ship. There had to be something for single people to do, though now that I thought about it, who went on a cruise by themselves?

To my left as I stood by the elevators, women entered and exited the Seaweed Spa. The women going in carried their shoulders tight and had pinched faces. The women exiting oozed out, their facial muscles so relaxed they appeared to be in comas. A quick peek at the price board made my wallet cry.

I took the elevator down to the Lido Deck. Who knew if I'd suddenly need a snack? Instead of turning toward the dining area, I wandered the hall in the opposite direction until it opened into an outdoor pool. There was a bar surrounded by tables with bright orange umbrellas. The Oyster Shack, a small grill and counter under a thatched roof, was responsible for today's free hamburgers. A burger sounded good, but the guests had crowded in, drawn there like zombies after a live body. Too many people.

"Where's your swimming suit?"

Robby leveraged himself up onto the side of the pool with muscular arms and swung his leg, also muscular, over the edge. He jumped to standing, picked up a towel for a quick rubdown, and came over. He had on fitted blue-and-white swim trunks, the type all men should wear to spare us from cheek-exposing Speedos.

"I'm like my cat," I said. "I hate getting wet."

He grinned. "That's right. It used to be fun to throw you in the lake and listen to your screams."

I nodded. "You were a brat."

He swept me up in his arms and took two steps toward the water. A clear, self-assured voice interrupted my shriek.

"Who was a brat?"

I rolled my eyes at the sound of Gina's voice, and when she swung her long legs over the edge of a deck chair and stood, Robby set me down. I said, "Give me a break," under my breath. Her entire bikini, in soft peach, used less fabric than my underwear, and the only bulges she had were in the right places.

She hooked an arm through Robby's, making certain to rub her arm against his tight abs. Like I said. Miss Touchy-Feely. "This sweet thing, a brat? He was always nice to me."

He grinned at her. "That's because you were taller than me until I had my growth spurt."

She threw back her head and whinnied, but then she

put a hand over her mouth in a demur gesture and said, "I suppose I should be more respectful after a death." She shivered her clothes-hanger square shoulders. "Awful, wasn't it?"

"I know. I was the one who found the body." Once the words were out, I felt a small amount of shame at getting proprietary over a dead body.

"It's not as if we knew the guy," Robby said.

"I wonder if there's anyone on board who cares that Marv is dead?" I said.

"His girlfriend," Robby said.

"And Bitsy," Gina chimed in.

"And his cats," I added. They both stared. "Animals get very attached to us. Haven't you ever heard of separation anxiety?"

"I'm going back in the water," Gina said, stretching one leg in front of her and rubbing it. "I'm getting goosebumps in the cold air. Are you coming?" She sauntered to the end of the pool and executed a perfect dive.

I shook my head and leaned it toward Robby. "The sign clearly says *no diving*."

Robby looked after her with admiration, so I told him to go play with the mermaid and I would amuse myself elsewhere. He took me up on my offer with disappointing speed.

That was okay because my mind was occupied with how I could get some private time with those cats. If they were with him when he died, a brief conversation might give me clarity about Marvelous Marv's last moments.

NINE

I did hit the restaurant portion of the Lido Deck. I took a corned beef sandwich on rye bread, fresh-baked brownies—two of them, but they were small—and a soda. Ordering a diet soda would have been hypocritical, plus I hated the taste of artificial sweeteners. I decided to eat in my room.

As the elevator doors opened to let me off on the fifth floor, I followed a steward carrying a tray with a silver-domed plate. He stopped at the first inside cabin and knocked, and when the door swung open, I recognized the black-haired witchy woman who answered. It was Marvelous Marv's girlfriend, Sonya. Wouldn't Marv's girlfriend inherit the kitties?

As she stepped back into her room with the tray, she caught my eye, and I veered over before she closed the door.

"I'm so sorry about your loss." It wasn't original, but it was appropriate since she was his girlfriend.

She narrowed her eyes at me. "Do I know you?"

Her voice had a throaty quality tempered by an accent. It sounded Transylvanian to my ears. I adjusted my plate and held out my hand. "Frankie Chandler."

She ignored my hand. "So, I do not know you."

"I'm not sure what's going to happen to the cats now Marv is dead, but if you need any help taking care of them, I'm good with animals."

She drew in a sharp breath as if I had suggested she was best friends with Bela Lugosi, and then she pressed her lips together and narrowed her eyes. "The felines are not to be my problem."

"But—" That's as far as I got before I was talking to the door. Marv's body had been found this morning, and yet her dry eyes reflected no sorrow. Maybe she was tough, but more likely, she didn't care. As soon as the thought formed in my head, I knew it wasn't fair. I'd known plenty of women whose boyfriends had been toads, but they still would have been upset had those boyfriends fallen from the top deck of a cruise ship.

I balanced my plate while I unlocked my door, and once inside, I sat on the couch and munched on my lunch, all the time wondering about the kitties. It was stupid of me to mention the cats to Sonya. They were probably with Bitsy, unless they kept them in cages with the cargo when they weren't onstage. That thought depressed me, so I cleaned my plate.

Once I had gathered the crumbs from the couch, I got up, arranged my napkin on the plate and set it on the end table, washed my hands, and then dried them on the towel in my bathroom. Then I straightened the towel. All of that took about three minutes. I had the rest of the afternoon to kill on my own, and boredom had already set in.

Sitting on the edge of my bed with the remote, I flicked on the television and scanned enough channels to remind me why I didn't watch television. I tossed the remote on the bed, stood, stretched, and headed for the veranda.

Outside, the cool air smelled pure, which meant no smell at all. No automobile smog. No stinky pet odor from a certain dog of mine who needed a bath. No barnyard fragrance like on Penny's family farm in Wisconsin. Just clean. How did the dryer sheet manufacturers recreate that smell?

I leaned on my elbows against the railing and inhaled a deep breath, but when my gaze wandered down to Marvelous Marv's last resting place, I imagined I could see a bloodstain on the lifeboat's orange tarp. Queasy, I sat down on the deck chair until the feeling passed. I would have to face Penny's wrath if both the best man and maid of honor were too ill to make the wedding.

In my lowered position, I caught sight of something gold crumpled on the floor. I leaned over and stretched out my arm until I could reach the object with my fingers. I held up a piece of gold fringe and thought back to the costumes Marv and Bitsy wore during the performance. It must have come loose when he fell. One last memory of Marv. I shoved it into my pants pocket.

The partitions on either side of me and the glass barrier under the railing blocked the wind. My skin warmed in the midday sun, and I put my feet up, leaned back and closed my eyes.

Faces passed through my mind, and they all had the potential to do Marv harm. I wasn't thinking murder. After all, everybody said it was an accident, but then again, everybody hadn't heard Marv's final words. *Why? For God's sake, don't!* I had difficulty believing those were the last words of someone talking to himself. So, if it had been an accident, there had been an unhelpful witness around. Although allowing a man to fall to his death without offering a hand might not get one arrested for murder, it would at least get you un-friended online.

The first face I brought up belonged to the victim; it was Marv with a leer getting ready to kiss Penny. Could Sonya have been jealous enough to refuse to help her boyfriend in his moment of need? She seemed a cold fish to me. Then again, with Marv alive, she'd have all the free cruises she could stand. Or did she? Did Sonya lay down money for the chance to hang out with Marv when he wasn't on stage? Personally, I'd need better motivation, but if she paid her fare like all the other passengers, she would expect to enjoy the trip. If Marv had made life on board unbearable...well, these cruises cost an awful lot.

What about Bitsy? Maybe their partnership wasn't as friendly as it appeared onstage. Or maybe she had designs on Marv. No. Then Sonya would have been the victim.

One of the crew members might have resented Marv. Was he such a bad tipper that his steward didn't feel the need to offer the extra service of lending him a hand? Literally? I frowned. Did the cash no-tipping policy apply to the entertainment, or was that rule just for the passengers who shelled out big money for the privilege of 24-hour room service?

After getting to know Sonny Street during the *Blue-Ribbon Babes* murder fiasco, I couldn't seriously consider him in the role of malevolent spectator. Still, I couldn't dismiss professional rivalry as a motive for wanting the cat trainer out of the way. What if Sonny wanted Marv's spot in the lineup?

Who else could have wanted Marv dead? A disgruntled manager? His manager wasn't on the ship to my knowledge. Was Marv blackmailing someone? From what I had seen of him, Marv was a toad capable of blackmail. But who? What if there was someone who coveted Sonya? I imagined her witch-like face and her Dracula accent and dismissed that idea.

I'd run out of plausible reasons for someone to stand by and watch Marv die, yet he was dead. Actually, there was one more face. Sharon Bradley. What had she wanted Marv to keep quiet about? And where had she been headed when she stepped into the hallway last night? I could have sworn it was her, and she returned to her room only after spotting me and Robby, which meant she didn't want anyone to see her.

Wouldn't it be just my luck to discover the culprit who watched Marv die and ruin Penny's wedding all in one swoop? Still, it wasn't as if Sharon were the groom or the mother of the bride. It wouldn't impair the ceremony if security hauled her off in handcuffs. Would they arrest you for not helping someone to not die?

Five furry faces wiggled their way into my thoughts. Those poor kitties. What would happen to them now? Would they continue as Bitsy's unloved performing slaves? Would they be adopted out to families who would let them spend their retirement eating tuna treats and getting belly rubs?

Fish treats and belly rubs reminded me of my own pets, Emily the black-and-white cat and Chauncy, the spoiled rotten pooch. Seamus from Canine Camp had agreed to watch them, and right now, Chauncey was playing his furry fanny off with the other dogs at Canine Camp. Emily was most likely ignoring them all. At least I didn't have to worry about them missing me. They loved Seamus—at least Chauncey did. Emily couldn't give a paw who she was with as long as they fed her on time.

My little fur babies. So sweet. Emily probably lazing

out in the warm sun right now, just like me. I stretched and shifted in the chair. So lucky to have me as their pet parent. Unlike those poor performing cats. Sad cats. Sphinx. Jinx. Sphinx and Jinx. What was the other cat's name?

I was still trying to remember when I drifted off to sleep.

TEN

The celebratory mood of yesterday's dinner had given way to subdued murmurs and gentle laughter. Even Gina reined it in when she responded to one of Robby's jokes with a giggle instead of a full whinny. I didn't have a lot to say because my mind kept drifting back to Marv's last words.

I may not have been talking, but Thomas Mohr kept my ears busy. Kemper's father told me everything I ever needed to know about kitchen cabinets. His company installed everything from etched glass doors and molded wood to simpler styles even I could afford. My only concern with my kitchen cabinets was that there was food available behind those doors, but I made an effort to nod as he talked and ask intelligent questions in the pauses.

I'm not sure when good taste gave way to gossip, but Marvelous Marv's nosedive to death wormed its way into the conversation.

"Done in by his cats," Robby said. "I wonder if his last thought was to send them all to the pound?"

"More likely he wondered if he had left anything unfinished," Kemper said, completely serious. When everyone stared at him, he shrugged his shoulders. "You know. Bills not paid. That kind of thing."

"That would be your last thought," Thomas said, though with affection. "You always craved order, even as a child. I remember you used to box up your toys by size and color, and if anyone threw them willy-nilly into the toy chest, look out."

"I don't believe it," Penny said.

"Trust me, dear," Christina said. "Don't mess up Kemp's toys."

Penny shook her head to clear away the image of her husband-to-be playing with building blocks. "That's not it. I meant I don't believe Marv was taking his cats for a walk. Who walks their cats?"

Judy Doud took a sip of her merlot. "I've seen people walking them on little halters in the summer. Not often, but I've seen it."

"I would think the night air would be too cold for them," Penny insisted. "And damp. Don't cats like to be warm and dry?"

Robby laughed. "Maybe he was taking them out for a drag."

Gina, sitting to his left, swatted his arm and giggled. "Maybe we should all go up on the Observation Deck and look at the scene of the accident."

"That does *not* sound like a nice thing to do," Sharon said, censuring her daughter's suggestion.

Gina twitched her shoulders in annoyance. "Maybe an interest in violent death is in my blood," she said. The effect of her words on Sharon surprised me. The Ice Queen paled and pinched her mouth into a thin line.

Her daughter repented right away and reached across the table to take hold of her hand. "I'm just joking, Mom."

"It does seem odd," I said. My words were meant for me alone, but they'd come out loud enough that everyone at the table turned to me with expectant looks on their faces. Embarrassed, I scrunched my shoulders up. "Doesn't it? I mean, how would a person wind up in a position to fall over a railing while walking cats?"

"Frances," Judy Doud said in crisp tones that brooked no argument. "I explained how he tripped over one of the kitties. That's what the security officer said, and he should know."

But the security officer wasn't there, was he? I kept that thought to myself because I valued my life too much to have a public disagreement with Judy Doud.

"What are you suggesting?"

Leave it to Gina to put me on the spot. My cheeks felt warm, and I slipped a glance at Judy, but she was digging through her purse and not paying attention.

"Maybe he had help," I said, trying not to sound over-confident.

That brought a response from the table. Fortunately, it was guffaws and giggles.

"You have such a vivid imagination," Penny said. Her laugh was missing joy and good cheer. She knew me well enough to take my suggestion seriously, but keeping Kemper calm was her priority. "That's why we love you."

Kemper didn't look as if he even liked me right now. Penny crumpled her napkin, dropped it on her plate and said, "I'm not letting anything spoil this cruise." She looked up at Kemper. "How about taking your fiancée for a spin around the dance floor?"

Kemper put an arm around the back of her chair and covered a yawn with his free hand. "Don't you need to save some energy for the reception? Why don't we take in a movie instead?"

Everyone jumped on that idea. I had to stop by the ladies' room first, so I told them I'd join them in the Pearl Theater. That was the plan, but by the time I arrived, an employee had placed a red velvet rope across the entrance.

"My friends are waiting for me," I said.

"Sorry. There's no saving seats, and the maximum number of people have entered the room. Safety regulations."

I wandered away, through the shopping arcade, where the prices hovered way out of my bank account's reach. At the Hardcastle collection, I paused for another look at the jewelry on display and tried to feel the pull precious gems were supposed to have on the gentler sex. In the few minutes I stood there, several passengers bought tickets for the auction.

Moving on, I eventually settled on a stool at the Seaside Bar. Since all purchases went on the room, and I knew that trying to pay for my expenses would have me in a fight to the death with Judy and Frank Doud, I ordered a club soda, the cheapest beverage they had. I wasn't sure if the drink card was intended only for coffee. I handed it to the bartender, and to my relief, the machine accepted it.

As I sipped my soda, I studied my fellow passengers. They all looked so happy. There were couples dressed up as for a date in their best outfits, holding hands and glancing into each other's eyes when the opportunity arose. There were families laughing it up and chatting. Everyone seemed to have someone, which emphasized how alone I was.

Penny's family considered me one of their own. Maybe it was their familiarity, such as the way I'd seen the outfit Judy wore to dinner tonight at the baptism I'd flown home for last year, that made me long for my own family in Wisconsin. Penny lived in Arizona, but she was going to be preoccupied with Kemper. That meant I was on my own. I didn't like crowds, but I did like company, or at least the opportunity to have company if I wanted it.

When Sonya took a seat at the end of the bar, my frame of mind moved me to get up and walk over. She was alone, too, at least for the rest of the cruise.

"How are you hanging in there?" I asked.

Her long nose twitched. "Where is it I am hanging?"

I slid onto the stool next to her. "I meant, how are you doing? It's been a rough day for you."

She narrowed her eyes at me. "Why are you asking?"

She had me there. Why did I care?

"I thought you might be lonely. Or in shock. Or sad."

Sonya ran her finger around the edge of her martini glass. "I am fine. It is polite of you to ask."

The woman was thawing toward me. I could see the ice melting as we spoke. I was trying to find a polite way to ask her if she could get me in to see the cats when she finished her thought.

"But I don't want to be your friend."

"I wouldn't dream of it," I said, sipping my drink to cover my embarrassment. Rejected by a Transylvanian witch. A new low for me.

"Are they going to send the kitties home now?"

She glowered at her glass. "The Bitsy woman will go on with the show."

"Seriously?"

"Contract." She spit the word out.

"Is she on stage tonight?"

"No. Young dancers will wiggle their bottoms to famous film music."

"That should give Bitsy time to work through the act under her direction."

"The show, it will be bad. She will fail." She curled the corners of her lips up in a satisfied smile.

On that cheery note, I finished my club soda, pushed the glass forward on the bar, and told her goodnight.

I could catch the replacement act tomorrow, but the thought of watching slim, beautiful, young people grinning and dancing their fannies off tonight had the appeal of a root canal. With nothing to do, I headed back to my room.

When I stepped onto the elevator, I paused before pushing five, and it was as if my finger had a little mind of its own. It pushed the button for the Observation Deck.

My first thought as I walked out of the elevator and onto the deserted deck was I needed a jacket. An icy breeze cut across the open area and chilled my bones, which is why strolling couples avoided this spot. Chattering teeth are not sexy.

I hugged myself as I walked along the deck past a large white dome with windows that loomed to my left. It reminded me of an atrium. Maybe the *Iso Kala* grew their own vegetables in case the ship got cut off from supplies during a storm.

When I reached the point where I thought Marv must have fallen, I looked out into the open water. I could *hear* the open water—the ship splashing through the waves—and I could feel the tiny droplets of spray as they hit my face and arms, and I could smell the brine, but I couldn't see diddly-squat. I couldn't even tell where the sky met the ocean.

Gathering my courage, I looked down. It was still early enough that lights still shone from the cabin windows below. Security lights illuminated the Lower Promenade,

Promenade and Upper Promenade Decks, as well as the lifeboats. I had enough light to see that Marv had great aim. Odds were one hundred to one that if I jumped over the railing with enough leverage to miss the jutting balconies below, I would miss the lifeboat under my window and splatter on the deck below. Had he been aiming for it? Had Marv, realizing his precarious position, swung himself toward the boat as he let go, hoping the tarp that covered the top would soften his landing? Mistake.

I ran my hand over the railing, searching for the spot where Marv's fingernails might have clawed away the polish before he went down, but the surface felt admirably smooth and hard.

This was the place where Marvelous Marv had breathed—or yelled—his last breath. I narrowed my eyes. If I was walking a bunch of cats on leashes, and I went over the railing, what would the cats do? When in fear, dogs run, but cats hide. I scanned my surroundings. There wasn't much to hide under up here except for the deck chairs. Of course, if I weighed nine pounds and stood about twelve inches off the ground, the space under those deck chairs would be cozy, but it was obvious after a quick survey that none of the felines were hiding now. The crew members must have collected the final strays.

The wind gusted, and I shivered. The dim floor-level spotlights designed to make walking safe left plenty of shadows, and after a day spent maneuvering the human traffic walking the hallways below, the lack of company made me nervous.

The doors on the Promenade floor opened, and I could make out strains of band music and laughter coming from the Jimmy Dean Lounge, which drove home how alone I was up here. What if Marv's fall hadn't been an accident?

What if the killer didn't have a personal vendetta against Marv but just enjoyed pushing people over the railing with the hopes of making another lifeboat bullseye? I headed back to the elevator, and the closer I got, the quicker my feet moved, until I jogged the last few yards.

When the elevator doors opened, the couple inside stopped giggling and paused before stepping out because the first thing they saw was me panting and jabbing the recall button. The man put his arm around the woman and pulled her close, and they both stretched their lips into fake smiles.

"The cold air is invigorating," I said as I pushed past them and pressed the button for the fifth floor. I shuddered and rubbed my hands together to make my point. The woman's forehead furrowed with worry, and the man grabbed her hand and pulled her outside to safety.

Back on the fifth floor, I dug through my purse for my key card. Just as I snatched it from the bottom of my bag, my head filled with a loud, static sound. I covered my ears with my hands, but the noise wasn't coming from the outside.

I was back on the Observation Deck, looking through the white bars that supported the railing. Marvelous Marv clung to the bottommost bar. I reached out with a trembling hand, desperate to help a man who only existed in my imagination. His eyes, aimed upward, were open wide in terror, and when he cried out his last words, I stopped breathing. My purse slipped from my fingers and the contents scattered on the rug. That broke the trance.

Panting and queasy, I knelt to gather my lipstick, wallet, and a few other items from the floor, searching the hallway as I did. There wasn't any sign of Felix. It took a few extra seconds to unlock my door because my hands were shaking, and when I got inside, I slammed the door and threw my purse on the bed. I jerked the sliding door open and stood on the balcony, gasping in the chilly night air until my lungs hurt. I worked up the courage to look down at the dim outline of the lifeboat below me. The lifeboat Marvelous Marv had landed on when he'd been murdered. Yes, I'd decided. I'd seen the fear in his eyes and heard the desperation in his voice. Only a monster would have remained unmoved. The person Marv had spoken to might not have pushed him, but to stand there and ignore his pleas was cold-blooded murder.

ELEVEN

"You're awfully quiet," Penny said.

It was our first site of civilization. Juneau, Alaska. We might have our own version of mountains in Wolf Creek, Arizona, but not the incredible green forest that covered the scenery. The city jutted out in a sprawl at the base of the mountains, almost as if the city had oozed out of the wilderness.

Penny, Robby and I stood at the guardrail as the ship maneuvered up to the dock, and then we watched the solemn procession as the crew removed the remains of Marvelous Marv on a gurney. They met with a medical examiner's van parked curbside, and the people from that department spent some time conversing with an officer from the ship.

A lone porter followed behind with a large traveling case that looked like something out of an old movie. He took this to a waiting station wagon. I assumed they were shipping Marv's stuff home, wherever home was. It would have been natural for Sonya to depart with her late boyfriend, but she wasn't part of the procession.

As they closed the back doors of the van and drove off, Robby offered a salute.

"It's nothing," I said in answer to Penny. "I just thought we might have a girly pajama party last night, but you got back after I was asleep. And today you've been busy." As soon as the words were out, I suffered a flash of guilt. I had slept in until almost noon, and it was now after one o'clock. Really, it was my fault we hadn't had any time together today.

"I'm sorry." She patted my back. "My mom wanted some alone time." She dropped her head to the side in an exaggerated show of exasperation. "You know how moms are. I'm the only daughter, and it was her one chance to pass on all the secrets of being a good wife."

I grinned. "Did she explain sex?"

"Watch it," Robby said. "My tender ears are burning."

Penny erupted in a fit of giggles. "She started to, and then she blushed. My mom, blushing!"

Robby snorted. "It dawned on her you and Kemper have already had sex."

She punched his arm. "We have not!"

Penny and I made eye contact, and a silent signal passed between us—one we hadn't used since we were kids and regularly ganged up on her older brother. Suddenly, she sprang onto his back and wrapped her legs around his middle and her arms around his neck, while I dove for the ground and untied his shoelaces. When he bent over to see what I was doing, Penny whooped and held tight. I sprang to my feet and put him in a headlock.

"Noogies!" I rubbed my knuckles on his head.

A steward walked by with raised eyebrows, and Robby turned and called out after him. "Help me. I'm being molested." The steward picked up his pace without looking back, and Penny and I broke out in shrieks of laughter.

Robby stood up and dropped his sister to her feet. She walked to me and gave me a hug. "Frances, I'm so glad you're here."

"Me too." I squeezed her tight.

With my head on Penny's shoulder, I was facing the Juneau port, so I was the first to see him. A man on the pier was joined by a steward who took his luggage and led him up the gangway. Even at this distance, his long, easy strides seemed familiar. My heart jumped into my throat, and I pushed Penny aside and leaned over the railing.

"It couldn't be."

Robby stood beside me and hung over the rail to get a better look. "You know him?"

I turned to Penny. "I could swear that's Bowers, but what would he be doing in Juneau, Alaska?"

She gaped. "It—it *does* look like him."

"Unless he has a twin, that's him."

Penny stepped back from the railing. "What a surprise!" But she sounded more worried than surprised.

"A surprise?"

"A coincidence."

"Uh-uh. Not a coincidence. There's no way Bowers suddenly got the urge to drop everything in Wolf Creek and join up with a cruise already underway."

"Does it matter how he got here? He's here to see you. Aren't you excited to see him?"

She moved to pass me, but I stepped in front of her. "How did Bowers know I was on this cruise?"

She twined her fingers together and cracked her knuckles. "I might have told him. You know, just talking about the wedding in general."

"You mean you emailed him from the ship right after the murder. That's why you were so quick to sign off your computer in the coffee bar when I sat down."

It was a free country. There wasn't a law against my best friend speaking to the man who dumped me before we'd formally gone out, but it still stung.

"Come on. Let's go meet him, and the two of you can talk about it for the rest of the trip."

"*You* meet him."

I stalked off to the one place that could offer me comfort. The Lido Deck. I wasn't feeling very sweet, so I skipped the ice cream bar and the cookie bar and headed straight for the sandwiches. Once I had a corned beef on rye and a bag of chips, I took a table in the corner, away from the chatting, happy tourists.

Detective Martin Bowers was here. Bowers! He, who with his black wavy hair and sharp deep-blue eyes resembled a model for a vacation poster—the before, not the after. The lines around his eyes from lack of sleep were usually visible, but they made him sexier. Why doesn't it work that way for women?

Ours was a strange history. We met on a murder investigation when I was a suspect, though not a strong one. I had just discovered my ability to communicate with animals via an image of a woman being murdered sent by Sandy the Golden Retriever. Not a good way to learn. I was confused and frightened and weirded out, and Bowers hadn't offered me sympathy. We met again when Petey the Cockatoo tried to tell me who killed his owner, and there was chemistry—with Bowers, not the cockatoo.

We had reached the stage where most people take their relationships from occasional flirting during chance meetings to intentionally arranging to spend time together.

Dating. But then I'd grabbed hold of his hand while receiving a disturbing message from Petey the Cockatoo, and Bowers had seen it too. Dating someone who considered holding my hand an act of terror didn't hold much appeal, and so that was the end of that. I'd caught glimpses of him on the streets of Wolf Creek, but we hadn't spoken.

I understood his fears, but part of me was angry that he didn't toss them to the wind and take a chance on us. I guess cops are better at keeping their emotions in check. And now poor Frankie had found another body, and Bowers was here to make sure she didn't make a fool of herself. Myself. It should have been romantic, but it was embarrassing, and it ticked me off. I shoved the last of the sandwich in my mouth.

"Take it easy or you'll bite off a finger."

I looked up into the eyes of Detective Martin Bowers. Maybe it was because his voice sounded so good to my ears after all this time. Possibly, the stress of the murder had built to the breaking point, and seeing his strong manly face gave me the confidence to break down. Or maybe it was because my mouth was so crammed with food I couldn't breathe properly let alone sound off with a pithy reply, but I hiccupped once and burst into tears.

"Frankie!" He sounded horrified by the sudden torrent of emotion, which being a man, he probably was. I would have liked to have helped him out by regaining control and dismissing my outburst as a bad case of allergies, but I'd been surrounded by Penny's family, who all called me Frances, and the more intimate sound of my nickname coming from this very sexy man made me realize how much I missed him. I cried harder.

He met the curious gazes from the passengers closest to

us, took my hand, and pulled me to my feet. I noticed he immediately shifted his hand to my elbow.

"Come on."

He led me out of the dining area, but a cruise ship is hardly the place to find privacy, so he asked me for my room number and led the way up the stairs. I gave him my key, and he opened the door and ushered me inside. I was ready to give him a piece of my mind, but his expression only held concern. It made me rethink my position.

Maybe I was being too hard on him. Was it possible Bowers had traveled all the way to Alaska to tell me he cared and couldn't envision life without me—or at least he wanted to have a shot at a relationship? Why else would a man drop everything and pay wads of money to see a woman?

We were alone for the first time since he told me anything beyond waving hello across the street was out of the question, and the first words out of his mouth were, "Show me."

Was this his idea of a come-on? I'd hoped for something more romantic.

"Don't be afraid," he soothed. "I'm here."

Certainly, he was here. Otherwise, what was the point? And I would have thought shy, or maybe nervous, would have been better word choices for a romantic encounter than *afraid*.

"Look at the bright side. At least he didn't land on your balcony."

I felt my face flush. Of course. Professional interest. With a final sniffle, I led him to the balcony and pointed.

"I assume he fell from the top deck, unless he was in another passenger's room and fell off their balcony," he said. He had both hands on the railing, and he turned his head to look up. "That must have been a real eye-opener. For you, I mean. Well, for both of you."

At this point, I could have crossed the small distance between us, put my arms around his neck, and told him—breathlessly, of course—how much I missed him, which was ridiculous and annoying because I didn't have any claim on him. Instead, I crossed my arms over my chest.

"So, is the Wolf Creek police force the official investigative branch of Finlander cruise line?"

His eyebrows shot up. "I'm not here officially."

"Then why are you here?"

He tapped my cheek. "Because I heard you were in trouble. Again."

My skin tingled where he touched me. So, he *did* travel all this way for me.

"Any time you're in trouble, things get interesting. It's irresistible to a cop. I couldn't miss it."

Okay. He didn't come from any personal interest but because of the potential for professional amusement. He knew how to make a girl feel special.

"How are things in the police world?" I asked. "Seen much of Gutierrez?"

Gutierrez, a detective colleague, could be described by neutral parties as drop-dead gorgeous. She also gave off the vibrations of a large reptile. In fact, her nickname with the guys on the force was Python.

His lips moved. A smile, I think. "We went away for a weekend."

"That's nice." My voice might have been strained.

He grinned. "It was a training exercise with about two hundred other cops.

I shrugged my shoulders to show it didn't matter.

"And you? How have you been spending your time?" he asked.

I leaned my back against the railing with my elbows hooked over—the picture of casual. "Oh, you know. Penny's always trying her hand at matchmaking."

That was the truth. However, I hadn't taken her up on any of her offers, preferring the company of my pets. I turned my head away from Bowers, but then he stepped in front of me and put each hand on the railing behind me so he had me trapped between his arms. I stopped breathing because it took too much effort.

"Things didn't go so well the last time I saw you."

"You shoved me out of your car. I think I still have the footprint on my backside."

"I was a little overwhelmed about your—thing."

He still couldn't bring himself to say *psychic abilities*, as if talking around it would make it go away. He ran his fingertips down my arm, took my hand in his and aimed those dark blue eyes at me.

"Since there aren't any animals in the vicinity, I thought we could—"

"About that." I cleared my throat. "The victim was walking his cats when he died."

Bowers threw my hand away and tried to cover it by scratching his head. He was saved from explaining by a knock on the door. Judy Doud rushed into the room, and she didn't seem surprised to see Bowers.

"I thought I would find you both in here." There was a note of censure in her voice, and I wanted to let her know we had no need of a chaperon. I was an Untouchable.

"Bowers wanted to see where I found the body."

She looked up at him. "Penny says you're a police officer."

82

"Yes, Ma'am."

"She also says she finagled it so you're a member of our party, since the ship is booked solid and there aren't any available rooms."

"Your daughter was very helpful."

She slipped a glance at the bed. "Well, you can't stay in this room."

Bowers said, "I wouldn't dream of it." When he kept his expression serious and didn't slip me a wink, I realized he meant it. "I was raised by seven older sisters after my mother died. They stressed the importance of respecting women. I'd have to answer to them." Now, he winked.

She immediately warmed. Her frown melted into a smile, and she took hold of his arm.

"You can share a room with Robby, my son."

"That's very kind of you," Bowers said as she led him from the room.

I closed my door behind them and leaned back against it. Bowers would be in the room next door. I didn't think I'd get much sleep.

TWELVE

I don't know how long I stood there fighting with my imagination. I told it that it had no business trying to decide if Bowers slept in a wholesome pair of striped pajamas, manly boxer shorts, or in the buff. The last option made my insides tingle. Oh, who was I kidding? Every option made my insides tingle, which is why I jumped and shrieked at the knock on my door. I pulled it open. It was Bowers.

"I haven't had anything to eat since breakfast. Since that's your favorite pastime, I thought you'd like to join me."

He didn't have to ask twice. I slipped my room key in my pocket and led the way to my favorite floor—number nine. Since he'd seen me polishing off the last of my sandwich, I limited myself to a piece of pie. Bowers got a steamed hot dog and fries.

We took a table near the entrance, and I struggled between the excitement at having him so near and irritation at my excitement. When we had parted ways, I'd cried myself to sleep. It might only have been for ten minutes or so before I dropped off to sleep, but I'd been fighting for my life that night with a murderer, so I was sleepy.

He didn't seem to have suffered any ill effects from our estrangement: no nervousness in his manner, no regret in his blue eyes. Nada. If he could remain detached, so could I.

"Did you have a pleasant flight?"

"It was fine. Is everything on schedule for the wedding?"

"Yep. Penny is having tea today with her mother and her mother-in-law. Then her father wants to have some daddy-daughter time together, so he's taking her shopping for something new. You know. Something old, something new, something borrowed, something blue."

"She sounds busy."

"She is." I tried to keep the disappointment out of my voice.

Bowers felt that was enough chit-chat, because he swiped a fry through a blob of ketchup and said, "Did you see the body fall?" He waved the fry. "If it upsets you to talk about it, just say so."

I grabbed one of his fries. "Thank goodness I didn't see it happen." Then I remembered the thump outside as I was trying to fall asleep. "But I might have heard it."

He paused mid-chew.

"The noises from the ship sounded eerie to me, so I was having trouble getting to sleep. Then I heard this thump, and I looked outside but didn't see anything." It was creepy reliving something that had happened so recently, especially knowing the deadly results. I said I'd skipped breakfast that morning and took a few more fries.

"Did you look down?"

"No, but I couldn't have seen much, anyway. The lifeboats are illuminated at night around the edges, but the top would have been in shadow. It was late enough that most people were in bed, so their cabin lights were off." I popped another French fry in my mouth and squinted, trying to focus on the details. "I did listen afterward, but since there wasn't any follow-up commotion, I figured I was being silly."

"What time was this?"

"We saw the show; I came back to my room. Then Robby invited me to get something to eat." It sounded better if it was Robby's idea. I didn't want Bowers to think food was always on my mind. "Then we came back upstairs and went to Robby's room." I didn't see a need to mention Robby had offered to let me spend the night.

Bowers' voice cooled ten degrees. "Did you really?"

"I had forgotten my room key, but Mrs. Doud called security and got them to let me in. That took about fifteen or twenty minutes. Then I tossed and turned a little. So, it must have been around one a.m. or so. Does that sound right?"

Bowers finished off his hot dog and wiped his fingers on his napkin. "Did you tell this to anyone?"

"I forgot. They were all running around, and then Mrs. Doud took me to Robby's room, so I didn't get a chance."

I left out the bit about Felix and the man's voice. If Bowers thought I was talking to cats, he might steal one of the lifeboats and head for shore. My gaze wandered from his face, and I caught sight of a man in uniform in the hallway. It was the security officer, Robinson.

I stood up and grabbed the last fry from his plate. "That is a great idea."

"What is?"

"I should tell the security officer what I heard."

Once in the hallway, I called out, but Officer Robinson must not have heard me, and I had to jog to catch up with him.

"Officer Robinson!" I called again.

He came to a stop and waited for me, which gave me time to study him. I thought he had been intentionally unemotional when I saw him with sobbing Bitsy, but under his white cap, he had a lethargic face, one that didn't look as if it changed expression often. There mustn't have been height requirements for his job because he was shorter than my five feet seven inches. He looked to be in his early fifties, but there wasn't any sign of belly bulge under his uniform.

"How can I help you?"

I pretended to catch my breath to give me a second to plan my approach. I couldn't very well ask him direct questions about a dead employee.

"I have information for you about Marvelous Marv. I didn't get a chance to tell you in the elevator because I didn't want to upset the woman you were with, but I think I heard it when he fell to his death."

"Um, thank you," he said. "That was delicate of you not to mention it in the elevator." And then he resumed his walk down the hall.

"You never asked me any questions," I blurted out.

He stopped and turned. "Such as?"

"My cabin is the one the medical team came through to retrieve Marvelous Marv's body."

His eyebrows lifted a fraction of an inch. "It was a terrible accident. I'm not sure what kind of questions you'd like me to ask."

A hand touched my elbow, and I turned my head to look up into Bowers' eyes.

"I'm sure she doesn't know, either." He reached out a hand. "Detective Martin Bowers."

As Robinson shook his hand, his eyebrows jumped

another fraction, and Bowers added, "Off-duty. I don't envy you, dealing with sudden death in a vacation environment."

Robinson seemed to relax in the presence of a fellow law enforcement officer. "It's a challenge. We must be very careful to keep it quiet. Can you imagine if the entire passenger list demanded a refund?"

Bowers put an arm around my shoulder, and I managed to keep from showing my surprise. "Are there any, um, safety issues? My girlfriend wanted to stroll around the Observation Deck, but she's worried."

Robinson moved his gaze to me. "No worries, Ma'am. Mr. Hodgekins—"

"Who?"

"Marv. He was walking the cats and one of them tripped him. He went over the railing. I don't suppose you're going to be walking any cats while you're with us." The right side of his mouth raised a fraction, so I assumed it was a joke.

"Was he alone?" I asked. "I mean, it would have been awful for Bitsy or his girlfriend to have witnessed the fall."

"Fortunately, the women—both his girlfriend and his business partner—were in their respective cabins. That *would* have been tragic," Robinson said, as if he hadn't considered that scenario.

"Are you sure that's where they were? Did anyone check?"

"Thank you," Bowers said to end the conversation, and he steered me ahead, his hand still on my elbow. When we were out of Officer Robinson's hearing range, he dropped the hand and said, "What are you up to?"

"I just thought it was odd he hadn't asked me for my version of what happened. After all, I was the one who found the body."

"But you didn't witness the fall."

"N-o-o-o."

"Leave it alone."

Fortunately, Officer Robinson was a conscientious soul, and he set aside whatever mission he had been on and offered to accompany us to the Observation Deck to put my mind at rest.

When the elevator doors opened, Security Officer Robinson motioned me to go first, and I led the way to the side of the ship where my room was located. At this hour, we had the deck to ourselves. Most of the athletes were down on the Lower Promenade jogging or walking in circles. I had a fear of slipping in the sea spray and sliding under the railing and into the ocean, so I skipped that pleasure.

After the "accident", I'd counted lifeboats so I could find mine from above. It was the third from the right. On our way over, I had an idea. Bowers would never listen to me if I brought up visions sent by kitties. I sidled up close to him. He looked down at me, smiled as I put my arm around his back, and responded by wrapping his arm around my shoulder, which gave me just the leverage I needed. As we closed in on the railing, I slipped my foot in front of his and shoved. The results were perfect. He lost his footing and pitched forward, slamming against the railing at chest height, with his arms draped over the bars.

"Why did you do that?" He managed to keep his voice calm, but Officer Robinson kept his feet at a safe distance.

"There's no way a kitty-cat has the ability to shove as hard as I did, and you didn't go flying over the railing. You fell against it, which is the natural response. And Marv wasn't even as tall as you are."

Bowers glared at me as he straightened up, and then he leaned against the railing and looked down.

"That's quite a drop."

"It is, indeed." Officer Robinson skirted around me to stand next to Bowers. "That's why we have this." He patted the railing with confidence.

The top bar was a fat piece of wood reinforced with three white-painted metal bars between the top railing and the floor, one running parallel to the floor and two criss-crossing at angles. Even on my skinny days I couldn't have wiggled between them.

I risked a peek down. There was my lifeboat, should I ever need it. I couldn't imagine being able to land on it without the skills of an Olympic diver, but Marvelous Marv had been lucky. Well, maybe lucky was the wrong word.

As I stood there, I ran my hands out over the rail to either side of me, and when I had a good hold, I gave a shove. Officer Robinson smiled.

"You're not going to move it, Miss. It wouldn't be much of a safety feature if you could."

"I think we'll just stay up here and enjoy the view," Bowers said. "Thank you."

Instead of walking away, as any sane man would have done, Officer Robinson moved closer to Bowers, shot me a look, and said in a low voice, "I was wondering...when you're through here...would you mind coming to my office? There's something I'd like your opinion on."

Bowers agreed, and Officer Robinson tipped his hat at me and returned to whatever he'd been up to before his detour to the Observation Deck.

"I can't believe you pushed me," Bowers said.

"I needed to demonstrate the physics involved. A person

doesn't just trip and then fly up and over the guardrail." I poked him where the railing met his ribs. "Marvelous Marv wasn't as tall as you are, so the railing would have met his armpit. Unless he took a Baryshnikov-style leap when he tripped, he wouldn't have gone over. Not without help."

"No," he said. "You proved that. But he *could* have leaned back against the railing," he suited action to words, "lifted his foot to avoid stepping on a cat and overbalanced." When it became obvious that scenario wouldn't have worked either, he climbed up and sat with his legs dangling over the deck.

"Don't do that." I resisted the urge to pull him down because I might accidentally knock him backwards. Instead, I twisted my hands together. "Get down. Please."

He hopped down and grinned at me. "The point of that demonstration was to show he might have been sitting on the railing and fallen backwards."

"Could be," I said. "Or someone could have pushed him."

"Tell me why anyone would shove a ship performer to his death."

I stood in front of Bowers, facing the ocean, because leaning against the railing made me nervous. "His girlfriend, Sonya, doesn't seem too broken up by his death."

He shot it down. "Some people don't put their emotions on display."

"But the night before he died, Marv kissed Penny in front of Sonya. Sonya his girlfriend," I repeated, in case he hadn't heard me the first time.

His eyebrows shot up. "Seriously?"

"Cross my heart. That gives Sonya a motive."

"To dump him, yes. To kill him...not so much."

"How about his business partner, Bitsy? She may have wanted the entire show to herself."

"Because they are obviously raking it in as a showboat act." Bowers turned around and leaned his elbows against the rail. "Any serious ideas?"

"Maybe he was blackmailing someone."

"That's a stretch."

Not if he had heard the argument between Marv and Sharon Bradley.

"Maybe he wanted to quit show business, and the cats belonged to him. That would have left Bitsy standing in the unemployment line."

"So, we're back to Bitsy as the suspect?" He lifted his arms over his head on a full body stretch. "I'm going back inside. The sound of the water is making me tired."

"You're not even going to look for clues?"

He sighed. "Like what?"

"Claw marks on the railing or skid marks on the floor." I moved my feet to look.

"That would be stupid."

He took hold of my elbow and led me to the elevator. "I can't trust you up here alone. You might fall overboard while acting out the scene."

I wondered if I should tell him about that other suspect. What had Sharon Bradley been doing out that night? And what had she been arguing about with the now dead Marvelous Marv?

THIRTEEN

Bowers left me in my room while he finished unpacking, so I had time on my hands. He told me not to wait for him because he would be going to Officer Robinson's office afterward, and I wasn't invited.

I didn't want to hit the casino; I wasn't in the mood to sit still for a movie, and there weren't any shows in the Neptune Lounge until evening. I didn't like exercise in my everyday life, and I wasn't about to check out a gym on my vacation. For once, I was too full to enjoy the offerings of the Lido Deck, and I was too broke to enjoy the spa. I wandered out to the pool on the chance of running into Robby.

They had crammed several booths into the open space and offered huge discounts on a variety of products: touristy shirts, chocolates shaped like salmon, and expensive purses and jewelry marked 25% off. The Oyster Bar had moved on from free hamburgers to free tacos and refried beans, and it looked as if everyone on the ship had gathered outside for a Mexican fiesta followed by a shopping spree.

I finally spotted Robby. He was next to the pool in a deckchair. Unfortunately, Gina occupied the one next to him. I put my ego aside, walked around Robby's chair, and made myself known. Gina raised her sunglasses.

"Aren't you going to put on a suit? The sun feels wonderful, and you're so pale."

Without thinking, I rubbed the skin on my arms, which according to Gina was pale, and when I noticed what I was doing, I pretended I had to scratch.

"Who's your friend?" Robby asked.

"He's a policeman from Wolf Creek."

"I got a peek at him while he was talking to Penny about getting a room. Dreamy. I wonder how he looks in a uniform," Gina said.

I curled my upper lip. "Detectives don't wear uniforms."

"They do at special events. Like funerals or parades."

My mind wandered to an image of Bowers in uniform.

Robby sat forward. "Detective, huh? Is he here to investigate Marv's death?"

Gina picked up a daiquiri from the small table next to her chair. "Don't be silly. It was an accident."

"Was it?" I said. "I think Marvelous Marv had help."

Gina, mid-sip, sputtered her drink.

Robby's eyes lit up. "Really? How do you know?"

"I don't *know*, but I'm not buying into the death-by-kitty explanation." I told them how I had given Bowers a nudge and he had fallen *into* but not *over* the railing. I waited for Robby's laughter to die down before I added, "Naturally, Bowers doesn't believe me. We're lacking suspects, but *somebody* must have wanted him dead. It's only natural. I bet each one of us knows at least one person who'd like to bump us off." I had to fight to keep my gaze off Gina. "And I don't know if you've noticed, but his girlfriend isn't too broken up."

"I thought we had decided Marvelous Marv was an ass," Robby said. Gina swatted his arm and told him not to swear in front of ladies. "I'm saying I wouldn't blame her if she did a happy dance."

"I wonder how he got along with Bitsy?" Gina said.

Robby gave me a mischievous grin. "Penny's been telling us all about your pet psychic business. Why don't you chat with the kitties?"

"Yes, Frances," Gina added, with a smile of pure condescension. "Aren't they witnesses?"

I didn't want to mention my one-sided conversation with Felix, so I said, "I haven't had time, but I will."

Robby stood up and held his hand out to Gina. "Speaking of time, we're going to be late for the salmon bake in Juneau."

Gina slipped on her flip-flops. "You have fun investigating your murder." Which meant she didn't believe me. If it hadn't been for Marv's last words, I wouldn't believe me either, but what was I supposed to do about it? Not a lot I *could* do.

I hadn't scheduled any offshore excursions, but that didn't mean I had to waste the rest of my day on the ship of death. And I would not spend any more time trying to convince Bowers something smelled about Marv's death. I had my dignity.

My wallet was in my room, so I went back up to retrieve it and take care of a few personal things before I delved into the Juneau tourist traps. As I left my room, I heard the click of a door farther down the hallway. Sharon Bradley had her back to me, so I slipped out of the hallway and left my door ajar just a crack, so I could see when she passed. It may have been my imagination, but I thought her movements were cagey—an extra glance over her shoulder as she moved down the hallway, hurried steps as if afraid of being stopped. It reminded me of her movements the night Marv died. If there were a simple explanation, I could cross her off my list.

She took the stairs instead of the elevator, so I was able to follow her to the second floor. Keeping my distance, I stayed tight up against the wall, and if the opportunity arose, I moved behind other people walking the same direction. Not that I expected her to turn around. She moved at a quick, determined pace, her focus on whatever lay ahead.

We passed the fancy restaurant, the Golden Pelican, and then several small bars and lounges. Sharon didn't strike me as a daytime drinker, so there had to be a more enticing target up ahead.

Right as we came upon a theater equipped with a kitchen where they held culinary shows, an elderly lady dropped her plastic bag, and the contents scattered on the floor. I had a moment's indecision—honor my girl scout training or keep Sharon in sight. With a sigh, I stopped to help the women scoop up her trinkets. Most of them were tiny charms of the state of Alaska.

"Thank you so much," she said, standing by while I did the scooping, though I didn't really expect a woman in her eighties to get on her knees alongside me.

"They are for my nieces and granddaughters and great-granddaughters. I had to find something inexpensive because there are so many of them, I can't keep count."

She laughed, and I laughed with her to be polite. When

I had them back in the bag, I handed it off, accepted her thanks, and then searched the hallway for my quarry.

No sign of Sharon. I could either spend my day looking for her or get off the ship and stretch my legs. I opted for the latter.

FOURTEEN

Since Sharon's appearance in the hallway had interrupted me, I had to return to my room for my wallet, identification, and a windbreaker. I slipped into the slow-moving crowd of people exiting the ship. Representatives from the different tours held up signs so passengers could quickly locate their guide. A short walk down Franklin Street took me to the Mt. Robert's Tramway station, so I parted with two ten-dollar bills and waited with a gaggle of excited tourists for the arrival of our tram. I wasn't as excited when I overheard the ascent went 1,800 feet up at a sharp angle, but I didn't want the hassle of returning my ticket. When a bright red tram came to rest at the terminal, I searched the faces of the people exiting. There weren't any signs of panic or fear, so I followed the flow and took a seat inside.

Our journey started with a mild jerk, and then we were airborne. The ride was smooth, though I kept a firm grip on the seat bottom, as if that would help me in a free fall. Three young women to my left chatted about a dinner they had attended the night before. Not a crease of worry on their youthful faces or a crack of fear in their voices. An older couple up front seemed preoccupied. The woman dug through her purse as the man looked on. The man's hands stayed in his lap. He wasn't clutching at the purse as if desperate for his wife to get hold of his anxiety meds, and when the woman pulled out a roll of mints and smiled, victorious, I wished it had been a bottle of *mother's little helper* instead. I would have borrowed one.

If I turned my head and looked down, I would have gotten a glimpse of how far we would plunge if the line snapped, so I didn't. Instead, I kept my eyes focused on the expanse of evergreens out the window across from me, so thick I could almost convince myself that, if we did fall, we would land in a soft nest of fat, green needles.

A woman's voice said, "Look!" I craned my neck to see what she was pointing at, and I drew in a breath when I spotted a bald eagle, perched on a branch. He seemed to watch us with a mixture of disdain and resignation. A bald eagle. In the wild. My heart gave a little jump, but it was only in part for the incredible display of nature out the window. We were coming in for a landing, and the tram had jostled, bringing back my fears of a snapped cable.

I let the rest of the tourists leave before I stepped outside, since many of them seemed to be in a hurry, and then I followed the line to enter the Mountain Complex. I bypassed the opportunities to eat, shop, and watch an award-winning, free film about the local culture. Instead, I moved right through the building to the trails outside, only pausing to grab a brochure.

Once in the shaded forest, the smell of pine filled my nostrils. The literature said this was a rainforest, but in my mind, a rain forest should be jungle foliage complete with parrots and monkeys. Monkeys reminded me of Bert, the friendly towel back in my room. I contemplated what I would do if I ran into a monkey here in the Alaskan rain-forest. That occupied my brain cells until the trail opened into a field of grass. Would you call them fields if they were on a mountain? A steady breeze blew my hair across my face, so I pulled up my attached hood and tucked my hair under it.

When I reached the first lookout point, I paused to catch my breath because I'd been making the uphill climb at a steady pace. Far below, the cruise ships looked like toys in a bathtub, but it didn't hit home how far up I was until I spotted a white bird flying over the water in a steady, unwavering path. Then I realized the small bird was a plane. I took a step back from the edge of the trail.

An older couple called out to me and asked if I would take their picture. After a few fumbles, I got used to the buttons on their camera and captured their vacation moment.

A little farther ahead I reached a gigantic cross. A plaque explained a Jesuit priest by the name of Father Edward Howard Brown had been instrumental in constructing the original trail up Mt. Roberts back in the early 1900s. I wondered what had possessed him. It wasn't as if this were an important trading route. Did people put out that much effort for the joy of trudging uphill?

This time when I looked down at the water below, a blanket of mist smothered the scenery and hid the ships. It floated in between the treetops below me like fluffy smoke. Still, when I scanned the surrounding scenery, everything seemed clear at my level.

As I continued to move forward at a slower pace, a movement to my left caught my attention. A large, furry animal rolled on its back in the dip of a small valley. I hoped it wasn't an undersized bear or a badger or any species that bit. If it was friendly, maybe I could lure it back to the ship and Bitsy could train it to perform tricks.

My focus turned back to the trail by necessity. The path had become steep and muddy, making it difficult to find purchase with my tennis shoes. I fell onto one knee when my shoe slipped off a large, smooth stone, and as I rubbed the sore spot, I noticed specks of blood coming through my jeans.

"This is for the birds." I stepped to the left of the trail and walked through the grass, thinking it would be easier. It wasn't. It was impossible to spot the jagged rocks hidden under innocent-looking layers of green.

I'd been so focused on my feet it came as a surprise when I looked up and noticed the mist had caught up with me. I turned a full circle and accepted my fate. I might as well have wrapped myself in a white sheet.

While waiting in line for the tram, I'd overheard a tourist talking about how beautiful Mt. Roberts looked when covered with clouds. Could I be walking around in a cloud? Tickled by the idea, I stood still and cast my mind back to childhood plane rides. I'd look out the window and wonder what it would be like to bounce around on those fluffy balls of cotton, and here I was, walking in a cloud. The thrill lasted about ten seconds. That furry animal, possibly carnivorous, was still up here, and I'd never see the attack with all this stupid cloud cover blocking my view.

Taking a few steps to my right, I searched for the original trail but couldn't find it. Turning so I faced downhill, I squinted my eyes, as if that would give me laser vision and allow me to spot a familiar landmark, such as the cross.

"Hello?" I called, hoping the older couple was still behind me. There wasn't a sound except the mournful horn of a ship far below.

I took a tentative step forward, feeling with my toe. Stupid, stupid, stupid. Everyone knows you're not supposed to swim alone, but who knew the same rule applied to hiking? Probably hikers did, but I never claimed to be an athlete.

When something hit me hard between the shoulders, I stumbled forward.

"Hey! Watch it!"

Attempting to catch my balance, I flung my arms outward, but forward momentum pitched me into the air. Right before I went airborne, I wrapped my arms around a small bush and held tight. It was more like the stump of a tree that had been growing sideways out of a rock, and that rock was at my eye-level, which seemed an odd place for it to be, especially as I wasn't flat on the ground. I still felt upright. I scrambled my feet for purchase but met with air. I'd fallen over the edge of Mt. Roberts.

"Help." It came out hoarse, like when you try to scream in a dream. That's because I was hyperventilating. Using my arm muscles, I attempted to pull my body up, but since my muscles have been on vacation for years, they declined to put out much effort. Besides, there wasn't a chance I was letting go of this plant to make a grab for the ground.

"Hello!" Whoever had run into me had moved on, or else why would they ignore my cries? I would have thought they would have noticed me when they made contact. Unless that contact had been deliberate. I swallowed— unsuccessfully because I didn't have any spit.

"Hello!" Someone else had to be walking this forsaken path. There had been dozens of tourists in the gift shop, and they must have come up here for something more than trinkets and a movie, so I put more effort into my calls. What if no one passed by? What if they had all turned around because of the fog? Would they ever find my body? Or would bears, or porpoises, or whatever stinking wild animal stumbled across it scarf up the battered remains?

And then it hit me. I had been pushed over a ledge, just like Marvelous Marv. If I hadn't been so busy fighting for my life, the thought would have pleased me. I wasn't making a big deal out of nothing. I was right. His death hadn't been an accident, and if I lived long enough, I would crow about my victory until Bowers begged me to stop. This was good. I had a goal, and it gave me a reason to keep fighting.

I wrapped one arm tight around the bush and risked letting go with the other to stretch out my hand. My fingers struck dirt, and I clawed at it, trying to get a grip. All I did was loosen a trickle of earth, so I grabbed back onto the branches with both arms. My hold wasn't as tight as it had been because I was losing strength in my arms. As I struggled to maintain my grip, my feeble arms slipped a few inches, and I yelped.

For the first time in a long time, I thought of God. "Hey there. It's me, Frankie. Long time no talk." A small branch pressed against my chest popped free and struck me across the face. "I don't want to be rude, God, but I have to cut straight to the point. I have a favor to ask. I'd really like to live, so if you don't have any other plans, could you help me out?"

A seagull cried out, and the shrill sound seemed to mock me.

"God? Are you there? Hello!"

"Frankie?"

God had answered! "Hello?" My voice came out in a squeak.

"Frankie?"

The voice came closer. It didn't sound like God. It sounded like Bowers.

"Over here!"

When two strong hands took hold of the collar of my jacket and pulled me up, I didn't even complain when they grabbed hair as well.

He looked down at me with his eyebrows furrowed and his hands on my shoulder. "What were you doing down there?"

"Taking a nap. What do you think?"

"This fog is pretty nasty." He brushed dirt off my jacket. "You need to watch your step."

"Someone pushed me."

He folded my hands together and held them in his. "Isn't it possible you took a misstep? It's hard to see where you're going up here." He turned me around to face the white blanket of mist. I spun back around and poked him in the chest.

"Then what hit me between the shoulder blades and shoved hard?"

"Your imagination?"

"Hardly."

He took my arm and guided me back to the path which he must have found by radar, and we began our descent. "Okay. Tell me why anyone would want to kill you."

"Search me."

He tightened his hold. "Have you been making noises about Marv's death?"

"Not really."

He caught the hesitation in my voice. "Tell me exactly what you said."

"Nothing. Just that I thought he had been murdered."

He said a naughty word. "And who did you tell this to?"

"Just Robby. And maybe Gina was there."

"Was she, or wasn't she?"

"She was."

I tripped, and he pulled me straight.

"Was there anyone else around?"

"About two hundred people, though none of them was listening. The Oyster Bar was shelling out free food." I gave a prissy sniff. "But I will say Robby didn't blow me off. He thought it would be a good idea for me to look into it."

"Really. And did you bring your detective kit with you? I understand toy manufacturers make one for children."

I would have stalked off, but I was depending on his arm to get me back to the tram alive. "I don't know what you're fussing about. It's not as if you can keep murder a secret."

"Not if you keep shouting it out in crowds. Marv's death was an accident," he said, but he averted his eyes and his voice raised in pitch when he said it. From my days of cold reading clients, that was a sure sign of a lie. Bowers thought there was something funny about Marv's death. I wondered what Officer Robinson and Bowers had talked about during their meeting. He went on, oblivious to the fact I knew he was lying, and I had to fight to keep the excitement out of my expression.

"Why is it so difficult for you to accept that bad things can happen without nefarious complications? Are you bored? Why don't you try dancing, or bingo, or eating?"

"I saw it."

He stopped walking. "You saw someone push Marv off the deck?"

I took a deep breath. "He was hanging from the railing and he said *Don't do it. Please, for God's sake, don't!* Words like that. You get the gist. And then he struggled and fell."

"What were you doing on the Observation Deck in the middle of the night?"

"I wasn't. I saw it through the cat's eyes."

He swore again, and I wondered if I should swat him and flutter my eyelashes like Gina did when Robby swore. Probably not. He didn't seem in the right frame of mind for flirting.

"Marv was talking to someone, which means someone was there."

"You just said the cats were there."

"He was looking *up* into the eyes of someone. If it had been a cat, he would have been looking down."

"Not if the cat was on the railing. What if it were about to step on his hands?"

I admitted this was possible but insisted people don't talk to their cats the same way they talk to people.

"They say *No. Bad kitty!* Or something like that. And everyone knows pleading with cats gets you nowhere. And now someone has tried to bump me off, too." I said this last bit with satisfaction and then realized it wasn't something to boast about. "And stop trying to convince me you think Marv's death was an accident."

He stopped walking again, pulled me around to face him, and squeezed my shoulders with unnecessary pressure. "You're not reading my mind again, are you?"

That had happened once, a complete accident, and Bowers still hadn't recovered.

I shook my shoulders loose. "Not in the way you think." I waved a hand. "You're easy to read, and I mean read in the same way your sisters can read you like a book. What did Robinson show you?"

He considered my question for a few moments. "Robinson saw bruises on Marv's forearms."

"You mean defensive wounds?" I threw the term out like a police pro, having heard it so many times on television crime shows.

"Not necessarily, but they concerned him enough that he took pictures."

"If he suspected something, why did he let the body go?"

"He didn't suspect something. He just wasn't comfortable. The doctor signed a death certificate, and there wasn't any reason to hold on to the body, so he took a few pictures in case there were questions. Besides, Finlander doesn't want a fuss, and Robinson works for Finlander."

"Too bad you didn't know this when you boarded the ship. You walked within three feet of Marv's corpse. You could have peeked."

"You saw me board the ship? Why didn't you come down and meet me?"

"Did I say I saw you?" It wasn't a lie. I hadn't said so. "You weren't on the ship when we left Seattle, so you had to come aboard in Juneau, and that's when they got rid of Marv. Anyway, it's not as if you let me know you were coming."

Just like a man, he tried to change the subject and put the blame for the tension in the air back on me. "Why did you go running off, anyway? I only left you for a half an hour. You ran off to avoid me, didn't you?"

I let out an unladylike snort. "How do you get that head through doorways? I didn't want to waste the entire day on the ship."

"Instead you decided to climb a mountain in the fog."

"It wasn't foggy when I left. And how did you figure out where I was?"

He smirked. "The tram was the cheapest tourist option,

and it didn't require any thought. The ticket booth was a straight path from the ship. I figured cheap and simple would be your top two criteria."

The fog thinned out as we entered the thick woods surrounding the Nature Center, so I let go of Bowers' arm. We passed through the tourist shop and got in line to board the tram. It was packed and just leaving, and my gaze landed on something that made me gasp. I grabbed Bowers' arm and pointed.

"See the woman in black?"

He searched the crowd. "You mean the one with the long hair?"

"That's Sonya, Marv's girlfriend."

Had Sonya tried to kill me? It was hard to imagine her traipsing around a mountainside in high-heeled boots, but that might have been envy. I can't walk in anything taller than a one-inch heel.

"This is a popular spot," Bowers said, and his tone had an edge of sarcasm that dared me to make further accusations against Sonya.

We had to wait for the next tram, so there wasn't a chance to ask Marv's mourning girlfriend what she was doing on a cruise ship tourist attraction, which when I thought about it, was just as well. It was a stupid question.

Because of the fog, there wasn't much of a view on the way down. It seemed as if we were floating through a cloud, which sounds romantic, but it wasn't. I was too irritated at Bowers.

I declined his offer to take me on a tour of Juneau. My legs were still shaky from my near-death experience. We made it back to the ship in one piece, and as we reached our floor, I said, "See you later."

"Not a chance. If there is a possibility you're right and

someone tried to kill you, I'm not letting you out of my sight."

"That's not necessary," I said, though his concern touched me.

He didn't agree. "Not for a minute."

"Even at night?" My face felt warm at the thought, so I joked. "Let's see what Judy Doud has to say about that."

Bowers conceded the point and suggested I ask Gina to room with me after the wedding.

"I'll take my chances against the killer. Besides, I have Bert to stand guard."

"Who's Bert?"

I didn't explain, and when he dropped me off at my door, I looked toward the window and discovered that Bert was gone. In his place, sitting in the middle of my bedspread, the stewards had left a sweet little elephant, cleverly shaped with a towel, probably the same towel that had given life to Bert. Poor Bert.

FIFTEEN

I found Penny in our room giving her dress another look. She was bordering on obsessive. All our dresses had come from a Wolf Creek shop, Dina's Dazzlers. Gina had hers shipped to New York so she could have her fittings done locally, and I admit I hadn't shown enthusiasm for my appointments with the dressmaker, but we had all tried on our outfits yesterday and they had fit perfectly.

"Maybe you should all try your dresses and tuxes on again."

I should clarify. Gina and I had tried our dresses on for Penny *twice*.

"Penny. Why did you email Martin Bowers?"

She pressed down on her lower lip with her teeth. "I've kind of been keeping him informed."

"On what?" I stared at her. "Me?"

"I emailed him yesterday and let him know you'd found a body outside your window. That's all. I swear I didn't know he would come. It's Alaska, for Pete's sake."

"You didn't ask him to come?"

She saw her way out of my bad graces and jumped on it.

"No. Cross my heart. My only intent was to share gossip. I never imagined...."

I waved a hand to show her it didn't matter now. "Your mother put him with Robby."

"They should get along. We'll find out. It's almost time for dinner."

While she changed into a beige twin set and black skirt, I reviewed the clothing I had brought along for the trip. Irritated that I would find my wardrobe unsatisfactory just because Bowers was here, I grabbed the closest outfit—black palazzo pants and a long-sleeved shirt in boring beige.

"I don't think so."

Penny stood behind me with a jewel-tone blue dress I'd only seen her wear a few times.

"Put this on." She shook the dress.

"I'm not wearing your clothes. You'll be naked by the end of the trip."

She snickered. "I'm sort of counting on that."

Penny was only a few inches shorter than my five-foot-seven-inches, but she had petite bones and a slim build.

"It won't fit."

She rolled her eyes. "It's a dress, not a bra. It'll fit."

Taking it by the shoulders, I held it up to me. I'd once threatened to steal this very dress from Penny's body. The color complimented my dark-auburn hair, and the skirt fabric swirled when it moved. It was a fabulous dress.

"Why are you doing this?"

"Because there's a certain someone on board who I bet would love to see the real you. Frankie the Woman. Not the Frankie you hide under jeans and sweats, especially when you run out in the morning without showering."

"Fine," I said. "I'll wear it to make you happy."

I went into the bathroom and changed in front of the

mirror. I filled the dress out more than Penny did, but in a good way. Sexy, or even pretty, weren't in my list of personal adjectives. Not that I thought I was an ogre, but I thought of looking grown-up and feminine as a privilege belonging to other women.

Penny knocked on the door, and when I stepped out, I felt awkward and shy, as if I were pretending to be someone else.

"Stunning. Let's go."

Bowers met us in the hallway. In deference to the dress code, he had on a dark-brown sports jacket over a royal-blue, collared golf shirt and beige slacks. He didn't say anything when he saw me. In fact, his neutral cop-face came up, and I blushed. Maybe he thought I was a pretender and looked foolish. I averted my eyes and put my attention on the great dinner awaiting us in the dining room.

The rest of our party were at the table by the time we got there. Bowers guided me to the empty seat next to Robby and sat on the other side of me.

"Don't you look nice," Judy Doud said, and I ignored the surprise in her voice and mumbled an appropriate response.

Tommy was still conspicuously absent. "He's going to come out of his room sometime, right?"

"I'm sure he'll be fine," Penny said. "Eventually."

Gina fixed her gaze on Bowers. "Aren't you going to introduce us?"

Her insinuation that I lacked manners got my hackles up, but I smoothed them back down and went around the table, naming everyone. "And this is Martin Bowers, a friend."

"How did the two of you meet?" Robby asked with a

grin, and alluding to Bowers' profession, he added, "Was Frances being bad?"

I lifted my chin. "We met during a police investigation."

"Was it a case of fraud?" Gina purred, and I knew she meant to suggest my pet psychic activities were fraudulent.

I answered lightly, as if it were no big deal. "Murder."

"Murder!"

I didn't know Sharon could yell like that.

Robby put his arm around my shoulder. "Was Frances your lead suspect?"

Bowers gave me a wry grin. "Hardly."

Gina snaked her slender arm across the table and took hold of Bowers' hand, allegedly to get his attention.

"So, what's it like being a cop in a small town?"

"Same as it is in a big town, I suppose."

Bowers had made his response polite, but the question was akin to asking a teacher what's it like to teach in the remedial classroom, as if it were a breeze. Pretty tactless for an international government employee.

Gina slid me a glance I recognized as her *I'm about to humiliate you* look.

"Did you come on board to investigate Marv's *murder?*"

When Judy Doud gave a small cry, Gina was quick to lay the blame at my feet.

"I'm only repeating what Frances said. She told me and Robby it was murder. Didn't you, Frances?"

The mermaid fell out of Robby's graces, going by the glare he shot her. "She didn't actually say that."

Gina put her fingers to her full lips. "Oh. I must have misunderstood."

Christina Mohr saved the day with a smile and a giggle. "Did we ever tell you about the mystery train tour of wine country Thomas and I took? It's how me met."

Christina's story couldn't have been better timed because she finished up just as the waiters arrived to serve us. Throughout the rest of dinner, I talked to Robby because Gina monopolized Bowers, though he didn't seem to mind. She was pouring out the charm, showing him every white tooth in her head when she laughed and blinking her long, dark lashes more than necessary.

Robby kept his arm stretched across the back of my chair and leaned in often to murmur humorous commentary on the conversations going on around us. Several times he had me laughing so hard I started to snort, an attractive Chandler family trait. Finally, Judy Doud asked if we had something we wanted to share with the rest of the group, and we both straightened up like disciplined children.

As soon as it was polite to do so, I left the dining room because I didn't want to be the odd woman out again when people started pairing off. I didn't stay on my own for long because Bowers was suddenly at my side.

"I meant what I said about sticking to you."

I waved a hand. "You're overreacting. As long as I don't look over any railings, I should be perfectly safe." I felt confident enough to make that statement on the ship surrounded by other passengers. I had already decided excursions on my own were out.

As we passed the Hardcastle Collection, I said, "If you want to keep me preoccupied, you could buy me a bauble. Say a ring. Then I'd sit at the bar and admire the way it winked at me under the lights."

"Sure. Just give me a minute to dip into my retirement fund."

I motioned to the jewelry display.

"You may not realize it, but you're in the presence of history."

As we crossed the hall to get a closer look, I explained about the famous jewels, adding my own embellishments— pirates and deathbed declarations about a curse—and finishing up with a sales spiel on the Pure Fantasy bracelet. "And it's authentic, too. You can tell by the flaws."

He cocked his head. "The flaws?"

"Well, I only saw one, and it's not noticeable."

Scanning the displayed items, he said, "Do women actually like this stuff?"

"Mrs. Doud stuck her nose up at it, but Penny might trade Kemper in for a nice pair of earrings."

"It's gaudy."

"Not all of it," I said, defending jewelry I'd never wear by choice. I stepped over to the next table. "Take this necklace. There can't be more than twenty tiny diamonds surrounding that one simple red rock. It's quite tasteful."

He hadn't moved from the Pure Fantasy bracelet. "Interesting."

He bent down and studied the bracelet, turning his head from side to side to check out every angle.

"I'm sure it's only noticeable under certain lighting, but it's the flaw that lets you know it's a real stone, rather than a cheap piece of fabricated goods."

Mistaking Bowers interest in the bracelet for an interest in owning the bracelet, Art stepped up and held out the clipboard. "Did you have any questions, sir?"

"This is the real bracelet?"

"Yes, sir. We have a copy available for only $600."

Bowers came out of his study. "Oh. No, thank you."

Art held out the clipboard. "Or you could purchase a ticket for the auction. Only two hundred dollars per ticket. It would make a nice gift for your girlfriend."

The security guard took his first good look at me and I

noticed the panic in his eyes. I tilted my head and studied his face. Crooked nose. Burgundy shirt and tie. Brown hair. It was the man I'd seen peeking out into the hallway after the lifeboat safety drill. He had probably been fraternizing with the passengers and feared I'd give him away. I winked at him to let him know it was our little secret, but he sucked in his bottom lip and looked away.

Bowers straightened up. "I'm sorry. My girlfriend refuses to wear anything but rhinestones." And then he led me away.

"Have I ever mentioned you're a snot?" I pulled my arm away.

"Several times, and it's still true."

I had a sudden thought. "Well, as long as you're here, do you want to catch a show?"

He studied my face, looking for signs of deceit. "Okay," he said, his tone cautious. "That sounds nice."

I'd already checked the ship's itinerary, so I knew the cat show was scheduled to go on in the Neptune Theater in ten minutes. This would be the Fabulous Feline's first performance since Marv's death, so the theater would be crowded with curious passengers. To keep Bowers from hearing any gossip before we got seated, I ran it close. We popped into the back row just as the lights went down.

The emcee went through the same routine he used last night with no mention of the late Marvelous Marv. The performing group had shortened their name to The Fabulous Felines, and this time, as the curtain went up, Bitsy held the whip.

"Cats?" Bowers leaned in and hissed in my ear. "You *knew* this would be the cat show."

"I wanted to see how they would handle Marv's

absence." I reached out and gave Bowers' hand a squeeze, just to watch him jump.

The vibrations in the room whirred on high. When animals communicate, it's often a hum or a buzz, and with all four cats talking at once, it sounded like white noise. They were in turmoil. Of course, I could tell that by their delayed responses to their new handler. Only Sphinx seemed unaffected. When he sprang off his stool to do his trick, he only had room in his brain for his fish treat.

I tried to zero in on the other cats as they waited, first concentrating on Jinx, then Jasper, and finally, Casper. I got the equivalent of a busy signal, though Jasper jerked his head up and looked out at the audience, searching for the source of the distraction. I silently called out to him, but he only flicked his tail and put his attention back on Bitsy.

I wondered how they would handle the big finish, since Felix wasn't there to take his bow. Either they hadn't found him yet, or he was too traumatized by events to go on with the act tonight. One minute's consideration about what it would take to traumatize a cat left me with an unsettled feeling about poor Felix's fate.

Bitsy got the cats to join her in a row and she took a bow in place of Felix. Then she left the stage with her furry companions and it was time for the comedy show. When the emcee announced Sonny Street, Bowers looked at me, said, "You've got to be kidding," and got up and left. Since I'd already heard Sonny's act, I followed close behind.

"This is like a bad dream," he said, refusing to slow down. "A dead body. Cats. And Sonny Street, for crying out loud!"

I stopped walking. "No one asked you to come," I called after him.

He spun on his heels and came back to me. "You're right. I'm an idiot."

"No argument here."

He narrowed his eyes. "I knew there would be trouble the minute I got Penny's message."

"Which she sent without my knowing a thing about it, just to be clear. What exactly did the message say?"

"That you'd found a dead body outside your room. That you were hysterical."

"Do I look hysterical?"

He admitted I did not.

"And did she ask you to come?"

His lips tightened. "No. I assumed from the tone of the message that—I assumed. A mistake."

"I'm surprised you braved seeing me in person."

He flung up his hands and walked away. "If I had known there would be cats on board, I wouldn't have." He took the stairs up two flights and then turned in toward his room, and since my room was one door down from his, I joined him.

"Look, Bowers. You paid a lot of money to join the cruise, so you might as well enjoy it. Just ignore me."

At that, he stopped walking again and took a step forward. I took a step back and wound up with my back against the wall.

"I wish it was that easy." He touched my sleeve. "You're hard to ignore." He sighed. "It's not your fault, Frankie. I heard you were in trouble and thought—well, I thought you might need me. I was doing the hero act." He traced my jaw with his finger. "My sisters always said I had a big head."

My voice was unsteady. "I thought you had decided I was an untouchable."

He nodded. "There is that." He took my chin in his fingers and lifted it. "Actually, you're very touchable."

"There you are!"

Bowers stepped back, and I closed my eyes to block out the view of Gina and Robby, headed our way. I opened them. My wish hadn't been answered. Gina was still there, and she tucked her arm through Bowers' and gave one of her horse-whinny laughs.

"You missed some great dancing."

"I'm not dancing material," Bowers said.

Robby grabbed my hands and twirled me around the hallway. "Frances is. I'm looking forward to the reception."

He dipped me, and I had to laugh at his enthusiasm, though I dropped my smile at the site of Bower's upside-down frown. When Robby brought me back up, I patted his shoulder.

"Too much energy for me. I'm going to bed."

"Hey!" Robby turned to Bowers. "Did you catch the show? Talk about silly! Who ever heard of trained cats, unless you're talking about tigers or lions, of course."

"Yes," Bowers said. "It was a stitch."

Robby let loose a yawn. "Are you coming, roomie? I have a bottle of scotch we can take to the veranda where we can keep a sharp lookout for falling bodies." He winked at me.

"Sounds promising," Bowers said, but Gina held onto his arm and puckered her lips into a pout.

"But that leaves me by myself with nothing to do. This is a cruise. You're all acting like old fogies."

Bowers sighed and patted her hand. "I am an old fogey."

"I'll save you a dance tomorrow night," Robby said to Gina, adding, "If you're lucky."

From the lack of enthusiasm she put behind her laugh,

that news didn't make Gina's night, but she gave in with good grace, and we all went to our rooms.

Except I slipped back out. Bowers and Robinson thought there was something fishy about Marv's death, and that was all the confirmation I needed. I'd already lost a day, but now that I felt certain it was murder, I knew just where to start my investigation. Once I brought Bowers some proof, Robinson would have to act.

The first night after the show, the celebrities had mingled with the passengers. I made my way to the Orca Lounge to see if anyone from the show remained, especially if that anyone was Bitsy. I was in luck. She stood in the center of the room, and fans surrounded her, most of them older gentlemen. I considered the best way to approach her and had decided on a plausible reason for asking about the cats, when I heard a voice in my ear.

"She's soaking up condolences like a sponge." Sonny Street stood at my side. "You would think she had been Marv's girlfriend instead of Sonya." He shrugged. "Maybe she was. Marv wasn't a considerate guy. I never understood what Sonya saw in him."

"Do you mean the other performers didn't like him?"

"Maybe I shouldn't say, now he's dead."

"Say. You know you want to."

He smirked. "We called him Marv the Menace."

"Did he threaten anyone?" I tried to keep the excitement out of my voice. Threatened people sometimes fight back.

"We didn't call him that because he was menacing in an evil way. He was annoying, like Dennis the Menace." He drew his brows together. "I guess if I have to explain it then it's not a good joke."

"So, there wasn't anyone he hung out with? Someone he might have spent his last hours with?"

"If there is, I can't name him. Or her. Sonya was around, though less and less lately. Of course, he had to work with his partner. Now Bitsy, her nickname is Banana Brain, and I don't have to explain that one."

"She got it together enough to go through with the act tonight. That was brave."

"It sure was. Not. She's been wanting to go out on her own for as long as I've known her. Granted, that hasn't been long, but she was vocal about it."

"Why didn't she?"

Sonny winked. "The Double C. Cats and Contract. The cats belonged to Marv, and she had a five-year contract."

"Interesting." I rubbed my chin.

He raised his eyebrows. "You think she helped him overboard to further her career?"

"It's possible his convenient death made her dream a reality. Now she's the headliner for the *Iso Kala*."

He shook his head. "That doesn't make sense. When Marv died, Bitsy tried to pack up the act and leave, but management held her to the contract and forced her to keep the act going without him."

"That *is* odd. By the way, who do the cats belong to now?"

"I have no idea," he said, looking at Bitsy with interest. "Marv must have had a will. Or maybe it's listed in the contract."

I hated to ask the next question because of the answer I might get. "Did they ever find Felix?"

"You mean the fat, dumb one?" He shook his head. "He hasn't turned up yet. Probably some old woman took him in." He nudged me in the ribs. "We should look for a passenger who has suddenly started ordering large quantities of fish from room service."

I was grateful he hadn't suggested Felix had gone overboard, and I appreciated his use of *we*. It made it easier to ask my next question.

"Where do the cats stay when they aren't on stage?"

"Well, as of this morning, the stars of the show are still in Marv's room with a couple of litter boxes. The steward brings them their food and cleans up after them. I assume they'll stay there for the rest of the cruise because Bitsy won't have them in her room."

"Why not?"

"Not a chance. She said she had an unpleasant experience with them once, and it left an impression. Personally, I don't think she likes cats."

I gaped. "Then why on earth did she want a solo act with them?"

"Let me rephrase it. She likes them as little dollar bills. She would as soon cuddle with them as you would pet your checkbook."

"The day Marv died, was he at rehearsal?"

He nodded. "The crew was moving his props onto the stage as I walked off."

"And he had an hour to rehearse?"

"That's how it works. Why?"

"I was trying to fill in Marv's last hours on earth. Maybe he met with someone and it didn't go well."

"The last time I saw him was in the Orca Lounge, after the act. You were there."

"And before that?"

"While he was waiting to go onstage."

"Do you remember seeing Bitsy or Sonya that night?"

"Not after Marv's exhibition with your friend."

Marv had rehearsed, and then he would have eaten dinner and changed for the show. That didn't leave him much time to tick off someone. I wondered how Bowers would trace Marv's movements. Probably interview everyone who knew him, but I didn't have that authority. I'd have to take a shortcut and ask the cats.

"Which number did you say Marv's room was?"

"I didn't."

"I was just thinking...."

"You want me to get you in to see the cats."

I was stuck. I couldn't sputter a protest because my next question was to ask if he could get me in to see the cats.

He laughed.

"It hasn't been that long since the *Blue-Ribbon Babes* fiasco. I remember how you work. Speaking of murder...."

I fluttered my eyelashes. "Who said anything about murder?"

"Give me a break. My good looks might fool you, but I have got a brain. It might be fun to be on the investigating side this time. Being a suspect wasn't that great. I'm not a suspect, am I?"

I made a deprecatory noise. "You're on the side of justice, which reminds me. Can you get hold of a master key for me?"

He tilted his head to one side. "Pardon me? I thought you said you wanted me to help you break into someone's room."

"It won't be breaking in if I have a key."

"No." His voice was firm but pleasant. "I can't risk it."

I leaned my head in and lowered my voice. "It's a matter of life and death."

He made the motion for gimme. "Spill it all or I won't even consider it."

"You're right. Marvelous Marv was murdered, and the only witnesses with anything to say are the cats. So, you see why I need the card. If you help solve a murder, you might get a raise."

He took hold of my arm. "My name stays out of this. I love this gig, and I'm not going to risk it." He let go and studied me until I started to fidget. "If this is for real, I don't see how I can stand by and not help bring Marv's murderer to justice."

"That's the spirit."

He sighed in a way that made me think he wished he had never met me. "I'll see what I can do."

"When?"

"For crying out loud, when I'm able. You just gave me a tall order to fill."

"Hurry it if you can. Remember, a life is at stake."

"If I can work it without risking my job, I'll let you know."

I gave him a puppy-eyed look, and he made a scoffing noise.

"I practice in the Neptune at noon. Meet me there."

Meeting Sonny Street backstage had another advantage. If the cats were being kept there in cages to wait for their time onstage, I might be able to get some face time. I dropped the idea of talking to Bitsy tonight. If I gave her too much attention, she would be suspicious if she saw me hanging around the cats.

I thanked Sonny and returned to my room.

I went through my nightly routine, which was minimal, threw on a nightgown and crawled under the covers. I'm not into television, so I lay in the dark, staring at the ceiling, and willing sleep to come.

A warm feeling spread through my tummy at the thought of Bowers dropping everything to respond to my cry for help via sneaky Penny, even though I hadn't given one. Was it possible he was still interested? Or did he feel sorry for me in the same way I felt sorry for homeless kittens?

Sleep came, but it was a light sleep, because the sound of giggles woke me up. Even at a lower volume, I recognized that irritating fake laugh. Gina.

I slipped out of bed and crept across the room. I managed to get the door open without making a sound, and I peered my head out in time to see Bowers letting Gina into the room next door.

SIXTEEN

Bowers meant it about sticking to me. I walked out of my door at eight o'clock the next morning and there he was, leaning against the wall, waiting for me. For a moment, I regretted rolling out of bed and throwing on sweats, but I wasn't awake enough to care for long.

"Breakfast?"

"Yeah. Sure," I mumbled. Before coffee and food, I'm unable to speak in complex sentences. That usually doesn't matter, since my cat, Emily, and my mutt, Chauncey, aren't conversant in English.

I dragged my feet, my shoulders hunched and my mouth stretched open in a yawn, until we stepped onto the Lido Deck. As the smell of bacon filled my nostrils, I transformed from shuffling zombie into an enthusiastic race-walker.

Once I had a plate of corned beef hash, extra potatoes, and an orange, I found a table. I was halfway through breakfast before Bowers sat down. He handed me a coffee with cream.

"Thanks," I said, taking a sip. "I'm starting to focus."

Fortunately, Bowers didn't chit-chat while we ate, which meant I could concentrate on my hash. Even better, he asked if I wanted to share his bacon, so I didn't have to lower myself to snatching a piece off his plate.

"What's on the agenda for today?" he asked.

I didn't want to mention a clandestine meeting with Sonny Street and a possible breaking and entering, so I pretended he meant the ship's agenda. "Tracy Arm. The captain is going to risk our lives to show us a closeup of some icebergs."

Both of his eyebrows shot up in surprise. "You're not interested in the glaciers? Glacier Bay National Park is a World Heritage site known for its unique ecosystem and its beauty."

"It's ice."

"Then what are you going to do all day? Shop?" He shuddered as he pronounced the last word.

I stood and picked up my tray. "Fortunately for you, I don't like shopping. Did you bring your swim trunks?"

He responded with a short and emphatic no. We got rid of our trays and started walking down the stairs without a destination in mind.

"That's too bad about your swimming trunks. I'm sure Gina would like to show you her tan lines."

"I'm sure she's showing them to Robert," he said. Since Bowers hated to be called Marty, he probably figured he was doing Robby a favor by refusing to use his nickname.

"Give me a break. She sneaked into your bedroom last night. I heard her. You want to tell me she couldn't stand to be away from her cousin?"

"They're cousins? Well, they were the only two talking. Apparently, they have a lot in common. Old horror movies are fine, modern romantic comedies are not. Seafood gets thumbs up, though sushi gets thumbs down. Historical novels—you get the point. I suggested they take it to the lounge, but they stayed where they were and whispered, which is worse. I've gotten a better night's sleep on a stakeout."

I snorted. "You're a guy which means you're oblivious to the manipulations of women. If she had stripped in front of you, you would have thought she was doing it because the thermostat was set too high."

"I'm a highly trained observer. She wasn't hitting on me. If she was and I missed it, maybe she wanted to make sure she had a dance partner, since you and Robert plan to dance the night away."

I chuckled. "I've got you there because I know something you don't know."

"What's that?" He really seemed interested. His detecting instincts had been on hold for two days and he probably smelled a mystery.

I stopped walking and took hold of his arm. "This is between you and me. Consider it a national secret." When he rolled his eyes, I shook his arm. "Promise me. I wouldn't want to hurt anyone's feelings."

He didn't cross his fingers or his heart, but he gave me a look that said I was starting to irritate him.

"Robby is a toe-stepper."

"You mean...?"

I nodded. "He is very energetic, and no woman's toes are safe around him on the dance floor. I lost the nail off my big toe when I was sixteen. A family wedding."

The corners of his mouth curled up. "So, this is what the ladies spend their time talking about in the powder room. Cruel gossip about the men who dote on them."

"Robby doesn't dote. In fact, I don't know any doters."

A blond woman in a pink satin suit, her lips looking as if they had never held any position except the broad smile she now wore, stepped in front of us.

"You're just in time! We're about to begin."

She motioned to a room filled with paintings on easels. Bowers' eyebrows wrinkled and his nose crinkled, and with that subtle change of expression, I knew it wouldn't be his choice to settle in for an art lecture. Normally, I would have agreed with him, but since he insisted on following me around, I said, "Great!" and took an empty seat. Bowers had two choices: to bail on his self-imposed assignment, or to take the seat next to me. I patted the chair cushion and grinned.

Thirty minutes later, I knew more about up-and-coming artist Santos Rivera's skills as an artist than I cared to know. Picasso would have envied his use of color. Rembrandt would have killed for his technique. He released all inhibitions when applying brush to canvas, which sounded to me like a lack of self-control. Yada-yada-yada. The cheery blond saleswoman moved in for the kill, offering us the tantalizing discounted price of $1,999.00 for three paintings. An elderly woman in the front row raised a hand laden with silver rings and asked whether there would be tax on the purchase. If you're going to spend two-thousand bucks on a picture, it seems petty to quibble about taxes.

Bowers got up and left, and since I wasn't ready to purchase an expensive painting I didn't like, I followed.

"That wasn't very nice," he said.

"Didn't you find it fascinating?"

"No. And neither did you."

I fluttered my eyelashes. "I was introducing you to some culture."

"Let me ask you something. What did you feel when you looked at *Geraniums in the Moonlight*?"

The question surprised me. "Sticker shock."

He nodded. "Great art, or even good art, will evoke an emotional response, or a memory. Those paintings were just pretty." Forgetting for a moment I was untouchable, he grabbed my hand. "Now it's time to do something I'd like to do. I am, after all, using up my vacation time."

Bowers and I got on the elevator, and when we exited, we were outside on the Sports Deck. It was still too early in the day to think about games, at least I thought so, but Bowers handed me a stick and suggested shuffleboard. It was a big, rectangle strip that ended in a triangle hopscotch board, but instead of hopping on it, players sent the puck flying into the highest scoring spot, which was the ten at the pointed tip. The only other people in sight were a couple who only had eyes for each other. They were trying to transform dribbling a basketball into a romantic event.

"Ladies first," Bowers said.

I stood sideways, placed my legs at shoulder width, pulled back with the stick, and swung hard. The little sucker flew fast and furious, just missing the woman by a foot.

"Fore," I yelled, too late. It didn't matter. Her back was turned. Her beloved's eyes popped open, he looked my way to see who could be trying to kill his woman, and then he left her to retrieve the puck.

"It's not golf," Bowers growled.

The man jogged up with my puck, his lady following close behind. I expected a string of expletives, but instead they both grinned at me like happy Labradors.

"You've got quite a swing!" He handed me the puck.

"I'm Josh, and this is Lindsey. You almost put an end to our honeymoon."

"How long have *you* been married?" Lindsey asked. "Because it's been a week for us. Seven of the best days of our lives."

It seemed they would forgive even a close call with a concussion if it gave them the opportunity to talk about the quagmire of love in which they were drowning.

I quickly clarified we were fellow guests at a friend's wedding. After we congratulated them on their bliss, Josh suggested it might be safer if we teamed up for a game. "Guys against girls," he called out as he picked up two more sticks.

Lindsey giggled and said, "You're on, Mister," which left Bowers and me without much choice.

The next hour was pure torture. My mind was frantically working on the problem of how to get hold of the key card, get rid of Bowers, and make sure I could get into Marv's room undetected, but it kept getting interrupted by the cutest couple on the ocean. They dripped the honey of happiness, and they wanted to share the sweetness. It was as if they were self-conscious about their own joy and felt obligated to pay extra attention to the two losers who lacked this special gift. Torture.

Bowers could have made our excuses, but he hadn't, so I wanted to make him suffer. After a few unsuccessful attempts to keep the puck from shooting past the board, I learned if I swung the stick with the same lack of enthusiasm Emily showed when I tried to get her to play with her latest catnip mouse, the puck slid half-heartedly onto the board and gave up somewhere around the middle.

My shot thrilled Lindsey. "That's another point for the girls. Woo-hoo!"

She seemed to think I was harnessing some feminine power to make the puck do my will. Feminine power. I pressed my lips together to keep from grinning. I knew exactly how to get rid of Bowers. My gaze went to him, and I caught him frowning at me. It was as if he could read my mind. I felt a need to explain the grin that escaped, so I pumped my fist in the air and said, "Go, Lindsey!"

Naturally, with my voluble support, she choked, and then it was Bowers' turn. You would have thought a man trained in marksmanship would have had better aim, but Bowers lacked the one skill necessary for shuffleboard. Patience. His shots all went straight, I'll give him that, but they either didn't make it to the board because he held back too much or, as in the case of his current move, the puck shot well past the board. Josh rallied to tie the score, but I blew him away by landing the puck in the 10-spot.

Lindsey jumped up and down, squealing with joy. Then she ran up to Josh, put her arms around his neck, and gave him a big kiss. You would have thought he had won the game. Maybe, with a happy wife, he *was* the winner. When they came up for air, Lindsey blushed.

"We thought it might ruin our honeymoon when that man died, but it hasn't made any difference in our trip." Lindsey blushed, realizing how self-centered her comment had been, but I felt for her when she explained. "I mean, I thought they might turn the ship around or something. We had to save for a year to afford this Honeymoon."

"They've already removed the body," I said.

She put a hand to her lips. "That's terrible."

"I'm sure Marv doesn't mind."

Lindsey slipped her hand around her husband's arm. "I heard he fell from up here." She looked around the deck as if expecting to see his ghost. "We were up here that night."

My ears perked up. "The first night of the cruise?"

The couple exchanged guilty glances. "We wanted to take a romantic stroll—a *private* romantic stroll—but there were so many people on the Promenade Deck. We decided to check it out up here."

"The place was deserted," Josh said. "Except for one other couple, but we didn't have much trouble avoiding them." He pointed to a spot of railing, and if he had moved his finger down, he would have been pointing at my lifeboat. "They never moved from that spot."

My stomach tingled. "Did they have cats with them?"

Lindsey blew out a sigh of relief. "I'm so glad you said that. There were shadows moving, and I thought they were giant rats."

So, Lindsey wasn't too bright.

"Then it was a woman with him?" Bowers asked.

Josh and Lindsey exchanged glances again, and Josh spoke for them. "We assumed, but we couldn't tell. The person had on a long jacket and a knit cap. Besides, as soon as we saw someone else up here, we turned and walked on the opposite side of the deck."

Bowers slipped into his non-threatening, smooth interviewer's voice. "How tall was the person with the man? Just a guess. As tall as him? Up to his shoulder?"

"They were leaning against the railing," Lindsey said. She squinted her eyes and looked in that direction, trying to bring the scene back. "I *think* shorter than the man, but not by too much. Not noticeable. Why? Is it important?"

Bowers smiled. "We're just curious." He shook Josh's hand. "Enjoy your honeymoon."

As soon as Josh and Lindsey wandered off holding hands, I said, "That's it then. It was a woman."

"You heard them as well as I did. They couldn't be sure. How tall was Marv, anyway?"

I thought back to when he kissed Penny. He wasn't as tall as Kemper's six-feet-two-inches, but he was taller than Sharon, and Sharon was around five feet six-ish.

"If I had to guess, I'd put him at five feet nine or ten."

"So, he could have been standing with a woman or a man the same height who wasn't standing straight. How tall is Sonny Street?"

"Around that height, but don't go bothering Sonny. I feel guilty enough about suspecting him of murdering the Blue-Ribbon Queen."

He didn't have anything to say about that, at least not out loud, so he changed the subject.

"I want it on record you cheated."

"At shuffleboard? How?"

"I don't know, but you're a klutz, you hate sports, and I don't think you've ever held a shuffleboard stick, at least not until I handed you one. There's no way you beat me without cheating."

I put my arm through his and led him to the elevator. "Cheer up, big guy. I'll buy you a free hamburger, or whatever they're serving by the pool."

But it was early yet, and they weren't serving. The next best thing to eating food is watching other people cook it, so we stopped by the Caribou Theater to watch a chef whip up a no-fail soufflé and a tasty vegetable stir fry. It reminded me of the *Blue-Ribbon Babes* taping I'd attended with my aunt. One of the contestants had been murdered, and the two of us had stumbled over the body on our way out of the studio. Hopefully, this cooking show would have a happier ending.

Just as everyone's eyes, including Bowers', focused on

the stage to see if, despite his confident assertions, the chef's soufflé had in fact fallen, I slipped a look at my watch. It was eleven-thirty. The chef finished to applause. I had to take his word that the final product was tasty because, unlike the Baking Channel's *Blue-Ribbon Babes* show, this event didn't offer samples. As soon as the show was over, most of this crowd would stampede to the Lido Deck, but for once, I had no interest in food. I wanted to get to Sonny Street and get that master key from him, but I couldn't do that with Bowers following me around.

The idea I had come up with for ditching Bowers would work, but it would cause me embarrassment. After running through a few alternate scenarios and finding serious flaws in all of them, I was about to employ my original idea when his cell phone rang. He answered, "Bowers," held up a finger to tell me to wait for him, and then walked away to take the call in private. It must have been work.

As soon as he turned his back, I ducked around the corner and made for the stairway. I jogged down one flight and trotted to the end of the hallway. The Neptune Theater wasn't locked, but it was in complete darkness. Sonny, wearing jeans and a polo shirt, stood in front of a microphone center stage. From the joke he told, I knew he was midway through his act, so I took a seat and waited for him to finish.

No sooner had I tuned out when something tuned in. I heard a low humming in my ears that meant the cats were somewhere close by. I headed for the side aisle and walked up a small set of stairs and toward the stage door with my head held high and my shoulders back, as if I belonged there.

Once I slipped through the open door, I was in darkness much blacker than that of the empty theater. They needed to put in a safety light. The humming increased into a static buzz, so I stretched my hands out in front of me and shuffled forward. When one toe hit something, the buzz rose in volume. I closed my eyes for a minute and opened them, which helped me adjust my eyes to the dark enough that I could make out shadows, like the large square in front of me. I put a hand down and felt the top of a cage.

Slowly, I crouched down and peered until I made out shadows moving inside, but I couldn't identify individual forms. I leaned toward the cage, opened my mind, and listened. There were too many voices to pick out one.

What was the name of the smart cat? Something Egyptian. Pharaoh? No. Sphinx.

"Here, Sphinx. Come here boy."

I almost jumped out of my skin when a wet nose touched my fingers.

"Good boy."

I reached my fingers through the cage and stroked his fur while I thought about Felix. Felix on stage. Felix running loose. Felix in my arms.

He responded with a long *Brrrrrrrrrr*.

Was Felix, lost and alone, feeling the cold? Another *Brrrrrrrrr*. I frowned. Was Sphinx trying to tell me *he* was cold? *Brrrrrrr*. Was Sphinx hungry? An excited *Brrrrrrrrr Brrrrrrr Brrrrrr* followed by images of kibble. The Ocicat rubbed his sleek body against the cage. And that's when I figured out *Brrrrrrr* was cat-speak for *duh*. Sphinx, the most talented and smartest looking of the performers was a kitty moron who would do anything for food.

I moved my attention to the other three cats. I thought if I focused on the entire cage, maybe I could communicate with all of them at once. Closing my eyes, I brought up an image of Marv and then connected it with my memory of the Observation Deck at night.

One of the cats growled.

I waited. A response finally came in words. *Gray Fur* hung in the air like a neon light. I sucked in a slow breath between clenched teeth, and my gaze went to Sphinx, the dark gray Ocicat. Was Marv's death an accident after all? Had Sphinx become distracted by a dropped treat and tripped his owner, sending him plunging to his death? If that was the case, why had somebody tried to kill me? I had to figure out which cat had sent the message, so I could dig for details.

"What are you doing?"

I twisted my head and looked up. Bitsy, dressed in a baseball cap, peasant blouse and black stretch pants, had one hand on her hip and a frown on her face. I stood up and cracked my stiff knee joints.

"I'm meeting Sonny Street after he finishes his practice, and I thought I would say hello to the kitties."

"No one is allowed back here except the talent."

The talent? I thought that was stretching it, and I was just about to say so, but just then, Sonny came trotting down the steps from the stage.

"I thought I saw you in the audience." He gave Bitsy a quick, impersonal nod and held out a hand to me. "Ready to go?"

I took his hand. "You betcha. Nice to see you again, Bitsy." I wiggled my fingers at her as we exited into the theater. As soon as we were out the back doors, I gave Sonny's hand a squeeze before letting go. Tingling with excitement from my new clue, I wanted nothing more than to have a long, uninterrupted conversation with those cats.

"Did you get a copy of the master key?"

"Hello to you, too," he said, though he didn't sound offended. "That was quick acting on my part, don't you think? I figured you didn't go there to talk to Bitsy. I'm cut out for espionage. I've got the good looks, and no one would suspect a comedian."

"Sorry about that. I'm grateful. She interrupted me just as I got started." I wasn't ready to share my new toy, *Gray Fur,* with anyone.

"Do animals really talk to you?"

"No. Not if you mean like 9Lives's Morris the Cat. I wish it were that simple. Now, what about that key?"

"I should be able to get it to you tonight. I'll drop by your room. There isn't any reason to check on the cats at night, so the coast should be clear."

I gave him my room number and then looked at my watch, sucking in a breath when I saw I'd been away from Bowers for almost twenty minutes. "I've gotta go. Thank you, Sonny. I'll wait to hear from you about the master key."

As he walked away, I called out, "What's the room number? Just in case we don't get a chance to talk before. you know."

"Four-two-seven."

I turned and ran into a wall. Bowers' chest. I raised my eyes to meet his gaze. His eyes were narrowed and aimed at Sonny's back.

"Why exactly do you need Sonny Street's room number?"

"It's not—" I paused. How would Bowers take it if I told him I planned to break into Marvelous Marv's room? Not well. I decided the better option was to let him think I was a tramp. I cleared my throat. "It's not any of your business."

His gaze held mine, and I'm proud to report I didn't flinch. Not that it was easy, especially when his left eye twitched, something that seemed to happen a lot around me.

"I came to get you because we're about to enter Tracy Arm. Unless you have other plans?"

"And miss a chance to stare at gigantic ice cubes?"

He took my hand. "I'm not missing this, and since where you go, I go, you're coming with me."

I made a face. "I hate crowds. They are all going to be fighting for the naturalist's attention and shoving to get a better view."

"Then we'll find someplace more private."

SEVENTEEN

"We are entering Glacier Bay."

With that announcement, we took our places in Kemper's room, where the wedding party had gathered. Since Kemper shared the room with Tommy, the best man joined us by default. He clutched at the veranda railing and leaned against the partition to the room next door. His smile seemed strained, but I gave him points for trying.

Kemper's parents, having taken the cruise before, had anticipated this momentous, ice-viewing occasion and ordered beverages and plates of fruit and cheese. After grabbing a few pieces of cheddar and a glass of wine, I decided there was too much weight out on Penny's veranda. Gina and her mother had nabbed the chairs, while Kemper, Penny and her mother leaned over the railings. I was happy to see Judy's rear end blocked Gina's view. Thomas and Christina stood at the rear of the veranda where they said they could see just fine, and Frank Doud stood with them.

"I think I'll watch from my room," I called. Bowers came with, of course, and Robby opted to join us.

"Wait for me," Gina called out, but at a sharp word

from Sharon, she stayed put. Mommy wasn't going to allow her to play with the bad children.

Robby grabbed the spot closest to the divider between rooms, and he hung over and gabbed with Kemper. As I watched the passing scenery, I tried not to point my gaze down at Marvelous Marv's last resting place.

The water had a creepy greenish-blue cast, and little white bits of ice floated on the surface. When one came close to the ship, I could see under the surface where the rest of the tiny iceberg spread out. Thoughts of the *Titanic* took over.

"Is this safe? I mean, couldn't one of those suckers tear a hole in the boat?"

"As slow as we're going and as small as they are, I doubt it," Bowers said.

Robby turned his head and winked at me. "Remember. If it's safe and convenient, I've got you covered."

A muted rumble came from the shore, where a waterfall cascaded down the side of a cliff—a spectacular rock face speckled with green. From here, it looked like a trickle of water, but when Robby handed me his binoculars, I could see an impressive, powerful flood of foam slamming against boulders as it danced down into the calm waters below. I handed the binoculars to Bowers.

"It's so peaceful here. I can't think why I was worried." I shouldn't have said it out loud.

"Look!"

The cry came from below, followed by shrieks from passengers on the surrounding balconies and those on the Promenade Decks below.

The ship was even with a small island in the middle of the waterway, and a figure stood in front of a large rock. He waved his hands over his head, but the ship's engines dwarfed his cry for help—if he in fact made one. We had been traveling at a crawl, but I felt a gentle lurch as they put on the breaks, or whatever they did to stop a ship. Though we didn't stop. Although we weren't going fast to begin with, we continued to drift past the island.

"How would anyone get stranded out here?" Penny said, leaning over the railing so far that Kemper hooked his finger through her belt loop.

I gasped. "Don't cruise ships go through here regularly? What if one of them sunk, and he's the only survivor?"

"Try again, knucklehead." Robby thumped my forehead.

Bowers didn't look amused. He still had the binoculars and was scanning the area.

The crew must have gone into action as soon as they spotted the man because they were lowering one of the lifeboats into the water with a crane. Two crew members stayed on board the lifeboat and headed for the island.

"At least we know they work," I said, but then I worried about what would happen if the crane were rendered useless by a spectacular collision or motor troubles. Did the crew have a backup plan to get the lifeboats into the water?

I nudged Bowers and took the binoculars from him, but when I looked through, all I saw was white fog.

"What did you do to them? Everything is a blur."

"You have to focus them for your own eyesight."

"You were the last to have them. Are you blind?"

"*My* eyesight is twenty-twenty."

"Oh."

Bowers took them from me and showed me how to adjust the lenses to bring them into focus. It took a few tries, but once I could see, I could make out a tiny, blurry man in a blue windbreaker, long, black exercise pants, and a black wool cap pulled down around his ears.

The rescue boat arrived, and the crew members gave him a hand as he climbed aboard. A small cheer went up from the deck below. One of the crew members got out and walked as far as he could around the island, but he came back empty. The lifeboat circled it once before they headed back to the ship. The man looked capable of telling them if he had been alone or not, but I suppose the employees had to make sure for themselves. He could have had a friend, fought with him, and then decided to leave his unconscious body behind, just to show him.

"I wonder if he'll have to buy a ticket?" I said.

Robby grabbed my hand and pulled me toward the door. "Let's check it out."

On the Lower Promenade level, Robby and Bowers watched as they helped the man aboard. Being shorter than them, I watched the backs of the people in front of me.

"He's lucky we saw him," Robby said.

"Yes. Lucky," Bowers responded in a flat voice. "Incredibly so."

"What are they doing?" I tried standing on tiptoe, but I still couldn't see a thing.

"Taking him inside."

I could have figured that out myself by the way the crowd broke up except for a few who remained behind to watch them get the lifeboat back onto the ship.

"If you rule out my theory that his ship went down, how did he wind up on the island?"

Robby grinned. "I'm sure we'll find out."

The news came via Gina, who had stuck her nose in as soon as the man set foot on the ship. She probably pushed herself forward and offered her services as an interpreter.

She met us on our way back to our rooms, and she bubbled over with news.

"His name is Trevor Grant."

I raised one eyebrow. "Trevor Grant? Sounds like a character in a romance novel."

"It is *such* a studly name, don't you think?" She paused to flutter her eyelashes at Bowers and then slapped his arm and let loose a hee-haw. "We girls are just terrible, aren't we?"

I didn't appreciate being included in her joke, but I slapped Bowers' other arm just for the fun of it.

Gina held up her palms as if we were the ones who needed quieting. "Okay. I'll stop teasing. Tyler was kayaking, and he came alongside one of those little icebergs, which aren't so little underneath. It tore a gigantic hole in his kayak. Can you believe it? He managed to row over to the island before the thing filled up with water, and then all he could do was stand there and watch as it sank."

"How terrible!" Robby said this in a girlish voice and pressed his palm on the center of his chest.

Gina poked his arm. "It *is* terrible. Or it could have been. Someone's guardian angel was on the job today! I mean, it was a miracle we found him."

Bowers muttered, "Something like that," under his breath, but I heard him loud and clear. "Who spotted him?"

"It was one of the jewelry guards. The guy. Everyone was on deck checking out the icebergs, so he wandered to a window for a look."

"He must have incredibly acute vision," Bowers said.

"You're telling me. Like I said. Lucky."

Gina leaned her head in toward Robby and suggested they check out the casino.

"That's a good idea," Bowers said. "You go with them. I have a few things to take care of."

"Like what? Stock up on groceries? Change your car's oil? You're in Alaska, for Pete's sake. What could you have to do?"

"Call the office."

"Oh. Are you on a big case right now? I don't remember seeing anything about a murder in the *Wolf Creek Gazette*." Not that I read the *Wolf Creek Gazette*, but I couldn't imagine what Bowers could do from here that someone in the office wouldn't be better equipped to take care of. I decided he was lying. "How does that work? Do they describe clues to you over the phone? Or is it a video call?"

He looked at his watch. "It's a quarter to four now. Dinner is at five-thirty. I'll meet you there."

Gina kept giving Robby glances I couldn't interpret. They weren't flirty glances, as her eyes were serious and her brow wrinkled, and he put a hand on her shoulder in a gesture that seemed geared to comfort her. Whatever they were trying to communicate to each other, it was obvious they didn't want to include me. I begged off and returned to my room.

I introduced myself to the new towel creation on my bed—a giraffe—and decided I might as well get ready for dinner early. Afraid to waste water, I couldn't enjoy the luxury of a long, hot shower, but I took my time choosing an outfit. My black palazzo pants paired well with a navy-blue-and-white print peasant blouse. The reflection that stared back from the mirror said "boring" even when I added a gold chain necklace. Clearly, I wasn't meant to be a fashionista, and I couldn't wear Penny's dress every day.

I opted for black flats for my feet, stuffed my room key

in my pocket, double-checked said pocket to make sure I did indeed have my room key, and headed for the fourth floor.

Gina and Sharon, the latter in a bathing suit, descended to our floor the same time I reached the stairway.

"I thought you and Robby—"

That's all I got out before Gina interrupted me. "Where's Martin?"

I had to think for a moment before I realized she meant Bowers. "Still working."

She goggled at me. "On a cruise? Aren't men just like that?"

I agreed with that general statement even though I could name five men from our own party it didn't apply to. What the heck. I figured I should choose my arguments. I also decided that since I was certain Marv's death was murder, I needed to investigate all leads. Listen to that. You would think I was the cop, not Bowers.

"Sharon," I said. "Could I ask you something?"

She told her daughter she would meet up with her. Gina hesitated, but then she went on ahead to their room.

"It's actually not a question. I wanted to offer my condolences."

The perfectly plucked brows went up. "Condolences?"

"About Marv. I didn't know you and he were friends."

"We weren't."

"But I overheard the two of you talking."

The ice queen's porcelain cheeks flushed an ugly shade of red, so I jumped in to head off an outburst, even though it would have been educational to see what a Sharon Bradley outburst looked like.

"Not that I heard what you were saying. I just saw you talking together, and it looked like you knew each other."

She regained her composure, though her lips hardly

moved when she said, "You're mistaken. I simply told the man he had behaved boorishly and if he did anything like that again, I'd report him to management."

I smiled. "So that's all it was."

"Yes."

"I thought, when I saw you slipping out of your room the night he died, maybe you had gone to meet him."

She stared into my eyes without flinching. "Of course, I saw you and Robby. I was going to look for Gina, but I assumed all of you young people were together, and if you were on your way back to your room, she'd follow shortly. You noticed I went back in my room, which means I didn't go anywhere." She smiled at me, though I wouldn't have rated it as one of the sincerest smiles I'd ever received. "I'm glad we cleared that up."

If I had been a suspicious woman, I might have thought the smile was because Sharon Bradley had just made me a witness to the fact she hadn't left her room that night.

I smiled back at her. That alibi wouldn't count for much, since she could have left again as soon as Robby and me and Mrs. Doud had gotten me back into my locked room.

I took the stairs down at a jog. It felt good to have my first solid suspect.

EIGHTEEN

There is something about wearing the appropriate outfit for an occasion that makes a person feel as if they belong. Dressed in my nice evening outfit, it seemed less likely the sales staff would take me for a hoodlum as I browsed their ridiculously high-priced merchandise. Not that I consider shopping an occasion worth dressing for, but there were plenty of guests wandering in and out of the stores who looked like they were taking part in their favorite activity.

I set up my base of operations in the general store, the only place where I could find something affordable as a pet-sitting thank you gift for Seamus. That limited me to tourist items like whale-shaped chocolates and Alaskan-themed t-shirts, mugs and snow globes. I finally settled on a gray rugby shirt with a picture of an Alaskan Malamute on the front. He could wear it to work at his doggy daycare.

I intended to stow my package in my room, so I wouldn't be stuck carrying it around all night, but I as I exited the store, a familiar face exited Nautical Knits—the shop directly across from me—with a shopping bag in one hand.

I stared at the man. He had brown hair leaning toward blond that went over the collar of his black turtleneck, and he was every bit as tall as Bowers. There *was* something familiar about him, and as I narrowed my eyes to think, his face became blurry and I had it.

"You're the man we rescued today. Trevor Grant."

He looked around until he spotted me staring at him. "Guilty," he said.

"You look bigger in person." I crossed the hallway. "I mean, bigger than through the binoculars. That is, through the binoculars, you looked short, though there wasn't really anything to compare your size to, except a rock."

I relaxed when he laughed. His deep dimples and white teeth reminded me of actor Josh Holloway, the good-looking blond guy from *Lost*.

"I'm Frankie."

Trevor shook hands with me and then we started to walk.

"How in the world did you wind up stranded in the middle of nowhere? It must have been frightening to be out there alone." I gasped. "Oh, my gosh. You were alone, weren't you? I mean you didn't—uh—lose anyone, did you, when your boat sank?" It was out before I had time to edit.

"My boat, which was actually a kayak, did sink. I must have gotten too close to one of the icebergs," he said, repeating what I already knew. "And I was alone, which was stupid."

"Let's say daring."

Trevor laughed. "That does sound better."

"How long were you out there?"

He puffed up his cheeks and blew out a breath. "Felt like forever, but it couldn't have been more than a couple of hours."

"You're lucky it was a warm day," I said. "I wouldn't have thought Tracy Arm was a place for kayakers."

"It seemed like a good idea at the time."

My shoulders shivered. "It wouldn't have been my choice. Of course, you couldn't get me in one of those things if you paid me. I mean, once you flip over, aren't you stuck in there?"

"Uh, no."

"You're wearing clothes." My impulse control wasn't working today. "Did the captain lend you some of his? Because, through the binoculars, it looked like you were wearing those long, fitted exercise pants. Definitely not slacks and a turtleneck and leather loafers."

"Fortunately, I keep my wallet in a waterproof package in my jacket, although I did lose my backpack. This is going to be an expensive mistake. It cost me seven dollars for a toothbrush in the general store."

"We'll be arriving in Sitka tomorrow. That's only one change of underwear."

He burst out laughing and told me I was priceless. "Actually, I have friends arriving in Victoria in a few days. Since that coincides with when the ship will get there, the captain allowed me to pay a pro rata fare."

I raised my brows, thinking about how Bowers had wound up sharing a room with Robby. "I thought the cruise was booked solid."

"They had a small room they let me have."

"Marvelous Marv," I whispered. There went my chance to search his room.

"What's that?"

Trever suddenly steered me toward the Hardcastle collection.

"I heard passengers talking about the Pure Fantasy bracelet. Do you mind?"

"Nope. Look away. I suppose thanks are in order, anyway."

"What do you mean?"

"Didn't anyone tell you?" I pointed at Art. "That guard there is the one who spotted you. If it weren't for him, you might have been fish food."

Art waved away any thanks, but Trevor insisted on shaking his hand.

"Anyone would have done the same."

"Not likely," I said. "Most of the eyeballs on this ship are closing in on the use-by date."

He gave me a feeble smile. "I guess so."

A man wanting to purchase a raffle ticket took Art's attention, so Trevor moved to the far end of the other table and bent over the display case. As for myself, I had seen all I cared to of jewelry, but I tried to look attentive to be polite. It was a strain because Trevor took his time. He hadn't said what he did for a living. Maybe he was a gemologist. Did they make good money? Because he had to make a good living to be so casual about shopping for a new wardrobe at cruise ship prices.

Finally, he got to the Pure Fantasy bracelet. Art gave him the spiel about the auction, and Trevor asked me, "Do you think I should take a chance?"

I shrugged. "I wouldn't."

"Of course not. A beautiful woman should be the recipient of the gift, not the purchaser of the ticket." Then, to my surprise, Trevor reached into his back pocket and pulled out his wallet. As he dug out some cash, he winked at me and said, "What the heck. You only live once, right?"

"Unless you're a cat."

He stared at me and then decided to laugh. As he filled out the form on the clipboard, I couldn't help noticing he came from Northern California. Sonoma. Wine country. Maybe Trevor owned a vineyard. He'd look good strolling through the grapevines, a glass of Pinot Noir in his hand and a border collie running ahead of him to chase away crows, or robins, or whatever threatened his annual crop. His handsome face wasn't what I would call rugged, but he looked healthy and fit, as if he spent time outdoors. And kayaking seemed more in line with the sporting interests of a grape grower, rather than basketball or shuffleboard.

As he exchanged the clipboard and money for his ticket receipt, he told Art, "Take care of that ticket. I'm feeling lucky."

The guard met his gaze and said with all seriousness, "You never know. It could be your lucky day."

Art looked at me and raised his brows, recognizing me from my trip there with Bowers. He probably thought I made up to strange men in order to get them to buy me tickets.

By then I was ready for a drink, and Trevor didn't let me down. We hit the Seaside Bar, and he told me to wait on the love seat, and when he came back from the bar, he held a margarita in each hand. As he handed me mine, he said, "Tell me about yourself, Frankie. What's Frankie short for? Francine?"

I took a sip and relished the sweet-sour mixture. "Frances."

"That's a lovely name."

He sounded as if he meant it, so I thanked him. He leaned back, crossed his legs, and stretched his arm along the back of the love seat in a move that seemed naturally possessive rather than flirtatious. Trevor had a confident air.

He was the kind of man who filled a space, though he did it without the aggressiveness of a tyrant. The move put him close enough to me that I could feel he was a warm-blooded animal.

"I won't ask you what you do for a living," he said, "because that's a boring conversation starter. Besides, it's not as if I'm looking for a job."

I wondered how bored he would be if I shared my experiences with Petey the Cockatoo or Sandy the Golden Retriever. "That's good, because you'd have to pay *me*." The skin on my face got warm. "I'm not complaining about money. It's just you said you weren't worried about money, and I, well, I'm not worried about it, but I don't have any to spare for an employee." I touched my fingers to my forehead to hide my embarrassment.

He set his drink down on the table next to the love seat, hooked his pinkie around mine, pulled my hand away from my face and took it in both of his. Then he leaned his face close to mine and lowered his voice as if he were sharing a big secret. "Never. Be. Embarrassed. About. Money. About having it or not having it. It's just money. You have it, you spend it. You don't have it, you can always use a credit card."

I thought he was serious until those dimples showed up again in a broad smile and he tapped me on the nose.

"Am I interrupting?"

Bowers hadn't made a sound as he approached, or maybe I'd been too busy noticing Trevor's hands were as warm as the rest of him. Hand now, since he was only holding on with one hand. Yes, we were sitting on a loveseat holding hands, and I was too embarrassed to move. Trevor returned his arm to the back of the couch, only this time, he wrapped his hand around my shoulder and squeezed. It felt as if I'd been caught in the act of cheating, but you can only cheat on someone you're committed to, right? And Bowers had been the one who had said we couldn't have a future together.

"Not at all," Trevor said. He picked up his margarita. "I'm Trevor, and this is Frances. Join us?"

Bowers finally moved his gaze from me to Trevor. "Actually, *Frankie* is going to be late for dinner if we don't get a move on."

Trevor didn't remove his arm or let my hand go, but said, "You two know each other?"

"We're here with a wedding party," I said. "I'm the maid-of-honor and he's—not.

After a pause, Trevor released me and sighed. "Dinner. The captain offered to put me at one of the smaller tables that had a free seat, but that would mean joining a couple. With my luck—and their bad luck—it would be people on their honeymoon or a couple taking an anniversary cruise. Maybe parents who had escaped the children for a week and were having their first night out alone in years." He grimaced. "I didn't want to be an unwelcome third wheel. I'll just have something sent to my room."

I jumped to my feet. I had just spotted Frank and Judy Doud in the hallway. "You stay right where you are. I'll be right back."

The Douds were delighted to have such an exciting guest to dinner. Since his rescue from the island, Trevor Grant was almost a celebrity. I brought them back to the bar with me to share the good news, and on our arrival, Trevor stood.

"This isn't permanent, you understand," Mrs. Doud said after she'd issued the invitation. "Once our best man,

Tommy, has his sea legs and joins us, we won't have a free seat."

"If you're sure it's not an imposition."

I laughed. "Please. You won't be interrupting any great romances. Penny and Kemper don't start their honeymoon until tomorrow night. We'd love to have you."

"In that case, I accept. Thank you."

I nudged him in the side. "You will have to pay for your supper with some exciting stories."

"I'll make them up on the way there."

Frank and Judy Doud monopolized Trevor on the walk to the dining room, probably with hopes of getting the inside scoop on his rescue. Bowers and I trailed behind.

"You certainly have been busy making friends," Bowers said. "Sonny, and now Trevor."

"Yeah, and? I'm human. I like company, sometimes. Okay, not often, but I'm on a cruise and you're supposed to meet new people when you're on vacation."

"Shipboard romances?"

"Sure. Why not?" A shipboard romance was not on my mind, as casual sex and regrets did not sound like a formula for a good time. I had enough trouble feeling good about myself.

Frank took the seat at the end of the table to make room for our addition. The guest of honor wound up between Penny and Gina, across from Robby, me and Bowers. Gina had donned a pumpkin-colored dress that accentuated her leftover summer tan and the reddish highlights in her blond hair. Her sophisticated style made Penny, in her pink blouse and a sparkling butterfly barrette, look like somebody's kid sister.

Gina's style may have been subtle, but her actions weren't. Already she had her hand on Trevor's arm, and her long hair made silky movements as she leaned her head in and nodded at his every word. When he made a joke, she even kept the whinny to a low, throaty chuckle.

Bowers, no longer the new guy at the table, sat quietly at my side, and Robby wasn't much better. They preferred to stare at the newcomer. Only Kemper didn't seem intimidated by Trever's good looks and charming personality, but Kemper is usually oblivious to nuances. And I suppose you have the right to expect your woman's unwavering devotion on the night before your wedding.

"Do you think you'll ever kayak again?" Gina asked. "After your awful experience?"

"Not alone, that's for sure."

Trevor's appeal wasn't limited to the ladies. The older men looked on him as a source of vicarious adventure.

"What happens when one of those things tip over?" Thomas Mohr asked. "I've heard you're trapped."

As Trevor explained kayaking 101, I peeked at the menu to make sure it still listed my favorite.

"Don't worry," Bowers said. "The kitchen hasn't run out of filet mignon."

"How do you know I wasn't going to try something new?"

He looked down at me, one eyebrow raised. "Seriously."

I held his gaze for the count of ten and then I crumbled into giggles and turned my menu face down. "You got me."

"I know you too well."

But was that true? We'd been through a couple of murder investigations together. Well, not *together*. He investigated; I got in the way, through no fault of my own. First, I was a suspect, since at Sandy the Golden Retriever's instigation, I had suggested the Peters' missing maid might be dead. I can understand how a cop might find that suspicious. Later, the killer resented my involvement and tried to kill me in my own living room, which is kind of rude. And it wasn't my fault I had literally stumbled over a corpse at the *Blue-Ribbon Babes* premiere. When my Aunt Gertrude was suspected of killing her rival in a very old love triangle, I couldn't just stand around and watch, could I? Bowers shouldn't be so judgmental.

"What's on your mind?" Bowers murmured in my ear. "The look on your face is intense, so it must be the dessert menu."

"I was thinking about how unfair you are."

"Unfair?" He sounded genuinely surprised.

"And judgmental."

He sipped his wine. "Unfair *and* judgmental. I sound like quite a catch."

"Then you'd better find someone who's fishing."

"I'd bite your ear for that, but I wouldn't want to upset your new boyfriend."

My gaze settled across the table at Trevor. "There you go again. Judgmental." I turned in my chair and looked Bowers straight in the eye. "I don't *have* a boyfriend. No love of my life. No special interest. I'm a free spirit."

I hadn't realized my voice had risen in volume, and now everyone was staring at me—Penny with pity, Kemper with fear that I'd cause a scene, and Gina with a smirk on her face. Robby looked surprised. I didn't like the amused expression on Trevor Grant's face.

Bowers broke into laughter. "That's awful." He laughed some more and then looked around the table to include them all in the joke. "Frankie was repeating the dialog from a very bad film."

"You should have been an actress," Mrs. Doud said. Her

sharp gaze never missed a thing, and I was certain she knew I had meant every word.

Thomas Mohr leaned forward to see past his wife. "What was the name of the movie?"

"Um." I squished up my face. "*Free Spirit.*"

"I haven't heard of that one."

"Lucky you," I said.

"I think I've heard of it," Penny said, trying to help me out.

Frank Doud chuckled. "Sounds like a stinker."

"It is." I nodded. "A real stinker."

When the waiter showed up, Bowers took pity and ordered the filet for me. I was too mortified to open my mouth.

After dinner, I excused myself saying I had a few things to take care of before the wedding. Bowers moved to escort me to my room, but I begged off and forced him to sit back down. There's nothing like making an idiot out of yourself to make you crave alone-time.

I made sure to go around the table and give Penny a hug before I left to assure her everything was fine. But everything wasn't fine.

Free spirit my fanny. I was lonely. Bowers and I had almost started something back in Wolf Creek, something I wanted. After he had experienced one, simple, accidentally transferred image of a screaming cat, he had declined to pursue the relationship. What a baby. He should try living in my shoes for a week.

Usually, I didn't mind being by myself. At home, I had my animal behavior business, U Behave, to keep me busy. If thoughts of Bowers' sensitive eyes, firm mouth, or even his sense of humor worked their way into my head, I could push them aside with a task, like washing the dog. However,

I was stuck on this boat, surrounded by Penny and Kemper, who grabbed every opportunity to make google-eyes at each other, and Gina, who pushed herself forward as soon as she sensed a Y chromosome enter the room. Robby was just Robby, a good-looking man who was off-limits because he was my best friend's brother.

Even the other passengers were paired off. The couple walking past me hand-in-hand. The elderly man and woman in front of me, moving like molasses. They had a lifetime of shared memories and finished each other's sentences, which might be annoying, but it meant they belonged to each other.

At the Seaside Bar, Sonya sat on a stool, alone. A kindred spirit. I didn't make any overtures, as I wasn't up to yet another rejection. Besides, she didn't count as a kindred spirit. She had been part of a couple until her other half had been murdered.

As I passed the door that led to the Promenade Deck, moonlight illuminated an embracing couple outside by the railing. Disgusting.

I took my time walking back to my room, dragging my feet in self-pity. To my surprise, I found Penny waiting in the room.

"Did you fly here?"

She ran over to me before I'd closed the door behind me and gave me a hug. "Frances. I can always tell when you're upset. What's the matter?"

We used to share every confidence, but Penny's attention belonged on her upcoming nuptials. It wouldn't be fair to bring up murder or morbid thoughts about how I was going to be alone for the rest of my miserable life.

"I'm just tired."

I sat on the edge of my bed and fell back, my arms out to

my sides. "I'll be fine." When someone knocked on the door, I stayed put and let Penny get it. "Come on in," she said, and I raised my head. It was Gina.

"Is the party in here?"

"Can't you tell?" I said, not feeling very friendly.

I rolled over on my side to face her. Gina stood with her hands clasped in front of her. She looked as if she wanted us to invite her to stay, which was an oddly vulnerable attitude, coming from her. I returned to laying on my back. Penny, who is heaps nicer than I am, told her to take a seat, and the two of them perched on the edge of Penny's bed.

"Do you have any plans for tonight?" Gina asked. "Because I thought since this is your last night as a single person, maybe Frances and I should take you out for a drink."

Penny threw her arms around her cousin. "That's so nice of you!"

"Great," I said, not meaning it. That meant getting up again. It also was a suggestion that should have come from the maid of honor, but she was too busy being selfish. I'd have to have a talk with her later. I hauled myself to my feet. "Where to?"

We wound up back at the Seaside Bar. They had piano music accompanied by a violin. The musicians were on a raised platform covered with the same carpet that was on the floor. Gina and Penny took the love seat I had occupied with Trevor Grant, while I pulled up a chair to face them.

We talked for a while about details of the wedding, assuring Penny our dresses fit, we had remembered to pack our matching shoes, and neither of us would forget our roles. We reassured her the musician would show up, and so would Father Basil.

"Oh my gosh." Penny paled. "I can't remember what I did with the list of readings."

I raised my hand. "St. Paul's Letter to the Roman's, chapter twelve."

"Book of Genesis, chapter one," Gina said. "Responsorial Psalm *The Lord is My Shepherd.*"

"That would be Psalm 23," I said, "followed by the Gospel of Matthew, chapter five. We've got you covered, Pen."

She grinned. "Have we gone over it that many times?"

"Yes, indeed." I took a sip of my margarita. "But you were sweet about it, so we forgive you."

She relaxed back into the love seat. "I'm looking forward to my wedding, and I take the ceremony seriously, but I can't wait for that part to be over and the fun to begin. I'm so stressed I'll trip or forget something or make a mistake with my vows."

I put on a serious voice. "I, Penny. take you Thomas Mohr—doh!" I slapped my forehead.

"That would be horrible. Kemper's father is already married."

"So, any regrets?" Gina said. "Now is the time to get them out of your system."

My sweet best friend furrowed her brow. "You mean like have I ever wanted to go skydiving?"

Here came the whinny, though since the musicians were playing, Gina covered her mouth to cut it off. "No, silly. Missed opportunities!"

When Penny squished up her nose, I put her out of her misery.

"She's talking about men, Pen. Are there men you wish you had gone out with?"

"You mean cheat on Kemper?"

"Let's say if you hadn't met Kemper."

Penny sipped her soda water. She had declined alcohol, saying she didn't want to be puffy on her wedding day. "No. No one."

Gina dropped her head to her chest and looked up through her lashes. "No one."

"Nope."

"Not even a movie star?"

"Nope. They might not be as nice in person, and then I'd never be able to watch them in a movie again."

"Huh." Gina took a swig from her bottle of beer. "I wouldn't mind having some alone-time with Mr. Trevor Grant."

Penny giggled. "He *is* good-looking." She turned her attention on me, maybe because I hadn't said a word. "How about you, Frances?"

"I'm not in a position to have regrets because I'm not getting married tomorrow. I'm not even attached to anyone."

"Is this a private party, or can anybody join?"

Robby grinned down at us and plopped down on the armrest next to Gina. Bowers remained in the background, leaning against the bar with his hands in his pockets and looking as if Robby had forced him to come against his will.

"This isn't a bachelorette party or anything, is it?" Robby waved his hands in the air. "Naked dancing men and drunken frivolity. Would it go with the classical music they're playing?" He tugged at his collar. "I could do a striptease. Oh, wait. It's *me* that has seen *Penny* naked before."

"Robby!" She reached across Gina and smacked his leg. "You're foul."

"Well I have. Somebody had to help mom change your smelly diapers. Poor woman. How she suffered." He leaned down and whispered in Gina's ear. "If you want to shut me up, buy me and my roomie a drink."

"Nothing for me," Bowers said. He looked at his watch. "In fact, I have to get going."

"Gotta call the office?" He rewarded me with his neutral cop-face expression.

"Something like that."

I stood. "You can walk me back to my room."

"And leave us with the reprobate?" Gina said.

Penny stifled a shriek. "Kemper's coming this way. He can't see me the night before the wedding."

"He saw you at dinner," Robby said.

I stood. "Men. Don't worry, Penny. Bowers and I will head him off." I hooked my arm through his. "We can drop you off at the office."

Fortunately, Kemper was in complete agreement about keeping his eyes off his bride. Besides, he was on his way to meet his dad for a man-to-man talk at one of the bars on the floor below. We walked him to the Atrium. Kemper went on ahead, and I stood at the top of the stairs.

"This way to Security Officer Robinson's lair. Isn't he your *phone call*?"

"That was just an excuse to get away."

The shopping arcade was up ahead, and Bowers said he shouldn't go back home without a token souvenir for the office. The general store was across from the Hardcastle Collection. He selected and paid for a snow globe, which took him about five minutes, and then he held it up for my inspection.

"I couldn't find a replica of an iceberg."

"I suppose you think you're funny."

"Moderately."

I should have laughed, but nothing seemed funny to me.

"There must be something wrong with me. Here it is a wedding cruise, but I'm not feeling very festive."

"It's not as if it's your wedding."

I shot him a sideways glance. "That's a selfish thought. Penny has been my best friend forever. I owe her more than that."

"Penny doesn't look like she's suffering from neglect. She's surrounded by loved ones, and if I may say so, she seems to be a naturally happy person."

"You mean she doesn't rely on her circumstances for happiness."

"Exactly."

"Unlike me."

We skipped the elevator and took the stairs to the fifth floor.

"I didn't say that."

"But it's true." I threw my head back and dropped my hands out to my sides. "I'm such a bore I'm boring myself."

"I would never call you boring."

"Thanks, I think."

We reached the landing and headed for our rooms.

"What would you call me? Strange? A pain in the side?"

"Sometimes."

I threw a half-hearted punch at his arm, and he rubbed the spot and said *ouch*.

"Faker. You're only doing that to make me feel better."

"Did it work?"

"No. What would make me feel better is—"

The hallway disappeared. I was back on the Observation Deck, and Marv's fingers clutched the bottom bar of the railing. *For God's sake, why?* My chest tightened, and shivers ran over my back, like tiny hairs standing on end. As

I watched, one finger slipped. Then the next. I turned my head, and a shadow stood by, watching Marv's struggle. Suddenly, he lost his grip and disappeared...without a sound. In his last moments, Marv hadn't screamed.

As the hallway came into focus, I fell to my hands and knees, panting. Bowers knelt at my side, one arm around my middle and the other on my shoulder.

"Frankie...Frankie."

I was aware we weren't alone, and I heard Robby's voice. "Is she alright?"

Though I couldn't see her face, I could imagine Gina's eye roll as she said, "Someone had too much to drink."

"She's fine," Bowers said, and he hauled me to my feet. He must have dug my room key out of my pocket. How else did he get my door open and steer me into my room? He shut the door on Robby and Gina's inquisitive faces, and once we were alone, he put his hands on my cheeks and forced me to look into his eyes.

"Frankie, say something."

My face crumpled. "It was awful."

"What happened?"

I reached up and grabbed his hands. "The murderer—he watched him die," I whispered.

"He?"

"He. She. I don't know. It was a shadow, but it stood there and watched him fall. And," I closed my eyes and took a deep breath, "Marv didn't even scream when he fell."

Bowers swore. He broke open the mini-bar and opened a whiskey. "Take a drink."

After one swallow, I coughed, made a face, and pushed the bottle away. "I'm fine."

He put his hands on my shoulders, and I shivered. His thumbs massaged in circles, and then he pulled me in and wrapped his arms around me. I put my arms around his waist and leaned my head against his chest. So solid. So warm. So protective. It took a few minutes, but my breathing returned to normal.

"I'm a wreck."

"Not a wreck. More like a fender-bender."

I sighed at the way his chest rumbled when he talked.

"You know, you haven't said once you were glad I came."

I lifted my head to look up at him, so he didn't have to adjust much to get his mouth to mine. His lips were firm and warm, and I was just getting over the surprise and starting to respond when someone knocked on my door.

Bowers put his hands on my shoulders, this time to move me back a step and look down at me. "Expecting someone?"

I gave a feeble laugh. "It's probably Penny's mom. I think she has a nookie radar."

I opened the door and surprised Sonny Street in the act of knocking again. He met Bowers' stony stare and looked a question at me. I think he wanted to know if Bowers was in on our secret, especially as he held a room key in his hand. I gave my head a slight shake.

"I was walking by and saw you left your card in your door," he said, holding the key card out to me. I stopped short of slapping my forehead because I thought that might be pouring it on a little thick, and I looked up at Bowers.

Bowers held out his hand. "I'll take that."

Sonny's smile faltered, and he darted a look at me, but then he gave the card up, tipped his fingers to his head in a salute, and left. Bowers stood in the hallway and waited until the elevator doors closed on Sonny Street. Then he held the key up between two fingers and said, "I unlocked your door. Your key is on the credenza." Then, with no offer to kiss me again, he returned to his room.

Bowers knew I had almost spent the night in Robby's room, he saw me holding hands with Trevor Grant, and now he'd witnessed Sonny Street knocking on my door in the middle of the night. Sonny had seen me alone in my room with Bowers. I was going to have quite the reputation by the end of this trip, but sacrifices would have to be made if I was going to track down the murderer.

Now, how to get the key back from Bowers?

NINETEEN

Early the next morning, the porter dropped off my bridesmaid's gown, which I had stored in the Honeymoon Suite. The bride had chosen royal-blue, a color that went with both my auburn hair and Gina's strawberry-blond coloring. My best friend was considerate that way. Nothing of Bridezilla hogging the limelight about her.

There wasn't a full-length mirror in the room, so after I slipped into the dress and performed the twists necessary to zip it up, the image staring back at me was only from hips up.

The fitted bodice was modest because of my insistence my chest remain private except where the neckline skimmed a hint of cleavage. At the hips, the tea-length skirt hung down in waves, and I had matching pumps. The nylons were a challenge. In Arizona, most people stick to sandals, since they'd melt in stockings. I lay on the bed and fought and wriggled to get each leg on. Pulling the waistband over my hips nearly gave me apoplexy. It was a good thing I'd left my hair until last.

Normally, I wear it down. The loose, natural curl gives

it body, and keeping the length just past my shoulders keeps it heavy enough to make the cowlicks behave. But today was special. I brushed my mop up high on my head and allowed the curls to do what they may, except for the ones that fell around my face. Those I beat into submission with enough gel to keep them in place. I fancied they looked like the loose tendrils I read about in romance novels. Tendrils. Sounded much better than stragglers.

I transferred my room card and my wallet into a small black clutch I'd purchased for the event, and when I stepped into the hallway, I found my watchdog waiting.

Bowers stared.

"I've never seen you with your hair up."

My hand went to touch the back of my head to make sure everything was in place.

"Or in a dress."

I brushed down the skirt and resisted the urge to pull the bodice up.

Bowers cleared his throat. "Robby went ahead with Gina. Will I do?"

Would he ever. His dark navy suit emphasized his eye color and his broad shoulders, and the white shirt and rose tie added a touch of sophistication.

His hands were in his pockets, so Bowers crooked an elbow out and I let him escort me to my best friend's wedding.

The rehearsal had taken place on the ship to allow us to practice our moves, but since the ceremony was a Catholic sacrament, it had to take place on consecrated ground. The bishops from the Phoenix and Juneau dioceses had given their permission for Father Basil to officiate the wedding, and our destination was St. Gregory Nazianzen Catholic Church.

Since the weather was in the cool sixties, most of the wedding party had decided to walk to the church, except for the bride, of course. She would arrive in a limousine with her stepfather. I did feel overdressed as we stepped off the gangway. Most of the tourists were in jeans and shorts, and here I was looking as if I was dressed for a prom provided nobody got close enough to see that my teen years were far behind me.

Robby and Gina waited on the sidewalk, and informed us the parents had gone ahead, along with Kemper and Tommy.

"I was a little worried about Tommy," I admitted.

Robby, who walked ahead of us with Gina, looked over his shoulder and winked. "He seemed happy to be back on dry land. He teetered the first few steps, but then it was as if he'd been walking his entire life."

It was a short stroll down Lincoln Street, and it seemed more like a funeral procession than a wedding march because I stayed silent most of the way. My thoughts were on what my life would be like once I returned to Wolf Creek, Arizona. Penny would still be at the Prickly Pear Bistro, the small diner she owned in Wolf Creek, but I couldn't expect to find her there all hours of the day if she had a husband waiting at home. We wouldn't be able to make spur-of-the-moment plans for a movie...again because of the husband waiting at home. And when children came along, I'd never see her, at least not alone. This wedding was bringing me down.

"Penny for your thoughts," Bowers said.

The unintended reference brought an ache to my throat. "I'm wallowing in self-pity."

He nodded and slipped his hand around mine. I was still depressed, but at least my hand was comfy and warm.

At least until we saw a squirrel or other animal and Bowers decided he needed his hand back.

We reached Baranof Street which we couldn't have missed because it was marked by a beautiful red structure, St. Peter's by the Sea. One block up Baranof, we turned down a short dead end that led to a simple wooden church. The brown paint, accented by a yellowish-beige door and window frames, reminded me of the buildings at the campgrounds where my childhood adventures took place. The forest-covered mountains from the other side of Crescent Bay made a marvelous backdrop, though the hulking cruise ship that passed by dampened the thrill a tad.

The nature theme continued inside, with wooden benches and wood paneling behind the raised altar. Several vases of white roses surrounded the altar, and white silk bows marked the first three rows of pews.

A simple crucifix hung from the wall over a beautiful gold box on a stand surrounded by vases of white flowers. To the left, a statue of the Sacred Heart of Jesus gazed down on us. I had to look away. It didn't take much reflection to realize I hadn't lived a life that deserved the love reflected in His expression. I could have dealt more easily with a scowling Jesus. In my discomfort, I tried to act casual.

"Look." I pointed to a red candle hanging in the window. "Kind of like a beacon to passing ships."

Bowers said in a strained voice, "That's the Sanctuary Light."

I glanced around. "Where's the Sanctuary? Isn't that where the priest gets dressed?"

"The Sanctuary Light announces the Real Presence in the tabernacle."

"Ah, the tabernacle." Bowers took me by the shoulders and turned me toward the beautiful gold box.

"Where they keep the Eucharist?" He wasn't questioning the purpose of the tabernacle. He was questioning the gaps in my knowledge. He knew my entire family was Catholic, and he seemed surprised at my ignorance. I felt I owed it to the team to come up with one smart comment. I pointed to a large bowl on a stand.

"And that's the finger bowl where the priest washes his hands during Mass." *Top that*, I thought.

He sighed. "That would be the Baptismal Fount, and the tall, pretty candle next to it is the Easter Candle." He took my elbow and escorted me up the aisle. "We've got to get you into a church more often."

Who is we? I wondered if he was in league with my mother. He did speak to her during the *Blue-Ribbon Babes* murder investigation, when he was looking for background information on Aunt Gertrude, my mom's sister. Maybe she had convinced him to join forces with her parish priest, Father Jakius, to drag me back into the Light.

Robby, Gina, Kemper, Tommy and Father Basil stood around the altar talking. Father Basil was decked out in white.

"Bet you don't know the name of the gown the priest is wearing," I said in challenge.

"His outer garment? It's a chasuble. He's wearing it over an alb, which means *white tunic*. That thing he's wearing over his shoulders," he grinned at me, "which you would call *his scarf*, is an amice, or a stole. Do you want to know what the altar server is wearing?"

"Thanks anyway. Showoff."

Bowers knew his faith. My mom would be proud.

Mr. Mohr waited patiently in the front pew with his wife. I guess the parents of the groom aren't required to fret as much as the bride's parents.

Penny had asked Frank Doud to walk her down the aisle. Her relations with her own father had remained cool since he cheated on Judy, something my Aunt Gertrude had discovered during an afternoon showing of *The Apple Dumpling Gang*. The scenario had been too embarrassing to share, so Aunt Gertrude had "read" the cards for Judy Doud, then Judy Newcombe, and revealed her husband's perfidy. Judy, a woman of action, had kicked her husband out of the house and filed for a divorce. A little investigative work revealed he had slept with a bridesmaid the night before their wedding, and since that showed he hadn't entered into the Sacrament with the right intentions, she was able to receive an annulment from the Catholic Church. She had been a free woman when she met the widowed Frank Doud, and she and her children had fallen in love with him.

Thinking of Judy, I didn't see her anywhere, nor did I see Sharon Bradley. I excused myself and went in search of the powder room. Sharon and Judy were inside, checking their makeup. Judy wore a chiffon dress in a muted shade of purple—a typical mother-of-the-bride dress. Sharon, almost to prove she wasn't old enough to have a married child, wore a sparkling silver dress on her slim figure and a dead animal slung over her shoulders. It was a silver fox stole, and it appeared to be staring at me, begging me to recognize the indignity of being draped over someone's shoulders instead of chasing bunnies in the wild. A gray fox with *gray fur*.

She saw me staring and paused, moving the lipstick away from her mouth. "It's not real, so don't try to talk to it."

"I don't know what you mean." I fumbled through my purse and realized I had forgotten to pack my lipstick. Judy Doud held out her own tube, and I dashed it over my mouth and thanked her. The doors swung open, and in stepped Gina.

She took a deep breath and announced, "She's here."

As the other two women scrambled to take one last look at their hair and makeup, Gina handed me my bouquet, a duplicate of hers filled with violets, pink carnations and roses.

With the somberness of funeral guests, we proceeded out of the bathroom and took our places. Sharon sat in the second row of pews, with Judy on the end leaving enough room for Frank to sit down after he performed his duties. The wedding party would sit in the first row.

I remained at the back of the church with Gina until a sandy-haired man in a dark suit put on a recording of *Pachelbel's Canon*. Penny hadn't been able to snag a musician for the wedding ceremony.

Everyone turned toward the back of the church. It wasn't my wedding, but with everyone staring in my direction, I felt the prickle of self-consciousness. I averted my eyes until Gina started down the aisle, because by then they would be looking at her. And they all were except one.

Bowers had his gaze fixed on me, and he didn't remove it once as I made my way down the aisle. I know because I kept darting glances his way when I wasn't looking at my feet. I had the crazy idea that if I kept an eye on them, they wouldn't trip me up before I reached the altar.

Pachelbel's Canon stopped abruptly and was replaced by the *Bridal Chorus*. Everyone stood, and I got my first glimpse of Penny as Bride. Her short-sleeved satin dress began in a neckline that came across her delicate collarbone in lacy waves and ended in a short train, also of lace. The same lace lined the tulle veil that covered her face. One hand held a bouquet of pink peonies—only available in

Alaska this time of year—and white roses, and the other rested on Frank's arm. He pressed his lips together in an effort not to cry, but his cheek twitched from the suppressed emotion.

When they reached the front of the aisle and Frank lifted the veil to give his stepdaughter a kiss, Mrs. Doud covered a soft sob with her handkerchief, and when Frank joined her, she kissed his cheek.

Because there were only eleven of us in the church, the ceremony had the intimacy of a secret wedding. Penny and Kemper sneaking off to get married with only their closest friends and family in tow. Or a shotgun wedding. I imagine those are pretty private, too.

I listened carefully to every word Father Basil said, trying to imprint them on my memory for those times when I would want to recall *important events* I had taken part in. I'd be eighty at the time and trying to justify my existence. *Yes, I did do something worthwhile, once, long ago. I witnessed a wedding.* That was my title on the certificate. Witness. It sounded so important. I wondered, would I ever be in the position to require my own witnesses?

My vision blurred when Penny repeated her vows, and when Kemper said his, a tear escaped. What I wouldn't give to be so loved by a man he would stand up before God and family and declare his intent to take care of me for the rest of my life, even if I became decrepit or insane. Of course, I would have to promise to do the same, and that part didn't sound as romantic.

Before I knew it, Kemper had Penny in his arms and he kissed her gently on the lips, and then we broke into applause and followed the newly minted Mr. and Mrs. Kemper Mohr out the door. Rice was forbidden. We didn't want any birds exploding. Instead, we tossed bird seed, which was immediately pounced upon by a gang of sparrows who had been waiting for us. They must have been regulars at St. Gregory's.

Penny and Kemper slid into the back seat of a limousine with a "Just Married" sign on the back and headed off for a tour around Sitka to see if anyone would honk at them. Since there were very few vehicles on the roads, I expected they would have a quiet drive.

Originally, Tommy and I were supposed to go with them, but since we would have been in the seats that faced backwards, and Tommy's tummy was still unstable, we both decided to bow out. It would have been awkward with just the married couple and me.

The parents and Sharon had a hired car waiting to take them back to the ship, so Gina, Robby, Tommy, Bowers and I headed back on foot.

Gina, a former drill team captain, kept tossing her bouquet in the air, spinning, and catching it behind her back. Maybe that was an important talent in New York, but I wasn't impressed.

I *was* impressed that the reception dinner took place in the Golden Albatross, which was the ultra-fancy dining room on board. We ordered drinks and then waited twenty minutes for the happy couple to show up. When Kemper and Penny swept into the room, still in their wedding garb, the guests at the other tables broke into applause. Since this was the fancy dining room, it was polite applause.

With their flushed faces and silly grins, the happy couple acted like carriers of a contagion that infected everyone. Even Tommy didn't notice the ship was back in motion, headed for Ketchikan.

The waiter served Champagne, and Mr. Mohr stood up and raised his glass.

"I'd like to toast the newlyweds, especially the bride. Kemper, you are one lucky man."

"Here, here," Robby said, and we all sipped.

Frank Doud went next, congratulating Penny on her choice of groom and wishing them both a happy marriage overrun with children, which made everybody laugh except Penny, who blushed.

The best man was obliged to say a few words, and he kept it short and sweet, and then some smart aleck named Robby insisted the maid of honor put in her two cents.

I got to my feet, raised my half-finished champagne, and said, "Penny, I've known you since we were children, and I've never seen you as happy as you are right now. If that ever changes, Kemper, I know where you live."

My toast got the biggest laugh, not that we were competing, and almost as a reward, the serving staff arrived with bowls of lobster bisque. My prime rib was so tender I cut it with my fork, and the whipped potatoes and skinny green beans must have been drenched in butter because I couldn't think of another reason why vegetables would taste so good. We finished off with a piece of white chocolate mousse cake.

Frank Doud stood and motioned, and a waiter approached the table carrying a box wrapped in silver paper. On top, next to the matching bow, little bells jingled with each step he took.

Frank and Judy held hands, and he waved Thomas and Christina over to join them.

"We want you to start off on the right foot."

Penny insisted they unwrap the gift together. When they lifted the lid off the box, Penny gasped and held up a plaque. A Recipe for a Good Marriage was written out in calligraphy and included *one cup of courtesy, two cups of*

praise, and one pinch of in-laws. That last one got a guffaw
from Robby.

"What's this?"

Penny peeled an envelope off the back of the plaque
and peeked inside. She squeaked, shoved the envelope in
Kemper's hands, and ran to her stepfather, throwing her
arms around his neck and kissing his cheek. Kemper pulled
out a piece of paper, dropped it, and joined Penny. He
pumped Frank and Thomas's hands and hugged the
mothers.

Robby slid the paper over, which was a check. After
reading it, he let out a long, low whistle.

"Twenty thousand bucks."

"It's difficult to start a family in this economy," Thomas
Mohr said. "We wanted to take some worry away. We know
it's not much in this economy...."

I raised my hand. "If it's too embarrassing for you, I'll
take it."

Thomas let out a hearty laugh, but he took the check
from the table and placed it in Kemper's hands.

Penny then insisted we go to the Jimmy Dean Lounge
and that her father honor her with a first dance.

I assumed with a name like the Jimmy Dean Lounge,
there would be a jukebox playing oldies music. Instead, a
DJ ruled the room from atop a raised platform, and from the
grin he sent our way as the wedding party entered the room,
he was expecting us. He cut off *It's Raining Men* mid-
chorus and put on *Wind Beneath My Wings.* Frank Doud
led Penny to the center of the multicolored, lighted floor,
and as he held one hand up and rested the other on her
waist, the squares on the floor shifted to a soft blue. After
the first verse, Tommy led me to the floor, and Robby did

the same with Gina. Soon, other couples filled the dance floor.

Robby grabbed me for the next dance. I glanced in Penny's direction.

"Hey, old man," I said. "You're next."

Robby sniffed. "There is no woman worthy of me. I'll be alone all my days, but don't feel sorry for me. I'll get a cat."

"You don't deserve a cat, you faker."

"What's that?" he yelled in my ear. "You want me to dip you?"

I looked around at the other couples and panicked. The dance floor wasn't big, and if Robby got ideas about fancy moves, I'd wind up slamming into Mrs. Doud and knocking her down. "Don't you dare."

He spun me and dipped, and I screeched and squeezed my eyes, waiting for my head to connect with the floor. To my surprise, Robby swung me around in one smooth move and brought me to standing.

He shook his head. "You have no faith."

"Did you have lessons? Because if I were dancing with the old Robby, that move would have been fatal."

"An artist never shares his secrets," he said, but I could tell he was pleased. So was I. I could relax and stop fearing for my toes.

We applauded at the end of the music, and then Bowers cut in for a slow dance. He held me in the old-fashioned way, just like Frank Doud had held Penny, with one hand clasping mine in the air and the other resting on my lower back. It may sound stiff and formal, but it was extremely sexy because it made me feel feminine. Adult. Respected.

"That was a nice wedding," he said.

"Yes, it was. Simple."

He shifted his arm, pulling me a little closer. "Is that how you see your own wedding?"

My wedding. That wasn't something I thought about, not even growing up. I'd known women who had every detail of the ceremony and reception planned and timed. Cut cake at 7 PM. Finish eating cake at 7:15. It wasn't that I was against getting married, but after my last experience with a man, I couldn't imagine trusting anyone that much again. I'd been foolish enough to move in with Jeff, buying into the oldest lie in the book—it would lead to permanence. Or it didn't matter if we had a certificate, as if marriage was a piece of paper. Living together wasn't a commitment, something Jeff had pointed out when he betrayed me in more ways than one with some floozy reporter. My cheeks grew warm at the memory of my humiliation.

"I'll give it some thought when I find someone worth marrying."

"And what qualifications would this worthy man have to meet?" His jaw pulsed when he said it, and his tone had an edge to it, as if he thought the worthy man wouldn't be getting such a prize.

Flustered by the question, I threw off a flippant answer about a cross between 007 secret agent Sean Connery and *The Avengers* Tom Hiddleston because I had just seen movies starring each actor and, well, what woman wouldn't want Sean Connery or Tom Hiddleston?

Fortunately, the conversation ended when Penny bumped into me, deliberately. Her smile exuded pure happiness, her blue eyes sparkled with love, and her entire being radiated a peace and well-being that demanded I respond in kind. I shouted out the first wedding-related thing I could think of. "Am I going to get any wedding cake?

Cause that dessert they served in the Golden Albatross doesn't count."

She made a face. "I guess you'll just have to fly back to Wisconsin for the Newcombe reception."

When the dance was over, Bowers and I slid into a booth, and by agreement, became silent spectators. He ordered a scotch, and I took a margarita to be polite. When Kemper asked me to dance, I couldn't very well say no, and then he passed me on to Frank Doud for the next dance. Tommy joined Bowers at our table, but before I could return, Thomas Mohr asked me to be his partner. My feet were throbbing by the time I slid into the booth next to Tommy.

"How are you holding up?"

He held up a tall glass. "Soda water. As long as I don't move too much, I'm fine."

Eventually, the inevitable happened, and the DJ put on another fast dance. Robby jogged over, grabbed my hand, and led me onto the floor. Though Bowers had expressed reluctance to dance to anything with a tempo faster than a waltz, Gina strong-armed him onto the center tiles.

I kept one eye on my feet in case Robby suffered a relapse and one eye on Bowers. He made a few halfhearted motions until Gina grabbed his hand and swung herself under his arm. She whispered in his ear, and he grinned, almost in relief that he had found a kindred spirit. The two of them broke into some kind of moderate swing dancing, with fast moving feet and twirls and kicks. They looked as if they had stepped out of the fifties.

I wasn't the only one who had stopped dancing to watch. Even Kemper and Penny moved off the floor to give them the spotlight. They were excellent, and as selfish as it sounds, that depressed me. When they finished with

Bowers dipping Gina to wild applause, I couldn't get up the enthusiasm to stay on the floor.

Robby ran over and high-fived his cousin, and he swept her into his arms for a slow dance. Bowers, out of breath, came up to me and held out his hand.

"Sorry. I'm not a professional," I said.

He took my hand anyway and jerked me to him. He had one arm around my back and held my hand against his chest. "This is more my speed."

"Don't be condescending. I stink at dancing and I know it, whereas Gina probably has it listed on her resume."

"Sulking doesn't suit you." He tipped my chin up with his finger. "You get this frown-line between your eyebrows."

"I do not!"

"Adds at least five years."

I tried to pull away, and he held me tighter. I could feel the rumble in his chest as he chuckled.

"You're a bone-headed brat."

"That's what my sisters tell me."

"They should know."

I gave in and rested my head against his chest for the rest of the number. When the song finished, the music returned to an upbeat tempo, and Gina swooped in for another dance with Bowers. What an attention junkie. She was obviously eager to get another round of applause. When she reached for his hand, he held both his hands up to wave her off.

"I only dance like that once a year."

Even if it was out of pity for me, it pleased me when he turned her down. Robby seemed happy, too, and I crossed my fingers that he would step on Gina's toes at least once tonight.

TWENTY

We spent the rest of the evening in the booth, sipping our drinks. Bowers had another scotch, but once I finished my margarita, I stuck to ginger ale. I hadn't yet felt the effects of the water's motion, and I didn't want to take any chances. Tommy had bowed out early and returned to his room, joking that he was eager to get to sleep now that he wouldn't have to listen to Kemper snore.

Around eleven o'clock, Penny and Kemper approached us holding hands and panting from a fast dance.

"We're going to get going," Penny said, trying to sound casual.

"Yeah," Kemper added. "We're pretty pooped."

I jumped to my feet and squeezed Penny in a hug. "You make him take care of you," I whispered in her ear, and she laughed. They dragged their feet almost to the door, since they were supposed to be pooped, but just short of their exit, their real state of mind broke through, and they took off at a trot.

Bowers had remained standing after shaking Kemper's

hand and delivering a quick, congratulatory kiss to Penny's cheek. He suggested we go for a walk.

"Sure," I said without much enthusiasm.

Out on the Promenade Deck, a mild wind blew my hair —mild in strength, not in temperature. I noticed the only other people out were a small group of smokers and a couple snuggling close enough to defy any drop in temperature.

I shivered. Bowers took off his jacket and placed it around my shoulders. "We'd better keep moving if we don't want to freeze." After a pause, he added, "What are you going to do now?"

"You mean tonight?" I said, even though I knew what he meant. I didn't want to think about Wolf Creek, and Bowers saw through me.

"It's not as if she's moving away. I've had a lot of friends get married, and I still see them."

"But not as often," I pointed out.

"No. They have their own lives, and trying to hang out with them all the time would be pathetic."

Would Penny and Kemper find me pathetic if I asked them to a movie? Or out to dinner? How depressing.

"There are benefits," Bowers said. "I'm an honorary uncle many times over."

I let out a long sigh, and he put an arm around my shoulder.

"Cheer up, Frankie."

I rested my head against his shoulder. "I don't want to. I want to have a pity-party and moan about how my best friend's happiness is causing me pain."

He gave me a slight shake. "That's the spirit. Have a goal. It always takes my mind off being lonely."

That stopped me in my tracks. "You? Lonely? You have

all of those guys down at the station." And I assumed a different woman every weekend.

He made a face. "Mere pups, most of them. They hit the bars after work and on weekends. I'm way past that stage."

I narrowed my eyes at him. "What do you do with your spare time? Origami? Bird watching? I know very little about you, mister. Maybe I shouldn't be alone with you out here."

"Maybe you shouldn't, because I know what I'd like to do with my spare time."

"What?" It came out a whisper.

He took my chin in his fingers, lifted it, and lowered his head. The first kiss was gentle, but then the pressure increased, and he took a step forward until I was leaning back against the railing. I slid my arms around his shoulders, and his jacket slipped off. He caught it and hung it over the rail with one hand without breaking our kiss. His hands slid over my sides, getting perilously close to what my grandma always called the "bits n' pieces", and when Bowers wrapped me in a tight hold and leaned in, the railing dug into my back—a railing just like the one Marvelous Marv had pitched over. Except instead of a lifeboat, I would hit the cold, dark waters below.

He felt me stiffen and pulled loose. When his breathing returned to normal, he said, "I suppose I should apologize."

I turned and started walking again. "No need." My breathing wasn't steady either, so it came out a squeak. "People always do silly things at weddings."

"Right. Silly. I forgot that you're a *free spirit*." He picked up his jacket and slung it over his shoulder, and he didn't move to take my hand again.

Silent, we turned the second corner and ran smack into

Bitsy and her four furry friends. Bowers shot me a glare, and I shrugged. I hadn't worked it this way, but that didn't mean I was going to pass up an opportunity.

"You did a good job on your own," I said.

"Eh?" She looked at me as if I came from another planet.

"The show. Without Marv. I assume you've worked together for a long time?"

"Oh. Yeah. Seven years this May. It won't be the same without him."

I looked down at the cats. "They don't look that old."

"These aren't the cats we started out with. I'll let you in on a secret. All of them came from the pound, except Felix. He was Marv's personal pet. Don't know what he saw in him. The cat didn't seem to like him much."

I squatted down, which was difficult in heels, and the little performers rushed me. I now knew Sphinx was a waste of time, and Jasper and Jinx were preoccupied playing with a loose thread on Bitsy's jacket. That left the black cat, Casper. As she rubbed her face on my knee, Bitsy scolded her.

"He'll get hair on your dress!"

"Casper is a girl."

"Whatever. She'll still shed."

"I have a cat, myself. Hair has become part of my wardrobe."

As I rubbed Casper's ear, I focused on her furry skull and imagined an information highway between her and me. She was by far the friendliest, next to Sphinx, and therefore my best chance to connect. In her relaxed state, she was ready to share. That didn't mean I could ignore Sphinx. I had to keep one hand busy scratching him behind his ears. I glanced up to make sure Bowers and Bitsy were still occupied.

"- walk them three times a day. I thought dogs were bad!"

Bitsy was on a complaint streak. Perfect. Bowers would have to keep his focus on her to be polite.

First, I heard the *Brrrrrr* from Sphinx, so I concentrated on the black cat's face, hoping to "tune in the channel", if you will.

I thought *gray fur*.

Casper's ears twitched. I had her attention.

Show me Gray Fur. I put emphasis on the words to show that gray fur was a title and not a reference to the hairs on Sphinx's back.

The cat encircled me, rubbing her body against me as she moved, and I had to lift the leash and duck my head under it. When she got in front of me, Casper turned and flicked her tail in my face.

I sneezed, and Bowers looked down at me with concern. With his attention off Bitsy, I didn't know how much time I had left.

Desperate, I called out, "Gray Fur!"

Casper spun on me and raked her claws down my arm. I cried out, and Bowers helped me to my feet.

"Bad boy!" Bitsy said, jerking the leash. "Are you okay?"

Casper gave me a baleful look and then returned to her fellow felines.

Bitsy leaned in for a better peek at the line of scratches on my arm. "A little peroxide will take care of that. I don't know what's wrong with them. They've been acting weird all day."

"Maybe they miss Marv."

"Could be," she said, but the way she pressed her lips together when she looked down at them with a complete lack of sympathy told me she couldn't care less about the *why*.

"We've taken up enough of your time." Bowers said goodnight, steered me away, and as soon as we were out of earshot, he said, "You knew they would be here."

"That was just luck. I thought they would be on the Observation Deck."

"Baloney. I bet they sent you little brain waves or something to let you know where you could find them."

I snapped my fingers. "I wonder if that would work." The idea intrigued me. Maybe I could use it to discover Felix's whereabouts.

Bowers brought me back inside, and we wandered the halls in search of members of our party but finally gave up. Because I was in heels, we took the elevator up, and during that quick trip, I started to fidget. Technically, Bowers had escorted me to the wedding, and he was now escorting me back to my room. Did that make him my date? Was this a date? Probably not. Dates were something you planned. I hadn't even RSVP'd that I'd be bringing someone to Penny's wedding, though since it took place during a cruise I couldn't afford to pay for myself, they most likely had me marked down as a single before they mailed the darned thing.

By the time we made it to my door, I had the key in my hand to eliminate any awkward goodbye moments. I faced the door as I slid the card in the slot and moved along with the door as I pushed it open. No room for guesswork. I halfway expected him to pull me into his arms and give me a kiss goodnight anyway, but when I glanced up, he had his hands in his pockets.

"Thanks for letting me tag along," he said.

"No problem."

Our eyes met, and I pressed my teeth into my lower lip. He looked handsome in that suit. His eyes, usually underscored by dark circles from too little sleep seemed clear and intense tonight, and—

"Frankie. You're going to have to spell it out. Do you want me to kiss you or not?"

I stepped back into the hallway. I couldn't come out with a yes because that would make me needy and put me at a disadvantage. Besides, just because he felt like kissing me goodnight didn't mean he wouldn't drop me the minute we got back to Wolf Creek. I already had too many powerful feelings about Bowers. Having to squash them down in three days sounded like too much trouble.

He placed his hands on my shoulders and looked down at me, and without warning, he pecked me on the forehead, turned me, and gave me a gentle push back into my room.

Was this what I could expect from him if I didn't beg for his favors? I turned back, my face flushed and ready to explain how any relationship between us would have to be a two-way street, until I heard him say:

"Good evening, Mrs. Doud."

She peeked into my room as she passed. "Good evening." She looked over her shoulder. "Are you coming, Frank?" She winked at Bowers. "He's not used to drinking. I expect you'll hear his snoring through the walls."

Frank came into view, his steps unsteady. Bowers took his arm, but Frank shook him off. "I'm fine."

Bowers took a firm grip. "I've been fine before myself at weddings."

The older man straightened up, his chin firm and an indignant spark in his eyes. Then he burst out in a fit of giggles. "You're right. I'm snockered. But I'm still on my own two feet. Just a little unsteady, that's all."

As Bowers navigated him to his room, he said, "I'm sure the motion of the ship doesn't help."

The ship was still. Even Tommy would have had difficulty getting seasick.

Bowers looked back over his shoulder and I wiggled my fingers at him and closed my door.

TWENTY-ONE

That night, after I had greeted my new towel roommate—a rabbit who I refused to name since he'd be leaving me tomorrow—and changed into my flannel nightgown, I sat in the middle of my bed and prepared for a new experience. I think I had decided to give it a shot as soon as I had seen the empty room. Empty except for the bunny. I didn't want to think about how I would never again have a slumber party with Penny. I know, I'm too old for slumber parties, but that's how I always looked on it when we would hang out all night, gossiping and dreaming and watching movies. Eating pizza and ice cream and calling it a balanced diet. Those days were gone.

I rolled my shoulders to loosen them up, took a few deep breaths, and cleared my mind. Animals emit a kind of white noise when they aren't trying to communicate with me. The best comparison I can think of is the static given off by a radio that isn't tuned in—all their voices and thoughts combined into a hum. To hear individuals, I must tune in, just as I adjust the knobs on the radio to focus in on a particular station. That is, unless they ambush me with a direct communication.

The interruptions to my own thoughts had become so distracting that I had come up with a mental barrier. A heavy, wooden door you might see in a horror movie, often used to keep torch-wielding villagers out. Closing that door kept the noise and voices out for the most part.

I shook my shoulders to ease my nerves. Opening that door often let in more than I was prepared to handle. I let it creak open, just a crack, and waited. A slight hum swept out and enveloped me, and my forehead tingled like it does when I have sinus problems.

I listened until one sound stuck out a little louder than the rest, and I put all my attention on that blip. As the noise became clearer, I recognized it. *Brrrrrrr.* Sphynx. I had just initiated contact with an animal that wasn't sitting right in front of my face. I giggled.

Adjusting the volume down on Sphinx's thoughts, I got it to the point where there were several other fuzzy channels at about the same noise level. Could these be the other kitties? They would all be the same distance away. The volume was about the same as someone talking on the phone a few rooms away. If I found out where they were being kept and then measured the distance between my room and theirs, then I would be able to connect the level of noise I heard with the distance between me and the source.

Who knew what possibilities this new talent held? Perhaps I could learn to recognize the signatures of specific animals. Maybe I could open a pet rescue and locate lost fur babies! But how would I recognize an animal's brain waves if I hadn't heard them previously? I'd have to think about that.

Suddenly, a song burst into my head. It was a joyful

sound, and it was loud, which according to my theory, meant it was close. Singing? What kind of animal carried a tune in its head? Singing cockroaches in the walls? Singing rats? Since the thought was being projected from nearby, and I knew neither Kemper nor Robby, the occupants on either side of me, had brought animals along for the trip, I slid off my bed and crept to the balcony.

My shoulders shivered as the chilled air hit me. When I listened, I could hear the murmurs of other passengers on their verandas. At the sound of a splash, I stared into the dark waters beyond the ship's railing. My first thought was the killer had struck again but his or her aim had been off. Then someone opened a door onto the Promenade Deck, and light spilled out. I narrowed my eyes into a squint. The song sounded in my ears again just as a porpoise—or would it be a dolphin?—sprang out of the water. I stepped back through the doorway, unable to breathe. I was hearing the voices of ocean life.

My thoughts were so caught up in my successful experiment I almost failed to catch another voice, one I should have recognized right away. Felix. As soon as I recognized him, I gave his "channel" my full attention. It came across as a deep purr, but what made me know it was Felix and not one of the other cats were the images of Marvelous Marv, waiving his whip, and demanding the cat take a bow. If there were such a thing as a disdainful purr, this was it. The purr was coming through loud and clear, almost as loud as the singing had been, which meant wherever Felix was hiding out, he wasn't far from me.

I opened the hall door and peered out. The coast was clear, so I stepped outside and let my door close. Since our wedding party ran down the hallway to my right, I turned and stepped softly to the left, focusing on Felix's wavelength. Right now, he wasn't emitting a signal, so maybe he had moved farther away.

"Frances?"

I squeezed my eyes shut and turned around. Robby leaned on the door frame of his room, still in his dress pants and white shirt.

"I thought I heard your door."

His eyebrows went up as he registered that I was in my flannel nightgown, but he was kind enough not to make any rude comments.

"I thought someone knocked on my door," I said with a laugh that sounded unnaturally high to my ears. I reached for the doorknob, turned it—or rather didn't turn it—and then bit my lip.

"I'm locked out again," I mumbled.

"Maybe you should tie your key around your neck," he said with a grin and opened his door wide.

Bowers, in a full set of green pajamas, leaned back against his headboard with a book resting on his chest, which he slapped shut when he saw me.

"What's wrong?"

"Nothing."

"Do you often wander the halls in your nightgown?"

Robby picked up the receiver and dialed. "She's locked out again. I think it was just an excuse to visit us."

"Wrong."

Bowers came over and stood in front of me. "Why were you in the hallway in your nightclothes?" His brow furrowed with concern. "Did something scare you out of your room?"

That sounded nice and feminine. Sure. They'd buy that answer. "I saw a mouse, and I opened the door to let it out. I jumped out of the way because I didn't want its furry little body to touch my feet, and the door closed behind me." I wondered if I should have shrieked on the word mouse. "Silly me."

Bowers grinned, relieved to find a simple explanation. It made me wonder how good of a cop he could be to buy such a stupid scenario.

"I thought you heard someone knock on your door," Robby said, and Bowers lost the grin.

"I got up to see who it was and *then* I saw the mouse."

Once he heard about a mysterious knocker, Bowers insisted on slipping his pants on over his pajamas, and once the porter showed up, he escorted me to my room and checked the bathroom, closet and veranda for lurking marauders.

"It was probably the wrong room number," I said, standing next to the open sliding doors. I wrapped my arms around my middle and shivered in the icy breeze.

He slid the door shut. "You're probably right."

"I, um, forgot something in your room." He moved to go with me, but I put my hands on his arms. If he came with me, it would ruin everything. "You stay right here. I'd feel safer if I knew you were watching over the room. I'll just be a minute."

The door to Robby and Bowers room was still open, so I breezed in and said, "Bowers might hang out for a while and he needs his room key."

All the while I talked, I made for his nightstand. Wallet. Car keys. Room key. Only one. I slid the drawer open and found what I was looking for. I palmed the card and took the second room key from the stand, waved, and closed the door behind me.

When I got back into my room, Bowers stood right where I left him. I held out his own room key and said,

"Robby didn't know when you'd be back, so he thought I should give you this."

His gaze ran over my nightgown. "Really." He took the card and turned it over, studying it. "What did you leave behind in our room?"

My gaze landed on the remote control, sitting on top of the television. I picked it up. "I thought I had this in my hand when I ran out of the room. You know, when I saw the mouse? Turns out, I didn't."

I avoided eye contact, turned my back on him, went to the door, and held it open. "We don't want Mrs. Doud dropping by, do we?"

At the mention of Penny's mother, Bowers moved to leave, but not without pausing before he stepped through the doorway. He held up his room key. "Seems like a waste of a good lie."

Once he left, I turned off the lights and slipped under the covers. With Penny now staying with her permanent roommate, I was on my own. Lonely feelings crept up on me, and my eyes grew warm and misty. I rolled over on my side and told myself to stop being such a baby.

I'd forgotten to close the curtains to the veranda, and moonlight filled the room and left the furniture in a shadowy outline. Moonlight. The stuff of romances. A perfect night to spend walking on the deck of a cruise ship with the one you loved.

I got up and closed the curtains.

Bowers had kissed me. I'd wanted him to kiss me, but did that make it right? When Jeff had sucker-punched me two years ago, moving out of our apartment and relationship to be with his new girlfriend, I'd resolved to keep my life free from entanglements with a high pain potential. I had been incredibly naïve in my twenties. I thought Jeff and I shared something special, and I'd believed him when he told me real love didn't need a piece of paper. Marriage was out of fashion. It all boiled down to Jeff preferred me to a blow-up doll. What a dope I was.

Now here was Bowers, a man who had decided not to pursue a relationship with me because my psychic abilities made it complicated. Yet, he kissed me. I decided it was a kiss of convenience. We were on the same cruise for a week and I was handy. It didn't mean anything, which meant I wasn't going to let it happen again.

But I had wanted him to kiss me goodnight, Evil Frankie said. Good Frankie countered, pointing out I had been caught up in the moment. Besides. Bowers had left it up to me. That meant he wasn't invested one way or another. That meant he wouldn't take the blame if something went wrong.

But he had paid an awful lot of money to get on this cruise just to see me, Evil Frankie whined. So, he should feel he paid for the privilege of using me? Excellent point, Good Frankie.

Good Frankie won the argument. I wouldn't let it happen again.

TWENTY-TWO

My first objective the next morning was to find an ideal situation to use my handy key card. It was burning a hole in my pocket. Since we were docked in Ketchikan today, I assumed most people would be off the ship and exploring the shops, leaving me to go through their rooms at will. Whose rooms? Sonya, the girlfriend, might have some of Marv's possessions. I might find a clue in Sharon Bradley's room pointing to her relationship with Marv. I might even be able to sneak into Trevor's room to see if the stewards had left behind traces of Marvelous Marv. The possibilities were endless.

Bowers had promised to stick to me like glue, and so far, he'd suited actions to words. I knew it would be easier to lose him if he never caught me in the first place, so I crept out of my room at the unheard hour of seven a.m. The Wolfe Creek detective was already on the job and waiting in the hallway. He looked me right in the eye without any sign of embarrassment.

"I hope you're hungry," he said, holding his arms above his head in a big stretch that reminded me of my cat, Emily.

"I rose for an early jog on the Promenade Deck, and I'm starved."

I scowled at him. "Don't talk about exercising first thing in the morning. It's obscene."

There weren't many passengers on the Lido Deck this early, so we had our choice of food stations without the bother of long lines. After we loaded up our plates, Bowers' gaze locked onto Trevor Grant, sitting on his own at a table for four by a window, and he steered our course in that direction. When we arrived, Bowers offered a friendly smile.

"Do you mind if we join you?"

"Uh, sure."

A newspaper lay open, spread out across the table, and Trevor gathered the pages and folded them up to make room for us.

Bowers pulled out the chair by the window for me and then took the seat across from Trevor. As he buttered his toast, he said, "How are you faring on your own?"

Trevor sipped his coffee. "Between us, I'm usually so busy that I'm enjoying the down time."

"What is it you do?"

I was happy Bowers had asked because I was dying to know. I checked my disappointment when the answer was *finance*. Such a vague term.

"How about you?" Trevor said. "What are you taking time off from?"

Bowers finished his bite of toast. "You don't really get time off in law enforcement."

Trevor picked up his coffee cup again, saw it was empty, and set it back down. "FBI?"

"Nope. Simple cop."

At this, Trevor grinned. "I can't imagine there's

anything simple about being a cop. My guess is you're not a patrolman. What's your specialty?"

"Wolf Creek is a small department, so there's variety, but my focus is murder."

I shoveled in the last of my hash and wiped my mouth with my napkin. "Today's the big day."

They both stared at me. Perhaps I had jumped topics too quickly, but the conversation bored me.

"The auction. The Pure Fantasy bracelet. Are you still feeling lucky, Trevor?"

Bowers paused in the act of sipping his juice. "You bought a ticket?"

Trevor grinned at me. "I was in the company of a beautiful woman and was showing off."

That made my face warm. "Don't blame me. I told you not to buy a ticket."

"Did you," Bowers said, and his tone held a note of interest. If he thought I was shallow enough to try to get strange men to buy me raffle tickets, he could lump it.

A pretty brunette and her blond counterpart approached the table. Both of them wore loose sweats that would have made me look like a slob, but they came across as fashionable and sporty.

"Are you the man that was stranded on that tiny island?" the brunette asked, and when he nodded, she squealed to her friend. "I told you it was him!"

"You were very brave," the blond said.

I looked at the situation from several angles and couldn't find anything heroic about kayaking solo, sinking, and then flagging down help. I rolled my eyes at Bowers.

He stood. "I hope you have a pleasant journey." Then he nodded to acknowledge the ladies and crooked a finger at me to follow him.

"Do you believe his story?" Bowers asked as soon as we were out of ear shot.

"Give him a break. He admitted he was stupid."

"I think it was too convenient."

I disagreed. "Tell me what's convenient about being stranded on an island in the middle of nowhere?"

"It's not nowhere. There are ships passing by all day long. And why was he alone?"

I chuckled. "Weren't you paying attention? According to the Barbie twins, he's very brave."

"Stupid, brave, or clever? He could have studied up on the *Iso Kala* and known her itinerary. There wouldn't have been much risk."

"What if we hadn't spotted him?"

"Don't you think it's a little too convenient we did?"

"Convenient for Trevor, who would have spent the night freezing his butt off. I'll give you that. And why would he want to get on the *Iso Kala* so bad? Why wouldn't he just buy a ticket like a normal person?"

"That's the magic question." Bowers halted by the elevator. "Where to?"

I spent the rest of the morning trying to ditch Bowers. Ketchikan's frontage street was built on stilts and lined with brightly painted, wooden buildings. They looked like houses to me, and I learned from the brochure that I wasn't far off. Back in the day, Creek Street was known as the red-light district. In fact, Dolly's House Museum-Gift Shop welcomed tourists to peek inside a former brothel, an offer Bowers declined, stating his time spent on the vice squad had forever ruined for him the more charming aspects of prostitution.

A wooden boardwalk ran between the shops and the Ketchikan Creek. The water level wasn't very high at the bottom of the waterway, and I couldn't help noticing several casualties floating by or stuck on rocks.

"I don't see any live fish."

Bowers looked to where I pointed. "This is a spawning creek, and those are the sad remains of salmon love. Female fish are just as difficult as female humans."

Nothing is more boring than shopping when you don't have money, so I followed Bowers around and pretended to look interested. I did perk up when he bought me a bottle of award-winning barbeque sauce, but I didn't take it as a token of his affection, since he bought one for each of his sisters as well. I picked up some Raven's Brew Coffee ®, and when we spotted a knick-knack store, I thought I'd found the perfect way to lose him. I hemmed and hawed over a display of handmade jewelry for twenty minutes and then walked away without buying anything.

He never left my side.

Not when I studied the ingredients on every food item in Sam McGee's, not when I read every t-shirt in the Troll store, and not when I took him through the Southeast Alaska Discovery Center and forced him to stand there while I tried to spot a goat through the spotting scope aimed at Deer Mountain. I finally caught a break when I let out a long, resigned sigh and Bowers misinterpreted it.

"Are you feeling alright?" He placed the back of his hand on my forehead.

Remembering my original how-to-lose-Bowers game plan, I let my body sag and willed myself to look pale and wan. "Not really. I think we should go back."

I would have been touched by how quickly he got me back to the ship, no questions asked, if I hadn't been busy gloating. He escorted me to my room, and it looked as if he had ideas about sitting by my sickbed, so I said, "I need some privacy."

"I'll wait out here."

"I'm going to be awhile."

He nodded. "I'll wait in my room."

I didn't have much experience looking demur, so I just pursed my lips and looked down at the floor. "It's feminine stuff." When he didn't react, I rubbed my stomach and sighed while putting on a face of pure agony.

I didn't imagine the two steps back Bowers took, nor the male panic reflected in his eyes. He'd been raised by a zillion older sisters after his mother passed away, so he knew exactly what I was talking about and how dangerous it would be to pressure me into rushing.

"Oh," he said, and all expression fled from his face. "Take your time. I'll wait for you on the Lido Deck." A grin broke through. "I know you can find your way there." Then he decided that joking about my eating habits at a time like this wasn't a good idea, and he dropped the grin.

I took my time opening my door, so I could watch him disappear down the flight of stairs. I pulled the door back, checked that it had locked, and strolled over to Sonya's state room. Since the stewards had cleared out Marv's room to make room for Trevor Grant, any of Marv's personal effects Sonya had decided to keep would be in here, waiting for me to pillage them.

After knocking several times and calling out her name, I slid the master key into the lock and pushed the door open. She had an inside room, and without a window to let in any natural light, the room was darker than the barn where Penny and I used to hide from Robby. I was preoccupied with putting the master key into my back pocket, and the figure was dressed completely in black, so when it plowed into me and sent me sprawling, I yelled in surprise. I landed flat on my back, and my head bounced off the floor, which was not as cushy as one might think from the appearance of the plush carpeting. The figure fled toward the stairway, so I rolled onto my hands and knees and looked up. Whoever had assaulted me was already down a flight of stairs by now. Then the elevator doors opened, and Bowers stared back at me, a surprised look on his face.

"Frankie!"

He helped me to my feet.

"What happened?"

"I-I don't know." Really, I didn't, but Sonya's door stood wide open as evidence *something* had happened. The card key on the floor might be more difficult to explain than the open door. Bowers stooped and picked it up.

"What's going on here?" he demanded.

"A figure in black plowed into me and knocked me down," I said in a small voice, hoping that would kick in his testosterone and make him want to save me, not kill me.

"From this room?" He moved me aside, told me to stay where I was, and reached inside to flick the lights on. The room didn't look too bad from the hallway, but that was coming from me, a confirmed slob. I followed close behind as he entered because it was possible the intruder who knocked me down had left company behind. When we searched the room, it was obvious a cat toy massacre had taken place. A catnip mouse on a broken fishing pole lay almost under my feet. Several stuffed animals were scattered on the bedspread and floor, little eviscerated corpses surrounded by stuffing, and a punctured ball, now deflated and flat, spread across one pillow.

The closet door stood open, with clothing in heaps on the floor, and Bowers stood sideways and pushed open the bathroom door with his fingertips. After checking the reflection in the mirror, he opened the shower curtain. Except for a pair of panties and a bra hanging on a clothing line, the bathtub was empty.

"You must have surprised them," Bowers said. "Come on."

Now that Sonya *and* the intruder were gone, I could have free rein for my search. Marv's effects had left the ship with him, but there could be other clues, such as a one-way ticket home for Sonya, showing she knew she'd be returning without Marv.

"Maybe I should go lie down."

He moved his fingers through my hair and pressed his lips into a thin line when I flinched. "After a doctor looks at you." He let me precede him out of the room.

"I'm fi—." The rest of the sentence hung in the air. Bowers followed my line of sight, and we both gaped. A fuzzy nose and sleepy eyes stared up at us from Sonya's door frame. We had found Felix.

TWENTY-THREE

"Are you certain you didn't see a face?" Officer Robinson asked me for the third time.

We were in his office in the bowels of the ship which was actually as nice as the rest of the floors.

Before beginning his interrogation, Officer Robinson had the ship's doctor look at my head. The medical man was a plump, cheerful man who I had seen before in my room after the discovery of Marvelous Marv's corpse. After a brief examination, he pronounced my head solid as a coconut. He was enjoying the excitement of the last few days. Murder and assault provided a welcome change in his routine, which probably revolved around dispensing constipation medication, diarrhea medication, and motion sickness pills. I could tell he didn't want to leave, but Robinson held the door open and he took his leave of us. Then the security officer jumped straight into an interrogation, with Bowers offering occasional commentary.

"It was someone dressed in black, and he or she ran into me and knocked me down. I can't tell you how tall the person was, or if it was a man or woman, or anything. All I saw was a black blur."

Officer Robinson held the master key in his hands. He turned it over as if hoping to find a signature or an identifiable mark, even though he hadn't found anything the first four times he looked at it.

"This master key was lying on the floor in the hallway."

I pursed my lips in a pensive manner. "The burglar must have dropped it when he or she collided with me. That card must be how the perpetrator got in."

"I'll find out whose card it is easily enough by checking it against the system, but I just can't figure out how a third party got hold of it."

"They probably stole it," I said, hoping to spare Sonny's source from harassment.

Bowers, his arms crossed over his chest, leaned against the wall. "Is that how you think it happened? Because I can think of other ways it might have gotten there."

There was something in his unwavering gaze that made me think he knew exactly how events had transpired. I blinked a few times.

"Well, what else? The perpetrator couldn't expect to kick in the door and get away with it. And a key card lock isn't easy to pick, is it? And someone bold enough to break into a passenger's room wouldn't be shy about lifting the card off a steward, or housekeeping."

"Or delivering it to the culprit in person."

I bit my upper lip and looked at my hands.

"She has a point," Robinson said. I didn't like the way he addressed Bowers. They were ganging up on me.

I rubbed the back of my head and winced. "I think this has been too much excitement for me. If you're through with me, I'm going to take an aspirin and a nap."

Officer Robinson became concerned, a worried frown on his face. "I don't think you should go to sleep so soon after a head injury. Did Doc say anything?"

He called the ship's medico Doc, just like on *Love Boat*.

"Nope. He gave me a clean bill of health."

Robinson tried again with a few more questions, but there wasn't anything else I could—or would—tell him. I stood and thanked him for his concern. The security officer made motions to Bowers, and after replying with a nod, Bowers held the door open for me and instructed me to wait for him in the hallway.

"We need to talk." He sounded just like my mother when she caught me sneaking back into the house at midnight on a school night. Fortunately, I wasn't a teenager, and he wasn't my mother. The more I thought about it, the angrier I got. It took a lot of nerve for him to get snippy with me. Here I was, the victim of an unknown assailant, wounded in the attack, and he wanted me to stand around waiting for him. I just smiled, and as soon as he closed himself in the room with Robinson, I headed for my room. I needed that aspirin.

I had my room key out, ready to slide it in the slot, when a door down the hall opened and a voice said, "You!"

Sonya's head stuck out through her doorway, and she crooked one finger at me in a "get over here" manner. There was no telling how she felt about my role in exposing Felix's whereabouts. She might be out for revenge, so I took my time walking over to her.

"Can I help you?"

She yanked me into her room and shut the door. Her cabin was similar to mine in the setup, except she didn't have a veranda, or even a window. I didn't realize how far sliding doors went toward making my room seem airy and spacious. With just a blank wall facing us from the other side of Sonya's bed, it felt like we were standing in a closet.

"Who did this?"

She swept her arm toward the space between the bed and the bathroom in a move that was as dramatic as her accent was thick, making her come across as an extra in a *Dracula* movie. On the floor stood a green, plastic chest with the lid up, and most of the cat toys that had been scattered around the room were now piled high inside of it. Most of the mess I'd seen consisted of kitty playthings. It was as if someone were looking for something, and I could think of one creature who would care about cat toys.

"Felix?"

She picked up a gray mouse on a broken string and tossed it into the box. "No. He is a very neat fellow. The thief most likely started there, thinking I had stored items of great value in there."

I know that would have been my first thought if I saw a green, plastic toy chest.

"Next they would have been putting sticky fingers all over my personal things." She lifted her chin and looked down her nose at me. "I want to know who, and you are only witness."

"I'd like to help you, but I didn't see who. The person dressed in black, so they blended into the dark room, and then they knocked me down and I hit my head."

She arched one brow. "You are claiming amnesia?"

"N-o-o-o. I didn't forget what happened. I just didn't see it."

I put on my most trustworthy expression as she studied me, and then she threw out her arms and sighed. "I will track them down and make them pay, but not tonight.

Tonight, I have to visit my Felix until the authorities come to their senses."

"*Your* Felix?"

"Of course. You don't think I kidnap strange kitties, do you?"

"But, didn't Felix belong to Marvelous Marv?"

She spit on the floor, thank goodness without spitting. "That man knew nothing of superior cats. I let him use Felix in his act, but my poor baby was too clever for the stage."

I stayed silent, remembering how Felix couldn't even take a bow without extreme prompting. Sonya's face flushed red, and she waved a finger in my face with great disapproval.

"I know what you think. You think my Felix is dumb cat, but he is like genius." She sniffed. "He was bored out of tiny but superior mind."

"That explains a lot." I know when I've had to attend meetings, family gatherings, and social events, I space out. I sympathized with the cat. "Why didn't you just tell Marv no more Felix?"

"Contract." She said the word with all the venom of a vegetarian looking at a rare steak, so the "c" sounded like she might be working up to spitting again. I sat on the edge of the bed, out of her line of fire.

"That Bitsy woman say Felix belong with her until contract run out." She shook her fist. "She tried to take his toys, but I tell her no. She think she can buy his affection with toys I bought him with love. Someday, I make her pay."

By this time, I thought it wouldn't be too judgmental to label Sonya as a vindictive person, or at least a vengeful one. But how far would she go in carrying out her threats?

"Did you see Marv at all the night he died?"

Her upper lip curled. "After his performance with your blond friend, I did not feel like sharing his company. I came to my room to sulk."

"So, you weren't around when Marv fell."

She twitched her shoulders. "Certainly not. To see something like that, it would have driven me mad. As it is, I am prostrate with grief."

"And yet you remained on the cruise instead of getting off with Marv's bod—er, with Marv," I pointed out.

She held up a hand. "Grief happens wherever you are, and I prefer to work through mine in surroundings of beauty. It is my tribute to my beloved."

"Is that why you went up the tram?" I asked. "To commune with the beautiful environment?"

She narrowed one eye. "You spy on me?"

The idea that I had followed her instead of the other way around threw me. She seemed filled with authentic resentment. I had to believe she was telling the truth. "No. I just happened to be up there, too."

"I had to escape craziness. *Sonya, how do you feel? Sonya, can I get you anything? Sonya, are you happy he's dead?* I just want to be left alone."

Her honesty made me think we might be bonding, so I ventured to ask a favor. "Did you say you're going to see Felix tonight?"

She drew her shoulders up. "Wild donkeys could not stop me."

"Do you mind if I go with you?"

"Why?"

Okay. We weren't bonding. I had to decide how much to tell her. Her appearance on the tram right after someone had pushed me made her a suspect, and her desire to get Felix back gave her a motive. Still, she didn't know I could communicate with animals, so she wouldn't suspect me of carrying trouble in my back pocket if I gave her a good enough reason to visit her cat.

I made my lips into a pout, but I couldn't work up any real tears, so I had to settle for a sniff. "I miss my own cat, and Felix reminds me of Emily."

She put a fist on her hip. "Of *Emily*? You think my Felix is a sissy?"

"Emily is very tomboyish," I assured her. Good grief. Cats were cats.

Sonya grabbed her sweater from the back of a chair. "Okay. I allow you to pet him." She thrust her pointer finger in the air. "But only if Felix does not mind."

I followed her to the elevator, and we descended to the fourth floor. Then we walked in silence toward the back of the ship, with me double-timing it to keep up with Sonya. We made it almost to the stairway at the end of the hall when she stopped and knocked, and as Bitsy opened the door, I had a memory of two eyes peering out to make sure the coast was clear. Almost certainly this was the same door Art had peered out of three days ago.

The pseudo-celebrity wasn't pleased to see us. I don't know how much it had to do with our arrival because she looked harassed when we got there. Her red curls were falling out of the bun on the top of her head and there were smears of something on her yellow t-shirt.

"Get off the bed!" she yelled, but Jinx, Sphinx and Jasper ignored her. "You should have called first," she said to Sonya, her lips pressed into a thin line.

The witchy woman dismissed her with a wave. "I have the rights of visitation until it is made clear you are unfit to be near my Felix."

"Did you bring his toys like I asked?"

Sonya dug a small fishing pole with a feather hanging where the bait should be.

"That's it? How am I supposed to keep him amused?"

Sonya shrugged. "It is his favorite."

"Marv said Felix liked some stuffed toy." She plucked at her lower lip. "Was it a mouse? No. It was a stuffed bear."

Sonya gave a broad shrug that indicated it wasn't her problem.

Bitsy turned her gaze on me. "And what are you doing here?"

"Moral support." She tried to block my way, so I bumped her shoulder when I walked into the room. It would be easier to bond with Felix if Bitsy wasn't standing over me, freaking out. "We can watch the kitties if you want to escape for a little while," I offered.

Bitsy looked at her watch. "I do have to pick up my costume from the dry cleaner. I'll be right back. Don't touch anything." And then she left us with her feline crew.

As soon as she left, Sonya held up the fishing pole toy and cackled. "This not even Felix's toy." She tossed it on the television set.

Jasper and Jinx sat on the bed with their furry faces glued on the television screen. Bitsy had it tuned into the weather channel, but they seemed to enjoy the wiggly way the animated sun's rays pulsed across the screen. Sphinx had fallen asleep on his back, legs splayed. In the corner, Casper cleaned herself with enthusiasm.

Felix plodded up to us, face upturned and purring until Sonya decided he was showing me too much favor and carried him to the couch, which suited me fine. While she preoccupied herself giving Felix tummy rubs, her attention would be away from me.

I relaxed, blew out a breath, and tuned into the Fabulous Felines. I expected the *Brrrrr* from Sphinx, and there were plenty of images of food bowls, kitty nip, and toys. I put out an image of a chicken treat just to warm them up and let them know I was friendly, and their response measured up to the enthusiasm level you would expect from cats. Jasper twitched an ear, Jinx gave me an extra blink, and Casper left her private parts alone long enough to turn her head in my direction. Only Sphinx jumped up and stretched out a paw at me from his position on the bed.

A few casual steps forward and I was even with Sonya and Felix. He lay on his back, eyes closed, and purred. Since he had given me the first message about Marv, I started a conversation with him. At least I think I did. I opened with a friendly greeting sent from my head to his noggin. Without moving a hair, he sent me back a short movie.

It was Bitsy's state room, the one we were in now. She sat at a small, folding table ready to dive into a dinner of pork chop, greens, and a baked potato. The view of Bitsy came from Felix, who peered around the bathroom door frame. Then he backed up into the room and took a flying leap at Bitsy's costume, which hung on the back of the door. It clattered to the floor.

"What now?" Bitsy shrieked.

Felix darted between her legs as she stomped to the bathroom, and while she was occupied, he deftly leapt onto the table and...he sat on her pork chop and massaged her vegetables with his feet. At the sound of her return, he jumped lightly to the bed, and while she focused on her dinner, pausing to remove a cat hair from her tongue, he rubbed his fanny and feet on her pillow.

I burst out laughing. "You clever little boy!"

He stretched his neck and meowed.

"You *are* a clever little boy," Sonya cooed.

Now for the hard stuff. I relayed the scene of Marv's last moments, including the dialog. The room became a mass of hissing and arched backs except for Felix, who only opened his eyes.

Sonya hugged him close. "What's wrong with them?"

"Dunno." I mumbled because I was trying to catch their responses. I could feel fear. Lots of fear. My chest tightened, and a queasy feeling ran through my stomach. They were definitely upset, but they didn't have information to pass on.

I projected an image of the faceless person who had watched Marv die along with a big question mark. Nothing. Then I made up a scene of Marv marching along on their walk the minutes before he'd taken a nosedive to death. That didn't get a response either. I sent an audio of Marv, skipping the images, and they reacted with fear and anger again.

Finally, I sent out the words *gray fur.*

Every furry body tensed, and every little head swung around to look at the door, as if expecting the monstrous Gray Fur to walk in, but they didn't offer any hints as to the identity of that monster. To calm them, I sent images of the toys I'd seen on the floor of Sonya's room, including the stuffed bear Bitsy had mentioned. Felix returned the image of the bear with a complaint. Apparently, it wasn't up to snuggly bear standards. Felix thought it was hard and uncomfortable and had crossed it off his list of favorite toys. I continued to sooth them with images of kibble and belly rubs until they returned to their former activities, or non-activities in the case of Sphinx.

The lock clicked and Bitsy walked in carrying her golden costume. "Time's up."

Sonya argued for a few minutes, and to cover my disappointment, I waited in the hall. What had I learned from my attempt to communicate? The cats were present at Marv's demise, but I already knew that. That Felix didn't like Bitsy. I might take that seriously except the cat had the same animus for his stuffed bear.

TWENTY-FOUR

I accompanied Sonya back to the fifth floor. Neither of us had much to say. Sonya was missing her Felix. I was bummed because I hadn't learned anything new. After a mumbled goodbye from Sonya, I returned to my room. My latest towel creature—a whale—wasn't the only thing on my bed. Bowers sat back against the headboard, his legs stretched out in front of him and his arms crossed over his chest. He reached for the remote and switched off the television, glaring the whole while.

"Where have you been?"

"Thanks for taking off your shoes before putting your feet on my bed," I said.

He stood. "I think I told you not to leave my sight."

"Kind of hard to do when you close the door in my face. Did you and Security Officer Robinson have a pleasant conversation?"

He set the remote on the bedside table. "Nothing pleasant about it."

I caught his tone. It had an official I'm-on-the-job sound to it. "What do you mean?"

He pressed his lips together, making the words fight their way out. "I mean you were right. Marvelous Marv was murdered."

"Get out of here!" I said this with wide eyes to emphasize the sarcasm. "What finally convinced you?"

"Officer Robinson got a call from the Sitka coroner, who also noticed the defensive wounds. He rushed a blood test and found sleeping tablets in Marv's system."

"He was drugged?"

Bowers nodded. "Probably to make it easier to push him over the railing."

"Well, you can't blame *that* on the cats." I sighed. "That's good news."

"Not exactly."

I gaped. "Why not? Now the ship's security, with our help, will look for a murderer."

Someone pounded on my door, obviously using a fist instead of knuckles. When I opened it, Penny flew into the room. She stopped short when she saw Bowers, and then she narrowed her eyes and clenched her hands into tight balls.

"How could you! After you came to my wedding!"

I looked to the crumpled bedspread, noted that Bowers and I were alone in my room, and assumed she was defending my honor. "It's not what it looks like."

Without taking her eyes off Bowers, she said, "It sure isn't. Kemper didn't kill anyone!"

"Kemper?" I cocked my head at Bowers.

"That's what I was trying to tell you. Kemper was Robinson's first interview. Apparently, he made a scene and threatened Marv the night he died."

Penny twitched her shoulders. "I wouldn't call it a scene. Kemper's not capable of causing a scene."

"But he did threaten the man?"

"Technically," I said, trying to be helpful, "he assaulted Marv, but he didn't threaten him. He told him not to kiss Penny again." I held my hands palms-up. "He didn't even say *or else*."

Penny dropped onto my bed. "It's ridiculous. Preposterous!"

"Is he under arrest?"

She rubbed her nose. "No. Security Officer Robinson took him to his office to question him after some tattletale told him the story."

I sat down next to her and rubbed her shoulder. "That's not so bad."

"But Marv *fell*."

Bowers said, "He had help."

"Oh." Penny's eyes widened. "Oh!"

"It will give you something to tell your grandchildren," I said, hoping a reference to their future together would calm her down. Instead, her bottom lip trembled.

"How can we have children if he's in jail?"

"Well, if he's in jail...I don't think you should stay married to a jailbird."

Her face flushed an angry red. "Wh—how—" and then I think she finally got the image of Kemper the jailbird because she burst out with a laugh. "It's so silly." She brushed her bangs back and stood. "I can't think why I let my imagination run away with me."

"Look at the bright side. You and I will get to spend time together while they're holding him. Does the ship have jail cells?"

Okay. That was a little much. Penny paled. "They wouldn't. They *couldn't*." And then she ran out the door.

"Does Officer Robinson have any other suspects in mind?" I asked.

"I'm sure he'll be talking to crew members. And Sonya."

"Is that all?" After blurting that out, I tried to look casual.

He cocked his head. "What aren't you telling me?"

"Since I'm not telling you, why ask?"

"Frankie. This is a murder investigation. You almost got your Aunt Gertrude arrested by trying to cover up for her after Elvira Jenkins was killed last year. If you're trying to cover for someone, why don't we make it easier and you tell me now."

"Penny will kill me."

"I don't think you can do much worse than accuse Kemper of murder." He raised his brows. "Unless it's about her mother or father. Is it?"

Did Penny even like Sharon? I'm sure she wouldn't want to see her carted away in cuffs, but Penny probably felt that way about most people. She was a nice person. I made my decision.

"I saw Sharon Bradley arguing with Marv the night he died. And Robby and I saw her coming out of her room later that evening, and when she saw us, she ducked back inside."

"Was this after the scene with Penny?"

"Yes."

"Did you ask her about it?"

"She said she had been warning him off, but that's not what it sounded like." I scrunched up my face in my effort to remember her exact words. "She said *if you ever say anything to her, I'll kill you.*"

"Which suggests he knew something about her he could repeat. Did they know each other before this trip?"

"She says no. So did Gina when I asked her."

"A daughter will protect her mother."

"I don't think that's it. Gina laughed it off." Now that I had said it aloud, I regretted sharing the information. "You don't have to tell Robinson, do you?"

"I'm only assisting him unofficially at his request. Officially, this is his investigation. And Finlander's. The lines are kind of fuzzy when the crime takes place on a ship at sea. I don't understand it, and I don't need to. But I do need to deal with him fairly, and that includes passing on any information I have that may help him."

"Could you wait and see?" I stood close to him, and trying my best to imitate the look Chauncey gives me when he wants a bone, gazed up with what I hoped were puppy-dog eyes. "Maybe you'll catch the murderer and won't need to share what I told you about Sharon."

"I'll at least have to talk to her myself."

"She probably wouldn't mind that." That was a lie. Sharon minded everything, but given the choice, she'd prefer Bowers to an official interview. "Thanks."

He put his hands on my shoulders and pushed me down to sitting on the bed. "Not so fast. We have to discuss a certain key card."

I blinked. "You mean the one the burglar left behind in Sonya's room?"

"No. The one you stole back from me and then tried to use to enter Sonya's room after lying to me about stomach cramps."

"Oh. That one." I grinned, but he didn't grin back.

He stood over me, looking down, and then seemed to decide what he had to say next needed an approach more personal than an intimidating glare. He sat next to me on the bed and turned his torso to face me. "We seem to need ground rules if we're going to get along."

"Were we not getting along?" I asked with a girlish giggle. Having him so close was scrambling my brain.

He held up his index finger. "One, don't even think about reading my mind."

I had once needed help when trying to communicate with a panicked dog, and I had grabbed the hands of the men standing next to me, one of them Bowers. Afterward, I read both of their thoughts. "You keep harping on that, but it was an accident. I don't even think I could do it again."

"That's good news. But don't test it." He held up another finger. "Two, don't steal from me."

"I didn't—"

"I knew you were going back to my room for the master key, but I wanted to see what you would do with it. You are completely transparent to me, and it's painful to listen to you lie and think you're getting away with it. We must trust each other. Which brings me to number three."

Here came the third finger. "Don't ever, ever lie to me, Frankie." He lowered his hand. "Please. Just don't do it. If you don't want to tell me something, just be straight with me. I'll never lie to you."

He was so sincere, it made me feel like a crumb to think of all the little untruths I'd told him since he boarded the ship. Obviously, he had those same untruths in mind because he said, "Is there anything you want to straighten out with me right now?"

Was this a ploy? Was Bowers trying to get me to spill my secrets? Was he a master manipulator? Or was he the most sincere, sexy cop that ever lived? Hard to tell.

"Why don't you ask me anything you'd like to know?" I said, cleverly putting the onus on him.

"Okay. Did you tell me everything the cats have shared with you?"

My eyebrows shot up. It wasn't like Bowers to treat kitty testimony as something worth considering. I related everything the cats had shared with me including Felix's attitude toward his toys and the ubiquitous statement *gray fur*.

"Gray fur." He rolled the idea around a few times, his eyes narrowed in concentration. "Do you think that might refer to the gray cat?"

I was surprised he'd taken note of the individual cats in the act, but he *was* a trained observer.

"No. I get a feeling it's something or someone else." Should I tell him about Sharon's fake dead fox stole? I'd already told him about her argument with Marv, so it probably wouldn't hurt, so I did.

"Okay. We'll file that."

"You're not going to question Sharon about it?"

"Did the cats have an opportunity to see Mrs. Bradley in her fox stole? I don't imagine she wore it to the Fabulous Felines show."

"Good point."

"Whose idea was it for Trevor to buy the raffle ticket?"

Bowers was full of surprises. "Trevor's. Definitely. Why?"

He shook his head. "I'm just gathering information. What did you want with Sonny Street?"

I looked down at my clasped hands. "Now we're headed into territory where I'm not going to want to share details." It wouldn't be fair to reveal how Sonny had helped me, especially if Bowers was going to pass on that information to Security Officer Robinson.

"Oh." He cleared his throat. "It's personal." He gave me a brief smile. "I should have guessed. You did ask for his room number, and you're a beautiful woman...without attachments. A free spirit."

JACQUELINE VICK

My laughter cut him off. "Me and Sonny?" I smacked his shoulder, and without my instructing it to, my hand lingered and my fingers gently massaged the fabric of his cotton shirt. "Give me a break. Sonny gave me Marv's room number. I wanted to search the victim's room, but before I had a chance, Trevor was rescued, and the captain gave Marv's old room to him."

Bowers covered my hand with his. "Don't do that."

"Why not?"

"It's distracting."

Hmmm. He hadn't yet asked me a general spill-all question, and I wanted to think about the implications of a Bitsy and Art relationship before Bowers started nosing around. A distraction might be a good thing.

"Sorry about that." I scooted closer and reached up with my free hand, so I could massage both shoulders. "How's this?" My brows went up. "Wow. Your shoulders are tight. Like rocks. Hard, muscular rocks."

With his face mere inches from mine, his gaze took on an intensity that made my insides shiver. It was the same way I looked at chocolate cake. He remained still, and his voice lowered when he said, "Are you offering me a massage?"

"Are you asking for one?" I matched his lowered voice in an attempt to sound coy, but to my ears, it sounded as if I were mocking him.

He placed his hands on either side of my waist and slowly moved them up my sides. The sensation made me suck in my breath. He kept going up my arms until he reached my hands, which he removed from his shoulders. "I don't think that would be a good idea." He stood. "In fact, I think I should get going."

I popped up so fast I bumped into him. "Where are you going? Because I'm going with you."

He smiled. "Of course you are because I'm not letting you out of my sight. Remember?"

There was a knock on my door, and our eyes met—mine innocent and his scowling.

"I swear I have no idea who it is," I whispered.

Mrs. Doud's voice called out. "The drawing for the Pure Fantasy bracelet is in fifteen minutes!"

Frank Doud's voice followed. "You'll need to hurry if you want a seat."

"I'll be right there," I called back. To Bowers I said, "Are we interested in the auction?"

He had on his cop expression, which meant no expression at all. "Yes, we are. We are most definitely interested in the fate of the Pure Fantasy bracelet."

TWENTY-FIVE

I didn't know they could fit so many people into the Orca Lounge. It was standing room only in the hallway outside, which is where Bowers and I wound up. Mrs. Doud wasn't in sight, so she and Frank must have slipped in and snagged a seat.

To me, the event had all the excitement of a doctor's appointment, but I was the exception. The chatter remained at a subdued noise level, as if the ticket holders were afraid their passions, if allowed to escape, might have them bursting into the bawdy shouts heard at racetracks. However, their bright eyes and barely controlled grins spoke volumes. They all hoped to win the prize.

Even Bowers kept his gaze fixed on the podium, or maybe he was watching the glass case that held the Pure Fantasy Bracelet. Art and Hannah stood at attention on either side of it, which was silly. No one could snatch the prize from under the gazes of so many people, and if a desperado had leapt on stage wielding a gun, there wasn't much Art or Hannah could do about it. I supposed it was for show.

A woman in her sixties with teased blond hair and enough bling on her fingers, neck and wrists to illuminate her seafoam-green suit in the dark stood to the side of the stage with a card in her hand. Once she received a nod from a man in a black suit, she approached the microphone and welcomed the guests.

"Isn't this exciting?"

The crowd responded with enthusiastic claps, but then she killed the momentum as she thanked about a hundred people for their participation in the event, ending with an ode to the generous Hardcastle family. By then I was asleep on my feet.

"Is it over yet?"

Bowers grunted a response. He wasn't taking his eyes off the stage.

The man in the suit approached the podium with a square covered in black cloth, which, once removed, proved to be a glass bowl filled with tickets. A drum roll sounded over the speakers and the woman reached her hand in. She glanced at the ticket, her gaze moved over the crowd, and then she broke into a broad smile.

"The new owner of the Pure Fantasy bracelet is Mr. Trevor Grant!"

A murmur traveled through the room, and necks stretched as heads turned to search the room.

"Oh, my, gosh," I cried.

Trevor, seated near the exit, stood up with a dazed expression. "Did you say Trevor Grant?"

People laughed.

"I certainly did." The woman held out her hands and welcomed him to the stage to the sound of polite applause. By then, disappointed losers had already begun to file out the door, so I had to stand on tip-toe to see. Trevor shook

227

hands with the woman and blinked as a flash burst from a photographer's camera, and the woman thanked everyone for coming.

"What a surprise," I said. "I don't know anyone who owns jewelry special enough to have its own name."

Bowers crooked his head. "Come on."

"Don't you want to stay to congratulate Trevor?"

"The ship's photographer will keep him busy for a while. We'll meet up with him afterward."

I followed Bowers down to the first floor to Officer Robinson's office. As he entered, Robinson looked up from his desk and Bowers nodded.

I looked from one man's face to the other. "What's going on?"

Robinson dropped his gaze down to the papers on his desk and said, "The captain will be along shortly to present the Pure Fantasy bracelet in person."

"Why do *we* need to be here?"

"You don't," Bowers said. He opened the door to let me out, but I ignored him and sat in one of the chairs in front of Robinson's desk.

Little conversation took place, I'm sure because of my presence. As a woman, I've dedicated my life to destroying long periods of silence. I asked Robinson what it took to become a security officer on a ship.

"Were you a policeman who got tired of the routine? Maybe you could get Bowers a job."

He laughed. "I don't think your friend has any desire to retire from detective work. As for me, I was military police."

The two men compared notes on their time in the army. I had no idea Bowers had ever been in the service, and I wondered if he still had his dress uniform. Then I gave myself a mental smack for my incredibly shallow view of our men in uniform.

Captain Milo must have received inside information on Trevor's movements because he arrived carrying an ornate, silver jewelry box just a few minutes before the guest of honor entered the room. Robinson stood on the captain's entrance and remained standing until Trevor Grant strolled in, his hands in the pockets of a sky-blue cardigan.

He raised his brows at me and Bowers on his entrance, but Robinson stepped forward and drew his attention to the forms he needed to sign. Something about transferring ownership. The captain waited patiently for Trevor to finish, and then he stepped up and shook his hand.

"It's a pleasure to present you with the Pure Fantasy bracelet."

Once the box had been handed over to its new owner, Captain Milo and Robinson exchanged salutes and left.

Trevor took the bracelet out and set down the box. His examination of his prize seemed perfunctory, as if he were only doing so because it was expected. "Beautiful," he said, reaching out to return it to the box.

Bowers grabbed his wrist. "May I see the Pure Fantasy bracelet?"

Startled, Trevor said, "Of course."

"Not that one. The one in your pocket."

Trevor didn't argue. He said, "Aw, hell," and reached into his pocket for a duplicate bracelet. Then he sat in the chair next to me and crossed his legs, giving my dropped-jaw expression a quick glance. "It's not as bad as you think, Frances."

Bowers and Robinson examined both bracelets, and when they were satisfied, Bowers said, "I don't get it. You switched out the fake for the real thing. Care to explain?"

"No, but I haven't got a choice now." He asked Robinson, "Do you have to repeat what I'm going to tell you?"

"Let's hear it first. It isn't my job to make more trouble than necessary."

Trevor gave me a sideways glance, and I'm happy to report my mouth was firmly closed. "My name is Trevor Hardcastle." My jaw dropped open again.

"When my siblings came up with the idea of lending the collection to a cruise line, I was against it. The collection is our legacy, and I thought they were asking for trouble. So, I switched the originals out for copies. The rest of my family doesn't know, but if word got out to Finlander they had fakes displayed on board, they might sue."

Robinson nodded. "That's entirely possible."

"It wasn't until after the ship had departed that my sister told me about the raffle. Accepting money for a fake bracelet is probably a criminal offense, so I had to get on board and make the switch. If I had come using my own name, I would have had to explain, and not to brag, but there would have been crowds watching my every step.

"Really?" I couldn't imagine wasting my time watching a famous person eat breakfast.

"Really. Instead, I sunk my kayak and waited until the *Iso Kala* came by before I signaled for the rescue of Trevor Grant."

"That was so, so stupid," I said. "What if the ship had had to change the itinerary or something? You could have been stuck on that island surrounded by freezing water all night. You could have died. You might even have been eaten by killer whales."

"Not likely," Bowers said without sympathy. "You probably had supplies with you, and I assume you had a cell phone."

Trevor gave him a pained look. "Yes, I did. It's not very heroic, but it's not criminal, either. I haven't stolen anything. I haven't committed a crime. And I was right about security! Even I, with no criminal experience, was able to steal—switch out the Pure Fantasy bracelet."

"What did you plan to do with it?" Bowers asked.

"Make up an excuse, such as a sudden breakup with my girlfriend—"

"You have a girlfriend?" I said. Men with girlfriends shouldn't have their arms around other girls. Having been a victim of a two-timer, I considered his deceit a greater crime than mere theft of property.

"She's more of a friend, but I don't think anyone would investigate our relationship. How could they prove it? Anyway, I'd make an excuse and then give the bracelet back for a second drawing."

Robinson's mouth had steadily compressed into a thin line. His brows had dropped into a glare, and his hands had squeezed together into fists. He couldn't contain his anger any longer. "You used this crew. Somebody could have been hurt during your fake rescue. There's always a possibility of danger in any unplanned use of the lifeboats."

I paled, and he added for my benefit, "It's a minimal risk. At the least, it was a thoughtless prank that abused our crew and our resources."

"I'm sorry. I never thought of it that way. You're right. As for the resources, I can make up for any losses. I'm not sure what I can do about the crew other than apologize to them."

"How did you rig the raffle?" Bowers asked.

Trevor leaned back and rubbed his mouth with his hand. "The tickets in the bowl had all been replaced with my information. That's all you need to know. I don't want to get anyone else into trouble."

"Let's put it this way," Robinson said. "If you don't give us a name, I'll make sure everyone associated with the contest is fired. They will all lose their jobs instead of just the guilty party."

Trevor only hesitated a few seconds before answering, but Bowers beat him to it.

"It was Art. The man who conveniently spotted Mr. Hardcastle."

When Trevor nodded, Robinson pushed a button on his desk, and a crew member entered the room. "I want to see the Hardcastle security guard, Art, here ASAP. Leave one of our men there as a replacement to assist the other guard."

"Yes, sir."

Bowers held up the two bracelets, then held one out to Trevor. "It's an excellent reproduction, except for the flaw." He threw me a look. "The one that makes it look authentic."

Trevor jumped out of his seat and grabbed the fake. "Chip? Impossible. I had the reproduction made from garnets. Since the bracelet stayed under glass, I didn't think anyone would notice." He leaned over Bower's shoulder to inspect the fake.

I frowned. "But I thought flaws showed the stones were natural. Like yarn."

"Yarn?" Bowers shook his head. "So that's where you got the idea."

"This is glass!" Trevor pushed the fake away as if he had been defiled by merely looking at it, and then he jabbed a finger at Bowers. "Someone has stolen my fake. It wasn't cheap. I want it back."

Robinson had no expression. Since he had been military police, I now assumed his lack of expression was a version of

Bowers' cop-face. "I'm not sure I want to allocate the resources to find the thief of a fake bracelet."

"The garnets are genuine enough."

"Have you thought about how I'd have to approach the problem? I'd have to tell my superiors I was hunting for a fake that had been substituted for the original bracelet, which would lead them to wonder about the other jewelry in the Hardcastle collection."

Trevor sat back down. "Good point."

Bowers said, "Do you mind if I hang onto this?" When he received permission from Robinson, he pocketed the glass reproduction.

Robinson straightened his shoulders in an official stance. "Mr. Hardcastle, are you officially handing over the original Pure Fantasy Bracelet for a second raffle? Assuming we find it."

With an impatient gesture of his hand, Trevor proved to me his fabulous net worth. "Of course. Do what you like with it."

There was a knock at the door, and the same crewman who reported earlier stepped into the room. "No sign of Art, sir."

"Maybe he's on break?" I said, but no one bothered to acknowledge my suggestion.

"Keep looking," Robinson said. "He has to be somewhere."

It wasn't until eleven o'clock that night we discovered exactly where.

TWENTY-SIX

Nobody seemed happy to see me as I approached the dinner table that night, even though I looked pretty good in my black palazzo pants and forest green tunic. They'd probably decided it was my fault Kemper had been interrogated, since I was the one who suggested murder instead of accident. Even Thomas Mohr had to force his smile when I took the seat between him and Bowers.

There was a moment when I thought I could stiffen my chin or upper lip or whatever it was that showed you were tough and let them think whatever they wanted. Once the truth came out, and the culprit was dragged off in cuffs, they could revise their opinions and thank me in the name of justice. Instead, I folded.

"The Juneau Medical Examiner's office told Officer Robinson that Marvelous Marv had been murdered. He found defensive wounds on Marv, and he had been drugged. That's what the medical examiner's office said. Isn't it awful?"

I knew they'd let Officer Robinson off without a slap on the wrist because who, on a ship of thousands with a killer on the loose, was going to risk alienating the man with the resources to come to their rescue should they be selected as the next victim? Let them blame an unknown civil official for Kemper's discomfort.

Bowers narrowed his eyes at me. I grabbed the glass of red wine in front of my place setting and took a gulp before whispering:

"You never said it was a secret."

"Silly me."

"All this talk about death is vulgar," Sharon said, which would have killed the topic had Sharon been queen of the table.

Christina Mohr leaned forward and took her son's hand. "Were they nice to you in the interrogation room?"

Bowers made a noise and covered it with a cough.

"It wasn't an interrogation room. It was an office. And they didn't use rubber hoses or a bright light, if that's what you mean." Kemper lifted his chin and looked down on the rest of us. "But it was annoying having to go over the scene again and again. Frankly, I was peeved at Marv at the time, and I couldn't really remember what I said to him."

Liar. He probably had this one fit of heroism emblazoned on his memory and would pull it out for a replay when he needed a confidence boost.

"It's okay, honey," Penny said, patting his other hand. "You just told him he was behaving badly, which he was." Her cheeks flushed, and she slid her hand away. "And then you told me the entire episode was my fault, but I'm sure that was the adrenaline talking."

Our waiter arrived just as Robby said, "Did they really think you might have killed Marv? Because that's just crazy."

Kemper's nostrils flared. "Why? Don't you think I'm capable of killing a man?"

"I'm sure you could kill anyone you put your mind to killing," Christina Mohr said, a mother showing her support.

Robby snorted. "Yeah. Kemper's a real ninja."

Our waiter left, murmuring something about giving us more time to decide.

Since I couldn't laugh out loud without hurting Penny's, or at least Kemper's, feelings, the conversation started to bore me. "Someone tried to kill me, too," I said. All eyes were on me including the party of six seated at the next table. In the middle of the silence, Gina broke loose with a full bray.

"Why on earth would anyone want to kill you?"

"I can think of a few good reasons," Bowers whispered in my ear, so I gave him a bright smile and grabbed hold of his hand.

Moving my mouth right next to his ear, I said, "I heard they're bringing the kitties into the dining room tonight." I held tight as he tried to jerk away. "Now, now. Don't cause a scene." Unless he wanted to throw me to the floor to break my grip, he had to sit there and take it.

"Did you or Robby mention I thought Marv had been murdered to anyone?" I asked. "You remember. When I talked to you, poolside."

Gina smiled at Robby. "That was right before the salmon bake." Apparently, I wasn't worthy of a smile because she lost it the moment she turned her gaze on me. "I had better things to do than repeat your insane ideas."

"Not so insane, since Marv was, in fact, murdered."

"Has everyone decided what they want for dinner?" Judy asked with a sharpness that meant she'd had enough of murder talk. We all looked at her in surprise, and then one by one we turned our eyes down to our menus in embarrassment for the obvious strain we had caused our hostess. I closed my menu because filet mignon was still available.

Fred held up a hand to summon the waiter who approached the table with a professional smile. You'd never have known we had scared him away just five minutes previously.

We placed our orders, but just as Bowers was handing the waiter his menu, he put a hand on my shoulder and said, "This lady would like to change her order to baked salmon."

My eyebrows shot up. "Wha—?"

Bowers had a nasty grin on as he leaned his face close and mouthed the words, "Don't cause a scene."

By the time dinner arrived, the topic had turned to the wedding, steered there by me. As the maid of honor, I felt guilty I had let the murder take precedence over Penny's big moment, so I joked and teased and made Penny blush like a good girlfriend should. Bowers showed his approval by spearing the salmon from my plate and replacing it with his porterhouse steak, though I noticed he kept back half of the mushrooms. As it turned out, he had to take back a large portion of the steak to finish it, but I'd enjoyed every morsel I'd eaten.

Thomas Mohr offered another toast to the happy couple, and then he pushed back his chair to leave.

"Headed for the Neptune Lounge?" I asked.

"There's a musical revue on stage tonight."

Christina grinned. "We're at the age we'd rather watch other people do all the dancing."

"Aren't the kitties onstage tonight?" Gina asked, oh-so-sweetly.

"They have the night off," Thomas said. "The entertainment director makes sure there is variety to suit every taste."

Thomas would know, since he and Christina had breakfasted that morning with the captain and select passengers. It was one of the privileges of being a Blue Whale member, the shipboard equivalent of a frequent flyer.

Kemper gave his wife's shoulders a squeeze. "Do you want to hit the dance floor?" He'd been kissing her fanny ever since she reminded him he had placed the blame for Marv's behavior on his innocent beloved.

Opting to be magnanimous, Penny begged off and said they should join his parents. Very smart. Deferring to the new in-laws.

"What about you?" I asked Robby.

He slipped a sideways glance toward Gina. "We're going to listen to the piano and violin duet in the lounge. Maybe you two would like to join us?"

Relaxing on a couch with a drink in my hand surrounded by soothing music sounded like a relaxing way to end the day, but Bowers cut off my reply.

"You two enjoy yourselves. I need to walk after a meal like that."

He pulled back my chair, and as I stood, my face felt warm. "I wasn't suggesting anything romantic."

"I didn't think you were. It just so happens I have other plans."

"Oh." I tried to hide my surprise and disappointment. Once again, I was the odd man out. Then Bowers grinned and jerked his head.

"Come on."

We walked side by side in a casual stroll, he with his hands stuffed in his trouser pockets, me with my hands clasped in front of me.

"Your family couldn't make it to the wedding?" he asked.

"Mom's supervising the Loon Lake reception," I said. "She doesn't like the water any more than I do."

"Huh. I thought retirees were drawn to cruises like," he smirked, "like Frankie Chandler to the Lido Deck."

"Funny. Not."

We slowed down as we caught up with a woman with a walker. A steady stream of people passed us on either side, making it difficult to go around her. I assumed they weren't all headed to the same place by the variety of outfits they wore. Some were in evening dress, others in jeans and t-shirts, and still others in shorts—a bit optimistic for an evening in Alaska. I had noticed an increase in their numbers, and then I realized we were closing in on the shopping arcade.

Since discovering there would be a second drawing, passengers were flocking to the Hardcastle collection to take their chances. I wasn't sure why the odds would be better the second time around, but to each his own. Robinson had assigned a security crew member to help keep watch over the jewels, but he made no move to sell raffle tickets, so Hannah had to hustle to keep up with their orders.

"Do you think there is a connection between Marv's murder and the stolen fake bracelet?" I asked.

"Hard to tell right now. Marv died the first night at sea, but we don't know when the Pure Fantasy was stolen. We need to find Art."

"He's been a busy boy," I said. "First helping someone steal the prize and then fixing the raffle. I wonder if the Hardcastles did a background check on *him* before they hired him?" I slowed my pace. "Maybe Trevor was the one to do the background check, and he saw that Art had experience with crime, which worked to his advantage. Maybe he had stolen from his employer before, or maybe there were only *suspicions* he had stolen from his employer before. Or maybe he had killed before, but everyone thought it was an accident." I grabbed Bowers' arm. "Could it be that simple? Maybe Marv caught Art helping the thief of the Pure Fantasy bracelet, and so Art, having killed before—and we all know from detective stories that once you've killed, it becomes a habit—maybe he murdered Marv in order to keep his job."

"That's your theory?"

If only the kitties weren't so reticent about showing me the killer's face. Was it a hideous face, twisted in malignant anger? Or did the cats, with feline indifference, just not care? Most likely, the latter.

"Couldn't Robinson do a room-by-room search for the garnet bracelet?"

"I wouldn't suggest that if I were you. Not unless you want to see a grown man faint."

I acknowledged his point. "There would probably be resistance. Complaints from the passengers and demands for refunds."

"Exactly. His hands are tied. We need to get to the bottom of Marv's murder and the theft, and it looks like we're on our own."

I stopped walking, certain I'd misheard. Bowers, the man who considered me a busybody and a nuisance when it came to his work, was asking me to join forces with him? Just to clarify, I said, "Did you say we?"

"You do have certain advantages over me. Trevor seems to like you enough that he might tell you things he won't tell me. The same with Sonny Street. Also, you've known Sharon a lot longer than I have, and she seems like the kind of woman who might react with a defensive silence if questioned by police, whereas she might not suspect anything if you brought things up in a casual conversation."

Should I mention that Sharon's idea of a casual conversation was silence and an ice-queen sneer?

"And as much as I don't want them to factor into a logical investigation, the cats might be able to tell you something."

"I'm confused." I said, my tone snippy. "Am I a slut, a simpleton, or a psychic nut job?"

Bowers' blue eyes opened wide in shock. "I didn't say to sleep with Trevor. Just meet him for a drink and talk to him. Ask him about his relationship with Art. And I'll have you within my sight at all times when you're talking to the suspects. Just make sure you stay out of the ladies' room when you're with Sharon."

Bowers put his hands on my shoulders and turned me around. "And here's your chance."

Dead ahead, Trevor Grant stepped out of the general store. I turned my head to say something to Bowers, but he had slipped away, like The Fog. Trevor's gaze landed on me, and he smiled and waved.

"Time to turn on the charm," I muttered, and then I snorted at the thought. When we met at the halfway mark, Trevor held out a hand in the direction I'd just come from.

"Shall we reclaim our spot at the Seaside Bar? Or am I tainted goods, now that I'm a wealthy liar."

How would a flirt respond to that? "Tainted goods. Sounds...tantalizing."

He looked down on me with a puzzled expression. "Really?"

I know my limitations. "No. Tainted goods remind me of a can of spoiled tuna."

241

"How does wealthy strike you?"

"Well, according to some, wealth is the ruin of modern society. We'd all be much better off scrounging for worms for breakfast. However, I've noticed the people who push this philosophy aren't exactly poor, or even middle class." I nodded. "I'm all for wealthy, as long as you're not *filthy* rich."

"Well...I could donate half my money to missionaries."

"It's a deal."

We shook hands, and he held onto mine and led me to the bar. Two women had taken our spot, but there was another, smaller loveseat in the room's corner. When he brought back our drinks and sat down beside me, our thighs touched, something I couldn't remedy unless I squirmed off my cushion and sat on the love seat's arm.

"I'm glad you're not going to hold my stupidity against me."

"You were just trying to keep someone from being cheated out of the bracelet."

He sighed with relief. "That's really all there was to it. I know it makes me look like a selfish ass for not trusting that the jewels would be safe, but they belonged to my father. We still have the properties, but the Hardcastle collection was special to him, and having it around feels like having a piece of him. Does that make sense?"

"Perfect sense. And if you could bribe Art, then anyone could."

"You're right. I'm either going to have to get over my fears, or we are going to have to pay for better security."

"Didn't you do a background check on Art and Hannah before your family hired them?

"My sister, generous as she is with loaning the jewels, is a skinflint when it comes to expenses."

"Security is probably not the right place to cut."

I prompted him to talk about the places he'd traveled, while I tried to think of a way to introduce *gray fur* into the conversation. When he mentioned Italy, it gave me an idea.

"Isn't Milan the center of the fashion world? I thought I heard it was all the rage to have fur-lined jackets and coats. Gray fur."

He looked down at his expensive sports coat and turned his palms up, as if he felt the need to apologize for spending money on nice clothes. "I know quality when I see it, but I don't follow designers."

My hand went to his lapel. "I wasn't poking fun. I wouldn't know a Dior from a...I can't think of another designer."

His hand covered mine and pressed it against his chest. "You are refreshing." His thumb caressed the back of my hand. When the musicians returned from their break and launched into a jazz number, he pulled me to my feet. "Let's take a walk. I don't feel like crowds tonight."

My mention of gray fur had gone over like a hairball. Expelled without ceremony. When we stopped in front of the elevator, I wondered how soon I could make my excuses and move on to Sharon. Once I had her alone, what would be the right approach? *Did you slip into your gray fur stole on your way to meet Marv on the Observation Deck the night he died?* Probably not subtle enough. Sharon wasn't an idiot.

Lost in thought, I stepped onto the elevator without paying any attention to where my escort was leading me, but when the doors opened on our floor, I raised my eyes, stepped back, and gasped. Trevor had brought us to the Observation Deck.

He switched positions so his right arm went around my

waist and his left took possession of my hand. "Don't worry. I won't let you fall."

A heavy mist had settled over the ship. The safety lights were mere orange glows trying to cut through the fog. As Trevor ushered me forward, I wondered what kind of person would want to walk around a ship's deck in these conditions. I glanced up at Trevor, expecting to find the determined look of a killer and was relieved to see he wore a smile. I don't know why that comforted me. Maybe he enjoyed killing people, and those curled up lips expressed the pleasure he received from other people's screams.

Steering me forward, Trevor passed in front of the empty deck chairs.

"There's something about looking out at the ocean from the up here that feels so powerful. No, that's not the right word. It's like all the walls and restrictions that follow me around daily fall away, and it's just me and nature." He stepped toward the railing, looked at me out of the corner of his eye, and grinned. "It's kind of creepy when you can't see anything, isn't it? But creepy in a good way."

"There's a good creepy?" I wasn't so sure.

I searched my surroundings for signs of Bowers, but I couldn't even see the windowed atrium I'd passed on the first day.

He leaned his forearms against the railing and soaked up nature, and I left him to his reverie for a few minutes before breaking in. Tiny droplets of moisture were coating my arms, making me shiver.

"You know," I said, watching his face for any change in expression, "this is where Marvelous Marv met his end."

"Who?"

I had a good view of his eyes, and they weren't trying to

avoid my gaze; neither did they stare, unblinking, like the eyes of an experienced liar. Then he glanced down.

"You mean the entertainer guy who fell? I've heard people talking about him."

"Yep. That was Marv." I pointed to the glowing lights that marked the lifeboats and explained the victim had landed right outside of my room.

He cocked his head. "So, that's your room?"

"All mine. Penny was sharing it with me, but now I'm on my lonesome."

There wasn't a hidden agenda behind my statement, but I should have realized how it sounded.

"That's a shame." Trevor's voice was low and husky, and he stroked my arm with his fingertips. It tickled, and I shivered. Another wrong move.

He wrapped his arm around my shoulder, pulled me in, and kissed me. It wasn't a bad kiss. Okay. It was pretty darn good. He'd obviously practiced his technique and scored high on the exams. I simply wasn't in the mood to kiss a murder suspect and confirmed twit. The stunt he had pulled, getting the crew to take out a lifeboat to rescue him, had been potentially dangerous. Not sexy dangerous, as in fighting with James Bond, accidentally falling onto the nearest bed and then being overcome by passion, but stupid dangerous. As in mixing bleach and ammonia when you're cleaning the bathroom.

My hands moved between us to his chest, and when I gave a light push, he took the hint and stepped back.

"Why don't we take a walk? I'm getting chilly."

He grinned. "Good idea."

When he headed toward the elevators, probably intending to take me back to my room, I steered him toward the atrium. The closer we got, the more certain I was that the building wasn't there. I stopped.

"Where did it go?"

"Where did what go?"

"The atrium."

"There isn't an atrium up here. There's a pool."

I snorted. "I couldn't have missed an entire swimming pool."

He nodded his head. "They must have had the cover on." He pointed to a white structure close to the elevators. "It's motorized. It comes out and covers the pool with a dome of windows, so people can enjoy their swim in foul weather."

"Huh. Imagine that." I took a tentative step forward and squinted. I could just make out the dark shape of the water.

"Did you want to go in?" His head turned for a quick look to make sure we were alone. "I'm not sure they leave out towels."

Jeepers. He thought I wanted to go skinny dipping.

"That's alright."

My first thought when I saw the large, floating mass in the water's center was a seal had gotten onto the ship and invaded the pool. In fact, I pointed and laughed, but then I wondered how a wild mammal had maneuvered the elevators, and then my laughter turned into hysterical screams. The shape was a man.

Trevor pulled off his jacket and dove in, and a second man, who came out from behind the pool cover housing, joined him. They dragged the body to the edge of the pool, and when I reached out a hand to help the second man out, I recognized Bowers. He had kept his promise to watch out for me.

He hoisted himself out of the pool without my help, and

while Trevor pushed Art's backside—because it was horrify-ingly apparent from the burgundy shirt and tie that it was Art—Bowers pulled at his arms. The security guard rolled onto the cement with the squishy sound of a waterlogged towel. Bowers crouched over him and checked his pulse, but he didn't even try to resuscitate him.

"Aren't you going to do mouth-to-mouth or tip him side-ways to let the water run out of his lungs?"

He pushed his wet bangs back and put his hands on his sides, breathing hard. "Body's cold."

While he took out his cell phone— waterproof—and called Robinson, I kept my eyes focused on his face and resisted an urge to look down at the corpse. He kept the conversation brief, and then he stepped over Art and led me to a deck chair.

"I'm sorry, Frankie. You're going to have to stick around for a while. I wish I could spare you."

Trevor sloshed up to us. "Lucky you were around. Lucky coincidence."

Bowers had his expressionless cop face on. "No coinci-dence. I was looking for Frankie."

Trevor looked from me to Bowers and back again, which seemed to confirm something in his mind. Then he rubbed the back of his neck. "Look. You know how impor-tant it is that nobody knows who I am, and I don't see how I can sign a witness statement without giving it away."

"Go on."

"You saw as much as I did, and you have Frankie here for a second witness. I hate to ask a favor—"

"Especially since I don't owe you anything."

"No. No, you don't. But the Hardcastle Trust does a lot of good. The money raised from the raffle will go to charity, and we do benefits all the time." He shrugged. "I don't want to mess that up with a scandal."

It made a good argument and took the edge off Trevor's cowardice. Bowers said, "I can't let you leave, but I'll talk to Robinson about keeping your name out of it."

Trevor had to accept that because Robinson and his crew marched onto the scene just then, followed by Doc. Three men and one woman fanned out and disappeared into the fog, apparently to search the deck, though I couldn't think of any place for a person to hide. Then again, Bowers had remained out of site behind the pool cover housing.

Robinson approached Bowers in the posture of one reporting. I expected him to salute. "I've stationed someone at each exit to keep anyone from coming or going. Doc can try to establish the time of death, though I don't know how easy that is when the victim has been in the water. Drownings aren't Doc's forte, believe it or not. We've never had one on the *Iso Kala*. What time did you find him?"

Bowers looked at his watch, which I assumed was as waterproof as his cell phone. "Eleven o'clock. But he was in the water for at least twenty minutes before that."

"Why do you say that?" Trevor asked, indignant. "Were you here? Were you following us?" The look he aimed at me wasn't friendly.

Bowers spread his hands. "How long were you up here? Did you see or hear him go in the water?"

Trevor's expression cleared. "Oh. I see. Good point."

For the second time during my ocean voyage, Robinson questioned me, and I didn't have answers. Unlike the episode outside of Sonya's state room, I wasn't hiding anything this time. When it became clear I had nothing left to offer, Bowers told me to wait for him in my room. He added please. When I got off the elevator on the fifth floor,

Penny was standing outside my door. I let her in, and we naturally drifted to our original beds and sat down.

"Another body," she said with a sigh, though her voice didn't hold the censure it had when the discovery of the first body pre-wedding.

"What can I say?" I sat up straight. "How did you know?"

"Kemper, me, Robby and Gina saw the movement of troops toward the elevator, and we overheard two of them talking."

"Great. How long before Gina is rubbing my face in it?"

Penny opened her eyes in surprise. "Gina? She works for the U.N. She has to be discreet."

"She's off duty, and you know she wouldn't miss a chance to make me look like an idiot."

"Maybe she's jealous," Penny said.

My optimistic friend. Always looking for the bright side.

"She's probably giggling over it with Robby, right now."

Penny's brow wrinkled. "They are close, aren't they?"

"They're like Siamese twins. Inseparable. Robby mentioned he hadn't seen her in a long time. Maybe they're catching up."

"It's silly. I mean, it's not as if they could date even if they wanted to."

My brows shot up. "Are you worried about future nieces with three ears and a nephew with an extra arm growing out of his forehead?" I hummed the theme song from *Deliverance*.

"Stop it!" Penny wrinkled her nose. "That's almost as bad as imagining you and Robby getting together."

I raised my hand. "Excuse me. Why would it be as bad? Do you think I'm not good enough for your brother?"

"It would be weird. My brother and my best friend...
you know." She shuddered.

"It's a good thing for you I had the same thought, young
lady, or I'd be offended."

When someone knocked on the door, Penny jumped up
and answered it. Kemper stood in the hallway, and I heard
him hiss, "Are you through in there? We need to get going if
we're going to meet my parents."

Penny, a generous soul, asked me if I wanted to come
with them. Ignoring Kemper's frown, I said I had my own
plans. As Penny stepped out, Bowers walked in with a nod
for Kemper. Since he had changed into dry clothes, I patted
the bed next to me, but he sat down on Penny's old bed
instead.

"Art was hit on the head with a blunt instrument. He
drowned, so we can assume the killer lured him upstairs and
attacked him next to the pool."

"Are you sure?"

"I can't see someone dragging his body through the ship,
can you?"

That didn't seem likely. "Did Doc come up with a time
of death?"

"More than two hours. After two hours, the body—just
trust me. He's probably right."

"Art was missing after the drawing. That took place at
four o'clock."

"But we didn't start looking for him until about half
past, or even a quarter to five."

"Could his body have been up there that long without
being discovered?"

Bowers rubbed his chin. "He must have spent time with
the killer somewhere private. Somewhere a search party
couldn't find him. Then, the killer lured him up to the

Observation Deck. He or she didn't necessarily kill him right away. It got dark around a quarter after seven, it's a new moon, and it's cloudy. There wouldn't have been much light, even before seven."

"And most people wouldn't want to stroll on the Observation Deck on a dark, cloudy, cold night. Or in the fog."

"Most people." His jaw muscle twitched. "Did you have to kiss him?"

"No, and I didn't. He kissed me."

He rubbed his forehead. "It's my fault. It was a bad idea."

"Bowers." It was time to tell him about Bitsy and Art.

His hands moved from his forehead to his eyes, and he rubbed them so hard, I thought he'd go blind. "What's the matter with me? Sneaking around a ship, following you when you're with another guy. I know we agreed to it beforehand, but it was demeaning."

"Bowers."

He dropped his hands to his lap. "You'd think I was a rookie, not an experienced veteran. What was I thinking, asking you to talk to a criminal? Even if the guy's not a murderer, he is a thief. And a liar."

I stood in front of him, took his face in my hands, and said, "Bowers!"

His dark blue eyes looked directly into mine, and he covered my hands with his. It felt as if a jolt of electricity passed between us.

"Frankie. I—"

In one swift move, he pulled me to him. One hand was on the back of my neck, pressing my mouth onto his, and the other was around my waist, hugging me close. He moved his leg and twisted me so I was on his lap, leaning back with my neck supported by his arm. My hands instinc-

251

tively clutched at his shoulders to keep my balance, but as the kiss went on, they moved up around his neck. When his hand rested on my waist, I was grateful my position on his lap was slightly awkward because it meant I had my ab muscles tightened. He might think I worked out.

Maybe just this once. What could it hurt? Evil Frankie was at it again. Unfortunately, Good Frankie's brain was in a scramble. She was incapable of putting together a sentence, let alone an argument.

Bowers raised his head and looked down at me. "We need to talk."

Warning bells sounded. Jeff used that phrase a lot. This was the moment when Bowers would tell me he liked my body and wanted to take it for a test drive to see if he liked it enough to stick around. Just like Jeff.

"But first, you wanted to tell me something."

"Did I?" I blinked a few times and brushed my hair back, disconcerted by his ability to just stop in the middle of kissing me and have a rational conversation. That confirmed my opinion that Bowers was just taking advantage of the moment without an emotional commitment. I jumped off his lap.

"Bitsy and Art."

I took a step back. As my mind cleared, fear of doing something stupid replaced any remaining desire. I took a deep breath.

"I saw Art coming out of Bitsy's room the first day of the cruise."

"You're sure?"

"I was taking the back way to the stairs after the lifeboat drill. A door opened, and someone peeked out. I recognized Art later when I saw him at the Hardcastle collection. Then, when I visited Bitsy's room with Sonya—"

"Why would you do that?" He sighed. "The cats?"

"I needed to talk to Felix."

"I don't believe I'm saying this, but what did he tell you?"

"That he doesn't like either Bitsy or his stuffed bear. Bitsy I can understand. She doesn't like the cats, and they can probably tell. His bear was his favorite toy, but I've seen Emily go gangbusters with a catnip mouse and then the next day, she acts as if they'd never met."

"Bitsy might have been in league with Art and stolen the original fake Pure Fantasy bracelet, but that doesn't give her a motive for killing Marv." Bowers turned his palms up. "We need a motive."

"Not necessarily. In the vision, Marv was asking *why*. Obviously, he didn't know her motive either. And you must admit. She could be the woman who was out on deck with him."

"If I'm going to take your kitty clue seriously, how does Bitsy tie in with gray fur?" Bowers stood. "Meanwhile, I'll ask Robinson to check on Bitsy's background and see what he can find out about her movements tonight."

"And what do I do?"

"Stay here. And I mean that. Promise me."

"Sure thing."

But it didn't count as a lie because I had my fingers crossed behind my back.

I changed into my sweats because my clothes felt tainted by death. Besides. After so many days on the ship, I didn't care if anyone saw me in my sweats.

As I tucked my key into my pocket, my fingertips met something soft, and I pulled out a piece of gold fringe. I'd forgotten about it. I tossed it on the television stand, and after checking the hallway to make sure it was clear, I left.

Sonny wasn't in the Orca Lounge, and when I asked two of the porters, I was told this was his day off. They only smirked at me when I asked for his room number, but then the younger employee regretted mocking one of the passengers and said Sonny gathered some of his best material in the casino on the second floor.

The Lucky Palace was the only indoor place on the ship where smoking was allowed. The air wasn't cloudy or anything like that, but it reeked of stale cigarette butts. Slot machines lined the walls, neon lights flashing out a promise of loads of cash. Throughout the center of the room, large round tables were manned by dealers dressed in black vests over white shirts. I recognized a game of blackjack, and that was the limit of my gambling expertise.

A large crowd gathered around one of the tables, and at the edge of the crowd, I spotted Sonny Street dressed in black slacks and a red turtleneck. I moved around to join him.

"Is it casual day at the office?"

He turned his head and grinned when he realized it was me. "People don't recognize me when I'm not wearing the tux. I needed a break."

I looked over the shoulder of the woman in front of me at a black-and-red wheel that spun as a white ball bounced over slots with numbers. The wheel slowed down, and the ball landed in the oo spot. The crowd cheered.

"Lady Luck is out tonight," Sonny said.

The winner leaned forward to sweep up her chips, and I said, "That's not Lady Luck. That's Sharon Bradley."

It didn't look like the cool, composed Sharon Bradley I knew. Strands of blond hair had escaped from her perfect French knot and stuck out willy-nilly, and her face was flushed a deep shade of pink. Her ice-cold eyes were warmed by a brightness bordering on maniacal.

"Mother!"

Every head snapped left to watch the approach of Gina Bradley. As Sharon set all her chips on number seven, she didn't even spare her daughter a glance.

"Don't be a party pooper. I'm having a good time."

"Yeah," some guy said. "Let the lady have her fun."

Gina took hold of Sharon's arm. "Come on, Mother. Let's go."

Sharon jerked away. "When I'm through."

The dealer said, "All bets in?" He looked at Sharon as he said this, and she nodded. He spun the wheel, and everybody held their breath. The ball bounced, the wheel slowed, and eight was the winning number. The crowd groaned.

Gina tugged on Sharon's arm, and this time, the mad gambler went along without saying anything. As they passed by, Gina's gaze landed on me.

"How could you!"

I watched her leave and then asked Sonny, "How could I what?"

"Search me." Now that the focus of excitement had been escorted from the room, the crowd around the roulette table drifted away, and along with it, Sonny's chance to pick up new material. "Buy you a drink?"

We found a quiet corner near a jazz trio and placed an order with the waiter. As soon as he left, I said, "You may have heard I've lost my key card."

He let out a laugh, but it was without humor. "Yeah. Jo —my contact was lucky he didn't get fired. Robinson took some convincing, but he doesn't like to blame the crew if he can help it. He bought the story of a sticky-fingered thief."

"I still want to get into Bitsy's room."

He settled his gaze on me. "I'm sure that's a joke."

"I think she might have stolen the Pure Fantasy bracelet."

He tapped his knuckles on my forehead. "Hello. Trevor Grant just won it in the auction."

It was a long story, but I told it as quickly as possible. "So, you see why I have to get into her room."

"Why don't you let Robinson handle it? I'm sure your boyfriend has already told him about it."

"He's not my boyfriend. Anyway, wouldn't they need a search warrant?"

"You've got me there. I don't know. I've seen customs board us, but I think contraband is their concern. Not robbery."

If I couldn't get into Bitsy's room, I could at least corner her and ask a few questions. "Where does Madame Kitty hang out when she's not on stage?"

"I haven't run into her in the casino. I know she hits the Orca Lounge after the shows, just like the rest of us. Other than that, I assume she's in her room."

"Maybe I can convince her to come out of her lair."

But what would entice a jewel thief and possible murderer to come out and play with me?

TWENTY-SEVEN

When I closed my cabin door behind me the next morning, I suffered a moment's disappointment. I'd gotten used to finding Bowers waiting for me in the hallway, but my body-guard wasn't in sight. Should I knock on his door? I dismissed that idea. He was probably sleeping in.

Since Sonya's room was a short walk away, it occurred to me that if the other kitties had come up with *gray fur* at Felix's instigation, then Sonya would be the woman to ask. He was her kitty. I thought she might be agreeable to an invitation to breakfast, but when she answered her door, I realized there were others who had it worse than I when the alarm clock sounded. She must have straightened her long black hair the times I'd seen her in public because the giant mass of curls matted together on her head stuck out in places. I couldn't tell if the swingy, black dress she wore was her nightgown or fit for daytime wear. If the crusties in her eyes were anything to go by, it was a nightgown.

"I thought you might like breakfast," I said. "I didn't realize you were a late riser."

She pushed a mound of bangs out of her eyes. "The

itsy-bitsy woman woke me late last night. She wanted to search the kitty toys to find one that would placate the beasts, as she called them. I refused. My toys are exclusive to Felix."

"As they should be. Since you're awake anyway, why not get something to eat? It always makes me feel better."

She agreed to accompany me so she could grab coffee and a bagel to bring back to her room, and when she simply picked up her key card and stepped into the hallway, I decided the nightgown must be multipurpose. I'd have to get one myself. The thought of rolling out of bed and out the door, giving me a few extra minutes of sleep, appealed to me.

As we waited for the elevator, because it would have been cruel and possibly dangerous to make her tackle the stairs in her *not fully awake* condition, I said, as casually as I could, "Does Felix have any gray fur on him? I haven't really looked at him closely."

She snorted, an unwise move before clearing the morning sinuses because it started a coughing fit. I moved to pat her on the back and she hissed at me. Sonya did not like to be touched. Kind of like Emily, my cat. When the coughing fit subsided, she dismissed my question.

"Felix is young and virile. He has no gray hairs."

"I wondered because I heard someone say gray fur in relation to the cat show, and I wasn't sure what they meant."

She shrugged her shoulders dramatically. "When do people ever mean what they say?"

When indeed. We arrived at our destination, and Sonya took a plain, boiled bagel. I did the same just to bond with her. A bagel for breakfast was like being on a starvation diet. When she reached for the lox and cream cheese, I suppressed a shudder. We each poured a cup of coffee from available carafes, and then Sonya said:

"We are finished."

And then she floated out of the room. Abrupt little cuss I thought as I left the bagel on a sideboard and rustled up a real breakfast. When my tray was full, I carried it to a small table, so I could have a think while I ate.

Bitsy had a connection to Art. I hadn't seen them actually snuggling, so I didn't want to call them lovers. Now Art was dead. The Pure Fantasy bracelet, the fake that boarded the boat, had been stolen. Did that necessarily mean Bitsy was involved? Maybe I was unfairly assigning her blame because I didn't like her attitude toward the kitties. Not every cat-hater is considered a criminal, though they should be.

Gina had seemed awfully protective of her mother last night, and Sharon Bradley had seemed...not herself. Was she in mourning for Marv and trying to hide it behind a good time at the roulette table? Or maybe it was guilt she was trying to put behind her.

Sonya didn't seem interested in anything but Felix. Then again, she had been traipsing around Mt. Roberts the same time a hand had shoved me over the edge of the mountain and nearly to my death.

I looked down at my plate, surprised to find it empty.

"Yoo-hoo!"

Only one woman alive hailed me that way. Judy and Frank Doud headed directly for my table.

"You're up bright and early. You've already eaten?"

I looked down at my empty plate with a pang of guilt.

"Good. It's ridiculous the way girls skip breakfast to keep their waistlines down. Sure as my name's Judy, that's a good way to let your blood sugar drop. Passing out all over the place, I wouldn't be surprised. Then they gorge to make up for it and wind up being asked when they're expecting. And they're not. They're just fat. Happened to my cousin Myrtle. Good morning, Martin."

Bowers walked up behind me, greeted them, and took a seat at my table as they left to graze at the buffet.

"When did you get here?"

He didn't smile. "I've been watching you this whole time. If you'd come up for air, you might have seen me."

He turned his chair so his back was against the window and he had a clear view of the entrance.

"Listen, Bowers. I asked Sonya about gray fur, and she had nothing to offer."

"Unless she's lying."

Funny, but it hadn't occurred to me that any of my suspects would lie to me. Not directly, anyway.

"Kind of like you lied about staying put last night."

He held my gaze without blinking, his mouth set and the knuckles of one hand rapping lightly on the table, as if he were controlling a strong emotion. Hadn't he asked me nicely never to lie to him?

"I meant it when I said it, but then I had to go out."

"You had to go to the casino and have a drink with Sonny Street?"

I gaped. "Were you following me?"

"I told you once—"

"That you would stick to me. I heard it the first time."

He crossed his arms over his chest. "When I say something, I mean it."

Warmth spread over my cheeks. "I thought you didn't like skulking after me," I said. The closed-cop face came down and Bowers looked at me without expression, though he couldn't control the twitch next to his left eye.

AN ALMOST PURRFECT MURDER

"Apparently, you no longer think someone tried to kill you on Mt. Robert's. That's a relief." He stood. "Since my services are no longer needed, and it's the last day of the cruise, I'm going to get some actual vacationing in."

Since his next move was to walk away, I assumed he didn't want to hang out. That played into my theory that I was a temporary good time but not someone he would take seriously outside of a case. If I'd been rational, I would have realized he was reacting to my derisive comment about skulking, but emotion had taken over and shooed off my brain cells. That probably explains my next move.

I marched straight to the elevator, took it down to the fourth floor, and walked up to Bitsy's cabin door. I only paused once, right before I knocked on her door, when Good Frankie tried to talk me out of doing something stupid. I rapped in an official manner and waited. And waited.

Bitsy finally answered, slightly out of breath, and when she saw who it was, she said, "What do you want?"

"To talk to you about the theft of the Pure Fantasy bracelet."

Her eyebrows went up. "Has somebody stolen it from Trevor Grant?"

I waved her words away with my hand. "Let's not pretend you don't know what I'm talking about. Marv is dead. Art is dead. Isn't it time we laid our cards on the table?"

A crash came from inside the room, and Bitsy whipped around. "Knock it off!"

I took advantage of the distraction and slipped through the doorway.

Jasper and Jinx looked up with wide-eyed innocence. Between them was a broken reading lamp. I knew they were faking the innocence because their tails twitched with excitement and there was a buzzing in my head of pure pleasure.

"I'll be so glad when this cruise is over," Bitsy said. She picked up the pieces of the lamp, looked down at the mess in her hands, and let it drop back onto the floor. "I'll call housekeeping and let them deal with it." She motioned to the small couch. "Now what were you saying about Marv and Art? Which one was Art?"

"One of the Hardcastle security guards," I said, taking a seat.

"Is he the guy that fell into the pool?" She shook her head. "So sad. Probably, he was drunk."

"He had a wound on the back of his head where someone hit him."

Bitsy put her finger to her lip. "Or, he hit his head when he fell in."

I hadn't considered that possibility. Could it be a coincidence his death came on the heels of Marvelous Marv's murder? And it was too early to tell if he had alcohol in his system. That would take blood tests, and we weren't getting into port until we arrived in Victoria, Canada, tonight. Really, Trevor Grant was the only connection I had between Art and someone on board.

Bitsy seemed to sense my resolve was weakening.

"I don't know why you think I would have anything to do with a security guard."

She *didn't* seem like the kind of gal to date a mere security guard. Maybe I was wrong about her and Art. Maybe— What was I thinking? Art had been in this room.

"The first day on board, I saw Art peeking out from behind your door. Why would he do that if he didn't know you?"

Bitsy shook her head as if she felt pity for me. "Not this room. You're mistaken."

"I saw it, clear as day."

She cocked her head. "The first day? You didn't know this was my room, not then."

"No, but I do now."

"Had you been on this floor before you came to my room with Sonya?"

"No, but—"

"You got a quick glimpse of a room, and then when you came up here days later, you made a connection. Sorry, honey, but you got it wrong."

I thought about my sense of direction and how I had gotten lost going around a block of one-way streets when I first moved to Wolf Creek, Arizona. Was Bitsy right? Feeling like a fool and a failure, I found a neutral topic that would help me leave with some dignity intact.

"What are you going to do when you get back to Seattle," I asked.

She gave the felines an unfriendly glance. "Without Marv, they're difficult to control. I'm considering something more glamorous, like singing. I was in the Madrigal group in college. You don't need animals with a singing act."

I stood. "Well, good luck with that."

She smiled. "Thanks."

"Maybe I'll see you in Victoria."

"Probably. I have some gifts I need to buy, since I won't be coming this way again."

I left with a desire to know more about Art's death. I would have to eat crow because Bowers was the only one I could ask.

I found him on the Lido Deck, sitting on the edge of a pool chair and talking to Robby and Gina. He was the only one fully clothed. He stood when I approached and waited until I'd taken a spot at the foot of the same chair before sitting again. As soon as Gina saw me, she clenched her jaw and looked away.

I spread my hands. "Look. I'm not sure what I did last night, but I'm sorry."

Gina huffed out a stream of air. "It's not your fault. You didn't know." She glanced at Robby and chose her next words with care. "My mother is drawn to games of chance, and she loses track sometimes. And she's not very good at games. She needs someone to look out for her."

Sharon Bradley had a gambling problem. "So, the night you and I saw her," I said to Robby, and he finished my thought.

"She might have been heading to the casino and then changed her mind when she spotted us."

"She thought you might tell on her," Gina snapped.

Did Marv know about Sharon's gambling and threaten to tell Gina? So what? Gina already knew. What else could Sharon have to argue about with a man she'd only met half an hour before? She must have known him. This information wasn't helping me.

I turned my head to look at Bowers. "Did you find out anything new about Art's death?"

"That's a question for Officer Robinson."

A dead end, since I didn't think Robinson would talk to me.

"So, what were you guys talking about before I showed up?" I asked.

Everybody's gaze shot away from me. Gina's went to the drink in her hand, Robby squinted his eyes as if there were something fascinating in the pool, which was ridiculous since Gina was sitting right next to him, and Bowers stared at his clasped hands as if they were about to reveal the name of Marvelous Marv's killer.

"Fine. Don't tell me." I stood.

"We're getting into Victoria at seven tonight," Robby said. "Dinner's being served an hour early."

I returned to my room to pack my things, leaving out my jeans and a burnt-orange sweater for tonight. I could wear them again on the trip home tomorrow.

After I changed, I headed to the shopping arcade for one last look at the Hardcastle collection. They were holding the second drawing at the start of the Mermaid's ball, and since I didn't have tickets or a Cinderella ball gown to wear to the dance, I didn't much care. I did notice a lot of passengers dressed in evening clothes— tuxes for the men and floor-length dresses for the women. At least somebody would enjoy the last night of the cruise.

Tommy made it to dinner. The last day of the trip and he finally got his sea legs and spent the day hanging out with Kemper and Penny. Without a chair to spare, Trevor Grant had to find someplace else to eat dinner.

The topics of conversation covered the latest show the elder Mohrs had seen, how Penny and Kemper were enjoying their first days as newlyweds, and what areas of the ship everyone wanted to hit one last time before returning to Seattle. Sharon didn't mention the casino.

It seemed like over six days since Marvelous Marv had breathed his last. In that time, I'd learned Trevor Grant aka Trevor Hardcastle had fooled his way on board the ship to exchange a fake bracelet for a real bracelet with the help of Art the security guard. Then someone had stolen the fake and replaced it with another fake, probably also with Art's help. Any of them could have considered Marvelous Marv a threat to their plans and removed him before making the switch.

Sharon had a secret gambling problem, and she had wanted to hide that secret or another one enough to argue with Marvelous Marv. Now Marv was dead, and all her secrets were safe. Bitsy, a closet cat-hater, had wanted out of her contract with Marv. Now she could do as she pleased. Sonya had suffered because Marv was a louse, and now she was free to move on and take Felix, her precious pet, with her. A lot of people were happier now that Marv was dead.

What else had changed? Penny and Kemper were happily married. Gina and Robby seemed inseparable. Bowers...Bowers was still a problem.

I hadn't made any progress, and as for proof? Forget about it. I wasn't even certain it had been Bitsy's room I'd seen Art peeking out of that first day. I wondered who else's room was in the vicinity. Maybe Finlander reserved a section on Bitsy's floor for all the entertainers to stay.

"Are you feeling alright?" Bowers whispered in my ear. "You haven't touched your dinner."

"Is that a crack about my eating habits?"

His jaw muscle twitched. "Yes. That's what it was."

"Because I could find plenty to comment on about you."

As if in a challenge, the corners of his mouth turned up in a petty smirk. "Really? Like what?"

I ground my teeth together, trying to think of a big flaw I could rub Bowers' perfectly straight nose in, but nothing came to mind.

"It's not polite to make fun of policemen." I kept my tone snippy to let him know if he was mad at me, I could be mad at him. Although, if he was mad at me, why would he care if I felt okay? I straightened my shoulders and my resolve. I would not give in to my friendlier impulses.

Frank Doud stood. "We can all share two taxis over to the Victoria courthouse and meet back there when the shops close at nine."

Everyone agreed that sounded fine except Christina and Thomas Mohr. They bowed out of going because they'd been there before and preferred to catch the final show—a musical review.

I dropped by my room to freshen up before I met up with my party, and after I closed my door, I knocked on Robby and Bowers' door. I didn't like feeling cranky, and I wanted to clear the air with Bowers.

Robby answered the door. He swung it open and walked back into the room, so I followed. His clothes were on his bed in neat piles, and he was transferring them to an open suitcase.

"You'll have to finish later. We have to meet up in five minutes."

"I'm not going."

I laughed. "You better be going. It's the last night of the cruise and your chance to walk on Canadian soil."

He shook his head. "I'm not in the mood."

Robby rarely fell into a funk, and it was unnatural to see a frown on the handsome face that could have been on a poster for happy, healthy, country living.

"It's a little late to get seasick."

He turned to me, clutching a sock, his forehead wrinkled, and his eyes filled with confusion.

"Frankie, why doesn't life make sense?"

I snorted. "You're asking the woman who gets messages from animals."

"I'm being serious."

"Right. Sorry." No need to explain I was perfectly serious, too.

267

"I find someone perfect for me in every way. Someone I could love, but there's not a chance it will work."

I thought of Bowers and sighed. "Love stinks." Then my eyes grew round. "You're talking about Gina."

He nodded and tossed the sock into the suitcase. "I've spent my life alone, you know? Not that I haven't gone out on dates. I'm not a monk. But they were just friendly nights out on the town, usually with a group of friends. I've never connected with anyone before. What's wrong with me? Am I a monster?"

"You better ask someone who doesn't know you as well as I do," I joked.

"I'm serious. I'm not bad-looking."

"You're a hunk."

He looked hopeful. "You think so?"

Amazing how people can't see their own gifts.

"You're sweet and honest and trustworthy, you have a great sense of humor, you're handsome. Robby, you're quite a catch. Any girl would be lucky to have you."

"Any girl?"

He stepped forward and kissed me on the mouth. His lips were soft and gentle, and he even smelled good, but this was Robby of my childhood, my best friend's big brother. When he broke the kiss, in my surprise I said the first thing that came to mind.

"E-w-w. Cooties."

He gave me a crooked Robby grin that reminded me of Penny, and then he laughed.

"Come here," he growled.

"You're not going to kiss me again, are you?"

He pulled me to him and wrapped his arms around my shoulders. "Not a chance, you little geek. Thanks for listening to me whine."

"It's okay," I mumbled into his chest. "We all need to get it off our chest sometime."

"Am I interrupting?"

It was Bowers, he with the perfect timing. Once again, he'd found me in questionable circumstances with another man.

"I just came back for my jacket." He took his windbreaker from the back of a chair and left.

Robby looked down at me. "Oops. Looks like you've got some 'splaining to do, Lucy."

I set my jaw. "I don't owe him anything." Any desire to make up with Bowers left me. If he didn't know me better than to think I would hit on Penny's brother, to heck with him.

"Are you coming?" I asked.

He nodded. "You might need a referee."

TWENTY-EIGHT

The taxi dropped us off in front of the British Columbia Parliament building, and I stumbled as I exited the taxi because I couldn't stop staring.

Architecture doesn't mean much to me, though I know what I like. Old buildings give me a rush of nostalgia and a flush of pride that people can create something beautiful. And the Parliament building was beautiful, historic, and impressive. It stretched out in two wings on either side of the principal building, which was topped with a green dome. Along the top of the wings were mini domes that looked like little caps. A wide set of cement stairs led up to an archway that covered the entrance, suggesting that to step through those doors would be to enter another world. The feature I liked best was most likely not part of the original construction. Bright, white lights outlined the structure and windows and made it look exactly like a Christmas card.

Visitors strolled across the lawn in front, some stopping by the fountain, while others tried to capture the moment in photographs of them posed on the front steps. These latter were optimists because the cloudy night sky offered little in the way of good lighting.

A crowded walkway ran parallel to an inlet of water that ended at the Empress Hotel, where Penny, Gina, Sharon Bradley and Judy Doud had booked a tea. I'd opted out of this treat, preferring instead to see as much as I could during my first time on foreign soil.

We walked there in one group, and I noticed Bowers stayed far away from both Robby and me. Then the ladies departed and left me with the men. The guys were itching to get a pint and enjoy post-wedding cigars, and though they didn't specifically say they didn't want me along, I could tell they wanted it to be a guy's night out.

"Why don't you fellas go ahead? I'm going to stay with Frankie." Bowers kept most of the regret out of his voice.

"I'm shopping for souvenirs," I lied. "I'm capable of doing that all by myself."

His brows knitted with worry and he took me aside. "Look, Frankie. I still don't think you should wander around on your own. You've been asking questions, which is partially my fault, and the killer might want to put an end to your curiosity. He or she has tried once before."

"I believe it was you who pointed out no one actually tried to push me over the edge of Mt. Roberts."

"Come on, Frankie! Let it go." He ran his fingers through his hair, and Mr. Doud slipped a quick glance our way. "It would be silly if you got killed just because you were sulking."

So now it was my fault. Typical man. And like a typical woman, my only thought was to cut him to ribbons with my sarcastic tongue.

"I don't need a bodyguard." I hissed the words out because now Mr. Doud was staring with frank curiosity. So were Kemper, Robby and Tommy. I put my hands on my hips and stepped up to Bowers, so we were eyeball to chin. Tilting my head back to make eye contact, I delivered the final blow. "I didn't ask you to come to Alaska, so you can take your hero cape and fly off with the boys. Read my lips. I don't need you."

The comment hit home. First, his eyes opened in a startled, hurt expression. Then he blinked twice to clear it away and the cop-face came down and wiped away any expression.

"Enjoy your shopping."

That was all he said, and then I watched his back as the men headed down a side street.

Why did I feel a huge wallop of regret over hurting his feelings? Bowers was just another guy ready to take advantage of a temporary situation that might make his vacation more pleasant. I was a convenience. My conscience twinged. It wasn't very convenient for Bowers to use up his vacation time on a ship with a bunch of people he didn't know that well, and this trip must have cost plenty. Would a man dip into his savings to take advantage of a gal who may or may not be willing?

I set my self-righteousness aside. It put up a struggle, but I won. Maybe Bowers really cared about me. Maybe this entire trip had been a sign in neon lights that Bowers thought I was worth the trouble. He hadn't ignored me after finding out about the cats on the ship. He had freaked out a tiny bit, but it had come as a shock. No, he had spent his entire trip watching out for me. Hadn't he followed me up Mt. Roberts? Every time I had needed him, Bowers had been there.

These past few months, Bowers invaded my dreams, often in the role of hero, and when he actually showed up to rescue me from the aftermath of finding a dead body, what did I do? Second-guess his motives. Give him a hard time. Insult him. I was an ass.

Then I got scared. Had I gone too far? Our attempts to have a relationship were tangled and confused, but at least there had been a possibility. Now, I might have squashed any hope with my ego. I'd have to find a way to apologize when we got back to the ship—if I could get him to talk to me after my behavior. With those thoughts, any desire to shop left me, but I still had two hours to kill.

I stuck to the main street, Government Street, because I once got lost for two hours traveling to a store one mile away from my home. I spied Roger's Chocolates across the street and decided there was only one way to heal a broken heart. It wasn't long until I was munching on a bar of maple chocolate. I'd already had several vanilla creams, but they were mini creams, so they didn't count. Employing great self-control, I promised myself to save the maple caramel sleeve until I got back to the ship.

My funds were limited, especially after my investment at Roger's, so I merely glanced into the art studio and cosmetic shop I passed. The only option open to me other than shopping was to eat a meal alone in one of the charming restaurants that overflowed with garrulous crowds. When I reached the Irish Times Pub, the people waiting outside consisted of groups of friends and couples. Not a single among them.

I always try to avoid looking pathetic when I have a choice, so I headed back to the Parliament building where our group had agreed to meet at nine p.m. and wondered how to kill the remaining hour. I crossed the street and headed back toward our rendezvous.

On my way, I passed by a tourist shop that sold t-shirts,

hats and knick-knacks. The front of the store was a long glass window through which foot traffic could look down onto an open lower level. My feet stopped moving when I recognized a pile of red hair.

Should I go in and accidentally bump into Bitsy, or should I wait here at street level until she finished her shopping? Turns out I didn't have to decide because she caught my eye when she looked up and then motioned for me to wait for her.

Ten minutes later, she burst out the front doors holding two shopping bags. She held them up. "Had to get souvenirs for family members, now that I won't be passing this way again."

We walked toward the government center. "You've dropped the cat act for certain? You don't think you'll regret it?"

"Not a chance."

"What's going to happen to them now?"

"Officer Robinson already came and took Felix away. I'll give the rest of them to a shelter, I suppose."

I might have shrieked. "I'm sure you could find homes for them."

"Who has the time for that?"

"I'll help you."

"If you want. It makes no difference to me. But how will you help?"

How would Emily and Chauncey take to four new brothers and sisters? And could I afford to feed additional mouths? I'd figure it out.

"At least Sonya will be happy to get Felix back," I said.

Bitsy reached into one of the bags and pulled out a stuffed killer whale. "His favorite toy was a stuffed bear, but Sonya couldn't find it. I got this as a replacement."

"Why would you bother?"

"For old times sake. He was Marv's favorite cat."

I didn't mention the only reason Marv held onto Felix was to irritate Sonya.

"I'm sure that will make him happy, which will make Sonya happy."

We had reached the large lawn in front of the Parliament building.

"Why don't we surprise her with it now?" Bitsy asked with a girlish giggle.

My watch read 8:30. "I'm meeting my group here at nine."

"Do you have a cell phone? Call them."

"I didn't bring it with me."

"Where are they?"

"The women are having tea at the Empress Hotel."

Bitsy pulled her cell phone out of her purse and pressed a button. She held up a finger to me as she waited, and then she asked for the number of the Empress Hotel, Victoria BC.

"They're connecting me. What's the name of the party?"

"Doud, probably."

When the hotel reception answered, they confirmed the arrival of the Doud party and promised to deliver Bitsy's message. We grabbed a taxi back to the ship and got on the elevator. Bitsy pushed four.

"I want to get rid of this stuff first."

When we got to her room, she invited me in and tossed the bags on the bed.

"Let me use the little girl's room and then we can go."

Bitsy closed the door behind her. I stepped farther into the room because lurking by the bathroom door when

275

someone is in there isn't an agreeable thing to do, for either party.

She had tossed her purse on the bed with the bags right next to her open luggage, and her cell phone had slipped out. How rude would it be to use her phone to call the Empress Hotel and confirm they had delivered the message?

I touched the call history button to get the number, clicked on the last number dialed, and waited. It rang three times and a man's voice answered with a grunt.

"Hello? Empress Hotel?"

"Wrong number."

The line disconnected. I stared at the phone. Did the Empress not wind up in her call history because Information had connected the call? Then why wasn't the last number in memory the number for Information? Something wasn't right.

"How's it coming in there?" I called out, and Bitsy responded she'd just be another minute.

My stomach tightened with a sick feeling as I lifted out the top layer of Bitsy's clothing. Underneath, I found the gold jacket from her costume, and I ran my fingers over the fringe. I felt the gap where a piece of fringe was missing just as the lock on the bathroom door turned. I shoved her clothing back in order just as she walked out.

"Ready?" Bitsy asked.

I nodded and preceded her out of the room, feeling better that we were walking public hallways. Once we were with Sonya, it would be two against one if Bitsy tried anything.

Outside of Sonya's room, Bitsy insisted I knock after pointing out that Sonya didn't care for her, which seemed reasonable. When Sonya opened the door, Bitsy pushed me inside.

"Hello," I said. "Bitsy bought a present for Felix." I didn't want to ruin the surprise, but the way Sonya was glaring at both of us made me nervous. A dinner tray rested on the bed. We had interrupted a steak dinner with a side of mashed potatoes. No wonder she was cranky.

"Why she would do that?" Sonya said.

Bitsy put on a smile, but not a convincing smile. The corners of her mouth pointed down. "He was Marv's favorite cat," she said. "I guess I was feeling sentimental. Marv always let him play with that dirty old bear. I thought I would replace it with a new toy. For old time's sake."

She held out the whale, and Sonya took it with a great deal of reluctance but then surprised me by shaking it and calling Felix with kissy noises. The cat trotted out from behind the bed, sniffed the toy, and sat down, his tail twitching.

"That was nice," I said.

"So, where is the bear?" Bitsy held out her hand.

Sonya sniffed. "I don't know what you mean."

"The bear. It was his favorite toy."

"Was. Now he hate it. I toss it away." She flung out her hand in a dramatic gesture to show she hadn't merely dropped the bear in the wastebasket but had thrown it with disdain.

"Why would you do that?"

At that moment, I glanced down and saw the bear peeking out from under the bed. Sonya and Bitsy followed my gaze, and Bitsy shoved me aside and snatched up her prize.

"You give me that!" Sonya bumped me aside and grabbed the bear back, and I went sprawling on the bed. My fingers landed in the mashed potatoes. Bitsy responded by scooping up Felix and grabbing the steak knife from the tray. She held him close, and with her left hand, she pressed the knife against his furry throat. Felix, whether because he sensed danger, or he was too lazy to struggle, just hung there like a very heavy rag doll.

"You." She jerked her head at me. "Get the toy and put it in my purse."

I wasn't close friends with Felix, but I didn't want to witness a kitty murder, so after licking off my fingers, I complied. Sonya, her gaze riveted on Felix, handed me the toy.

"You hurt baby cat, you die."

"I won't if you do what I say. We're going for a walk."

Sonya turned away. "It is cold. I get his jacket."

"Get back here! The cat will be fine. That's what fur is for."

Bitsy made us walk in front of her to the elevator, and when we stepped on, she told me to press ten. The Observation Deck.

Most passengers were in Victoria, packing in their rooms, or enjoying the Mermaid Ball. They weren't on the Observation Deck, except for a handholding couple who leaned against the railing, the woman with her head on the man's shoulders. When we got closer, I recognized the honeymooners, Lindsey and Josh.

When Lindsey saw me, she smiled. "We're just enjoying our last—"

"Move it," Bitsy snapped. "We're having a private memorial and you're not invited."

Josh put his arm around his wife, and they both sent me searching glances. How could I send them a message? I wrinkled my eyebrows and moved my gaze from their faces sideways to where Bitsy stood, trying to point with my eyeballs.

"Come on," Lindsey muttered, with a frown for me. "They've ruined the mood, anyway."

Once we had the deck to ourselves, Bitsy told us her plan.

"I need a head start, which I won't get if either of you talk. You," she said, pointing the knife as Sonya, "are so distraught over Marv's death that you throw yourself over the railing. And you," she jabbed the knife at me, "are going to die trying to save her." She tightened her hold on the knife at Felix's throat.

Sonya and I stared.

"Really?" I said. "You expect us to kill ourselves to save the cat? That's a stupid plan."

"Oh, yeah?" Bitsy's lip curled. "Somebody's going down, and it's not going to be me."

And that's when the fight broke out.

Sonya leaped for Bitsy's hand—the one that held the knife—and when she got hold of the wrist, she bit it. I jumped on Bitsy's back and wrapped my arm around her neck. She thrashed from side to side, and then Sonya grabbed her hair. She jerked her hand, Bitsy cried out, and Sonya was left holding a large pile of red curls.

Underneath the wig, Bitsy's real hair was short...and gray.

"Gray fur!" I shouted.

Maybe I should have explained because Bitsy took offense at what she obviously thought was a derisive comment about her age and being ticked off gave her extra energy.

"Of course it's gray," she said between gasps as she jerked backwards and repeatedly slammed me against the railing. "Hair. Dye. Is. Bad. For. You." With the final slam, I lost my grip. She grabbed my legs and flipped up, and I went over the railing.

My hands caught the middle rail, and my feet scrambled against air. I squeezed my eyes shut, refusing to look down at Marvelous Marv's final resting place. Would I be lucky enough to hit the lifeboat? Luck being a relative term. I risked peeking down at my feet. Below were private verandas, but there wasn't a chance in heck I would hit one as I did a free fall toward the deck far below, unless I slammed into the veranda railings on my way down. That thought didn't cheer me.

Since my head was lower than the edge of the deck, I couldn't see what was happening, but I heard grunts mingled with cries and thumps.

"Sonya, will you please lay her flat and help me out?" I said, my voice cracking. Bitsy may have been an insane killer, but nothing beats a mother when her baby is in danger, even if it's a pet parent.

To my left, a hand shot over the ledge and the movement on deck stopped, probably because that hand held Felix by the scruff. He blinked at me, bored.

"Take one more step and I'm letting go."

Sonya's voice rang out, fearless and proud. "Felix, he would never forgive me for being coward. Aiiiiii!"

As the hand released Felix, I swung my left leg up. The cat grabbed hold and hung on.

"Ow, ow, ow!"

Using me as a climbing post, Felix scrambled up my jeans and sweater. When he reached the top of my head, he tensed and then sprung through the railings. I heard the thump as he landed.

By then there were running footsteps, too many for

Sonya and Bitsy. I heard a male voice call out, "Drop the knife."

"Where's Frankie?" Bowers sounded more puzzled than concerned.

"I'm right here!"

Two hands grabbed my armpits and lifted me, but only so far before they jerked to a stop.

"Frankie, honey, you need to let go of the railing."

I squeezed my eyes shut and shook my head.

"Frankie. Look at me."

I cracked open one eye and bent my head back. He leaned over the railing and held my gaze. Though he had a twitch in the corner of his left eye, he was trying for a cool, calm expression.

"I've got you. Let go."

"No."

"On the count of three."

"No."

"One. Two."

He jerked up, and another hand grabbed the waistband of my pants, and as they pulled me over, the hands clutched at whatever body part they could until I landed on the deck in a heap. I gazed up and blinked, dazed. The second pair of hands had belonged to Robinson. Considering the body parts he had grabbed to haul me up, his face held no expression, which saved us both from embarrassment.

Bowers crouched down. "Can you stand?"

Without waiting for an answer, he pulled me to my feet. My knees buckled, and I leaned against him and buried my face in his chest. After a few deep breaths, I felt steady enough to peer out and review the carnage. Except there wasn't any carnage.

Several security officers surrounded Bitsy, who was face

down on the deck with her hands cuffed behind her back. Sonya, holding Felix, sported a tiny nick on the hand that rubbed his scruff. My own scars, for they would probably turn into scars, given to me by Felix, were the only signs of violence, and I couldn't see them because they were on my face.

Bowers lifted my chin and said, "Hold still. You've got blood on you." He licked his thumb and wiped at my forehead.

"That must be where Felix used me as a launching pad. I'll be scarred for life."

He patted my shoulder. "You can wear bangs."

Sonya's gaze met mine. I pulled away from Bowers, and we both marched over to Bitsy and delivered a one-two kick to her behind.

Robinson pulled Sonya back, and Bowers did the same for me, though neither of us put up a fight. Tousling with a killer took a lot out of a girl.

"Ladies. We've got it covered," Robinson said, but I noticed the female security employee covered her mouth to stifle a laugh and then offered us subtle congratulations by pushing the brim of her cap up with her thumb.

"Something the matter, Connors?" Robinson asked.

"No, sir," she said. "Nothing at all."

Felix mewed, and I saw that Officer Robinson was holding the toy bear.

"The cat stopped liking his toy," I said.

Robinson looked at the bear. "Okay."

"Because it was suddenly too hard and lumpy."

He squeezed the toy and his eyes opened wide. He pulled a multi-purpose tool out of his pocket, flipped open the knife, and slit the bear's seams. The Pure Fantasy bracelet sparkled in the beam of his flashlight. That is, the first copy of the Pure Fantasy bracelet made by Trevor sparkled in the beam of his flashlight. Robinson scratched at a stone with the tip of his knife and grunted with satisfaction.

"Didn't leave a mark. This must be the garnet copy Trevor Grant had made."

Bitsy whipped her head toward him. "What do you mean copy?"

He held up the bracelet. "This is a fake."

The guests on the Promenade Deck below must have heard the scream.

"You mean I went through all that for a fake?"

"Yes. You killed two people—almost four people and a cat—for nothing," Bowers said.

I walked over to Bitsy. Robinson blocked my way, but I held up my hands to show I didn't intend to do violence. Looking down on her, I asked, "Why Marv? Did he discover what you'd done?"

But Bitsy had decided not to talk.

TWENTY-NINE

I'd gone directly to bed as soon as Robinson had finished with his questions last night. This morning, I had time to take a shower before Bowers herded me into Robby and his stateroom and directed me to the couch, which I now shared with the detective. We weren't alone.

The Douds, the Bradleys, the Mohrs, and Tommy had crammed into the small space and taken their places on the edges of the two beds and were waiting to receive an explanation for the delay in exiting the ship. The short answer? We had to wait for the local police to arrive and escort Bitsy to her new residence.

We had special guests this morning. Sonya cradled Felix in her lap, while Trevor Grant stood in a corner of the room looking relaxed and casual. They to convince Sonny Street to come. He was afraid his role in stealing the master key card might come up, and he wasn't taking any chances with his job. Sonya had finally talked him into it, and he sat next to her on Robby's bed.

I'd just finished explaining why I hadn't met my party

in front of the Parliament Building when Penny, who held a place of honor on my left, asked a question.

"I still don't understand. Why did Bitsy kill Marv?"

Bowers answered. "She needed a way to get the bracelet off the ship. If Marv died, they would drop his body off at the first port they came to, and she thought she could exit with him. She hadn't counted on Finlander Cruise Line holding her to the contract."

Sonny sputtered. "She killed him for her convenience?"

"Evil, evil woman," Sonya said.

"How much was the bracelet worth?" Robby asked.

Everyone looked to Trevor Grant, now that they knew he was Trevor Hardcastle. He grinned. "The real one? About two hundred thousand dollars."

Penny gave a little shriek. "And Art helped her steal it?"

I raised my hand. "I saw Art in Bitsy's room the first day after the safety drill. I assume she found out who would be the security guard for the Hardcastle collection and—," I met Judy Doud's gaze and toned down my wording, "made his acquaintance."

"And he helped this woman he hadn't known that long steal a bracelet he was supposed to guard?" Robby snorted. "That was stupid."

"We don't know he was part of the theft," I said to be fair to a man who couldn't defend himself. "I can imagine Bitsy convincing him to let her have a private peek at the jewelry before the passengers boarded, maybe asking to try it on and then making the switch."

"But why steal such a high-profile piece of jewelry?" Gina asked, showing off her superior deductive skills. "Why not steal one of the lesser known baubles?"

Robby looked at her with admiration. Knowing how he felt about her, it was pitiful.

"The Pure Fantasy got a lot of publicity because of the auction, which gave her the best opportunity to make a copy," Bowers explained.

"My sister insisted on it," Trevor said. "Unfortunately, buyers, even buyers of raffle tickets, want to know what they're getting, so the description was very detailed, down to the weight and measurements of the stones."

"And she didn't think anyone would have the bracelet valued right away because it wasn't as if they had bought it retail," Bowers said. "She figured by the time they got it home and handed it over to their insurance agent, it would be too late. Or at least it would be the Hardcastle family's problem."

I picked up the story. "She hid the stolen bracelet in one of Felix's toys."

Sonya looked up. "When I spy my baby cat wandering the cold hallways, alone and frightened, I bring him into my room, and I know just what he need to cheer up. I sneak into cages backstage and bring back his little cuddle bear. It was his favorite, but no more."

"That's because it was hard and lumpy with the bracelet inside." Everyone was looking at me, and I thought it best not to explain Felix had told me so. "At least, that's what I assume. Anyway, I bet it surprised Bitsy to find her prize gone."

"She keep pushing and pushing for toy, but I don't give it to her," Sonya said with grim satisfaction, adding, perhaps unnecessarily, "I don't like her." She bent her head and tickled Felix's belly. "Do we baby cat?"

Sonny reached out a hand to stroke Felix's head. When the cat allowed it, Sonya said, "He has exclusive taste. You must be quality man."

I swear Sonny blushed.

Trevor cleared his throat. "I feel like Art's death is my fault."

All the women cooed, and Robby and Bowers exchanged a male version of an eye roll. Thomas Mohr twisted his head to look at Trevor.

"How do you figure that?"

"If I hadn't switched the bracelet in the first place, then I wouldn't have had to get on board to make the exchange again. And I think it might have been the commotion I caused that got Art killed."

"What commotion?" Bowers said, one eyebrow raised. "We kept it quiet."

"From the passengers, yes. But you can't tell me the crew didn't gossip. They couldn't have had the full story, but they must have known something fishy was up with the Pure Fantasy bracelet, and that probably panicked Bitsy enough that she killed the man who might have remembered her interest in the bracelet."

Bowers said, "True," the same time Gina tossed her hair and said, "No." Her eyes held a challenge. "Bitsy's responsible for her own actions. I'm so tired of people assuming women are too dumb to be accountable for their actions."

"Here, here!" That came, surprisingly, from Judy Doud.

Before Gina could arrange a march for women, Frank leaned in and pecked his wife on her cheek. "I can't imagine you ever doing anything wrong."

She jerked her head in a nod. "That's right, Mister, and don't you forget it."

Gina looked at her watch and jumped up—gracefully, of course. She swooped to her feet like a delicate bird, ready to twinkle across the stage in a production of *Swan Lake*.

"I want to double-check our room to make sure we didn't leave anything behind."

As her mother joined her, I debated leaving it lie—sleeping dogs and all that—but curiosity got the better of good manners.

"Sharon. Now that it's over, do you still say you never met Marv before this trip?"

Her face muscles went stiff. "I don't understand why you think so."

"Come on. You were arguing with him. You told him if he ever said anything to *her,* you would kill him."

Her upper lip twitched.

Gina gazed down at her mother. "Her? Am I her?"

Sharon wouldn't meet her daughter's eyes, and Gina shook her head so that her long, reddish-blond locks swayed from side-to-side.

"You mean you didn't want him to tell me I'm adopted?"

Sharon cried out and clutched Gina's arm, but that was nothing compared to the range of emotions that passed over Robby's face. First wide-eyed shock, then a worried frown, and finally a broad grin.

"Calm down, Mom. Daddy told me years ago."

"That ba—"

"Mom! He thought I had a right to know. He told me my mother was a friend of yours, and that she had stabbed her boyfriend when he tried to force her to have an abortion. After that, she was kind of unstable. Not because she tried to stab him to keep him from killing me. That was a good move, and anyway, he lived. Daddy said she was always a little *off,* even before then. Anyway, she didn't have the means to raise me, and you took me in."

Gina had put an arm around her mother's shoulders, but now she dropped it. Her skin turned pale, and she looked a little sick. "Marv wasn't my biological father, was he?"

"Heavens, no! He was a friend of—" she sucked in a breath, "your *real* parents. He hung around at the time. A real jerk." Sharon sniffed. "He actually hit on me years ago."

"Well, you and Daddy are my *real* parents. That's all that matters."

"Not quite *all* that matters," Robby said. He spun Gina around and planted a kiss on her mouth, which she enthusiastically returned.

Sharon cried out, and Judy said, "Oh, my," but then the world's most practical farm woman gave them her blessing.

"They aren't related, you know. Not even second cousins. I had a cousin who married her second cousin, and they just celebrated their fortieth anniversary. Had several children, too. Smart as whips and not an ugly one in the bunch. And it's not as if Robby and Gina share the same last name. Yet. And think of how you'll get to condense the guest list for the wedding, since people will be related to them both."

"Ah, sweet romance," I said to Bowers. "Makes you want to leave the room, doesn't it?"

"Yes, it does." He stood, gave me a hand to help me up, and led me out to the veranda. He closed the doors and pulled me behind the portion of the window blocked by the curtain.

"When I got to the Observation Deck and didn't see you there, I thought I'd lost you."

Since he was an observant Catholic, I joked, "And then you prayed to St. Anthony and found me."

"Actually, I went straight to the Father. I didn't have time to mess around with intercessors."

That shocked me. I don't think I'd ever had someone

pray for me, except of course my mother, who prayed constantly I would stay out of trouble and turn back to my childhood faith—not necessarily in that order. I couldn't think of a catchy comeback, so I said nothing.

"Frankie," he said with an expression so serious it was hard to meet. "Did you mean what you said in Victoria? That you don't need me?"

I fidgeted. "I was angry."

He sighed. "Are you glad I showed up?"

In my discomfort, I snorted. "You bet. Especially when I was hanging onto the railing for dear life."

He took my hand. "I'm serious. I need to know where I stand."

A warm flush traveled up my cheeks. "You have a lot of nerve. You told me you were afraid to go on a date with me, as if my ability to communicate with animals was contagious. Which, if I'm fair, it was, but only that one time. And every time I see you in Wolf Creek, you run the other direction."

"Guilty. But I've had time to think. And time to miss you."

He squeezed my hand. That's right. He was holding my hand even though there was a cat in the next room.

"What if I've changed my mind?" His brow wrinkled. "Is it too late?"

I squinted one eye. "I like things clear. Are you saying the few, um, moments we've had on this trip weren't an attempt at a vacation fling? That you would seriously like to spend time with me outside of a murder investigation?"

In answer, Bowers cupped my face in his hands and kissed me. My insides tingled, and I stepped back.

"Is that a yes?"

He stepped forward and put his arms around me. "Yes. Now kiss me."

I wrapped my arms around his neck and pulled his mouth onto mine. He responded by tightening his hold until I could hardly breathe, not that I was getting much air, anyway. Bowers' hands started to move, caressing my back. I wanted to feel them all over—in places Mrs. Doud would disapprove of—and Bowers must have had the same thought because he lifted his head and let out a sigh.

"Frankie, I have something very important to ask you."

I was ready to say yes to whatever it was. Only my self-respect kept me from opening my mouth.

"That is, I want you to do something for me. With me."

I clamped my lips down to keep from responding. He wasn't making it easy.

"I enjoy being with you. It's the best part of my day, except when I'm putting the cuffs on someone I've been after for weeks. The thing is...when we get back to Wolf Creek, will you—that is, I'd like you to—"

I pushed against his chest to move him away. This sounded suspiciously like an invitation to live together.

He laughed.

"This is harder than I thought. When we get back to Wolf Creek..."

We would never get back to Wolf Creek at this pace. "Just spit it out."

He kissed my hand and gazed at me with an eager expression that made him look ten years younger.

"Frankie, I want you to meet my sisters."

A Note from Jackie:

It began with a cruise to Alaska for my parent's 50th wedding anniversary. Twelve hours into the trip I wondered, *"What would happen if someone were murdered during the cruise?"*

The noises a ship makes at night creeped out this land-lubber and suggested several delicious scenarios for murder.

Since this is a pet psychic series, I had to come up with an animal that might be on a ship. A service dog was a possibility, but then I realized I hadn't yet heard from a kitty. The entertainment on board is typically limited to singers, dancers, and comedians, but I wondered if a cruise line would ever hire performing cats. This is fiction, so the answer to that question was YES!

The 50th anniversary became a wedding and the story developed from there.

It just goes to show that everything is fair game to a mystery writer.

Jackie

ACKNOWLEDGMENTS

Albert & Beverly Voirin took me on my first Alaskan cruise without which this book wouldn't exist.

Many thanks to Father Andy Sensenig OMI of St. Gregory of Nazianzen Catholic Church in Sitka, Alaska, for taking the time to answer my questions and for suggesting Basil as the name of the priest character.

Many thanks to my support group of brave souls willing to read proof copies and give me feedback and advice, especially Mary Grant, Andrea Voirin, and Gayle Bartos-Pool.

Thanks to my hubby for his unwavering belief in me.

Finally, thanks to the Mystery Buffs, a community of readers who love mysteries and laughter as much as I do.

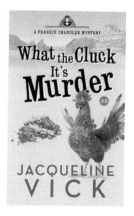

Pet psychic Frankie Chandler finally (and reluctantly) agrees to meet Detective Martin Bower's family. All she has to do is impress the pack of sisters who raised him. Not difficult, right? The only thing at stake is her relationship with the man she loves.

The weekend at his eldest sibling's farm surpasses her worst nightmares. His former guardians excel at finding her faults. Even the chickens have it in for her. Then her first moment alone with Bowers on a romantic stroll ends with the discovery of a murdered farmhand.

Now the marshal is fixed on Bowers' sister Dymphna as the chief suspect. On a homestead overrun with animals, there must be a witness. The broody hen? The carrot-obsessed horses? The suspect's self-involved dog? As she wrangles information from animals both furry and feathered, the case against Dymphna worsens. Should Frankie's loyalty be to the truth? Or to Bowers' family?

BOOK CLUB QUESTIONS

An *Almost* Purrfect Murder

Do you think Frankie was exaggerating the effect that Penny's marriage would have on her social life? Have you had a similar experience? Did it turn out well? Or were your fears justified?

Detective Martin Bowers arranges to meet the ship in Juneau. Would you appreciate or resent this if your loved one "came to your rescue"? Why?

Frankie has difficulty seeing herself as a Woman, and all that that implies. Have you ever struggled with this? What are some examples?

Frankie's first impression of Sonya is that she is a "witchy woman". Did you find that Sonya grew on you as the story went on? Did you sympathize with her? Or do you think she chose Marv with her eyes open and that's just too bad?

Sonya is caught up in a contract that gives away her rights to her Baby Cat. Have you ever made a seemingly benign promise and found that you had given away more than you intended?

Frankie asks Sonny Street to steal a room key for her. Have you ever been asked to do something that might put you or your job in jeopardy? Did you do it?

At the end of the last book, Bowers was afraid to get close to Frankie because of her "gift". Do you think he deserves a second chance?

ABOUT THE AUTHOR

Jacqueline Vick writes the Frankie Chandler Pet Psychic mystery series about a woman who, after faking her psychic abilities for years, discovers animals *can* communicate with her. Her second series, the Harlow Brothers mysteries, features a former college linebacker turned etiquette author and his secretary brother. Her books are known for satirical humor and engaging characters who are reluctant to accept their greatest (and often embarrassing) gifts.

Find out more at jacquelinevick.com.

Made in the USA
Columbia, SC
08 August 2024

40170055R00183